THE OXFORD BOOK OF
Canadian Military Anecdotes

Edited by Victor Suthren

Toronto   Oxford   New York
OXFORD UNIVERSITY PRESS
1989

Oxford University Press, 70 Wynford Drive, Don Mills, Ontario, M3C 1J9

Toronto Oxford New York Delhi Bombay Calcutta Madras Karachi
Petaling Jaya Singapore Hong Kong Tokyo Nairobi Dar es Salaam
Cape Town Melbourne Auckland

and associated companies in
Berlin   Ibadan

To the men and women of the Canadian armed forces

CANADIAN CATALOGUING IN PUBLICATION DATA
Main entry under title:

The Oxford Book of Canadian military anecdotes

Includes index.
ISBN 0-19-540711-3

1. Canada - History, Military - Anecdotes.
I. Suthren, Victor, 1942-   .

FC226.O93 1989   355'.00971   C89-094517-9
F1028.O93 1989

CONTENTS

ACKNOWLEDGEMENTS

WILL R. BIRD, *Ghosts Have Warm Hands* (Clarke, Irwin & Company Limited 1968). Reprinted by permission of Stoddart Publishing Co. Ltd, Toronto, Canada.

ERNEST G. BLACK, *I Want One Volunteer*. Reprinted by permission of McGraw-Hill Ryerson Limited.

JEFFRY V. BROCK, *The Dark Broad Seas*. Used by permission of the Canadian Publisher, McClelland and Stewart, Toronto.

ALAN D. BUTCHER, *I Remember Haida*. Used by permission of Lancelot Press Limited.

DANIEL G. DANCOCKS, *Legacy of Valour* and *Spearhead to Victory*. Used by permission of Hurtig Publishers Ltd.

TED FERGUSON, *Desperate Siege: The Battle of Hong Kong*. Copyright © 1980 by Ted Ferguson. Published by Doubleday Canada Ltd. Reprinted by permission of Doubleday Canada Ltd.

FRED GAFFEN, *In the Eye of the Storm*. Used by permission of Deneau Publishers.

MABEL TINKISS GOOD, *The Bridge at Dieppe*. Used by permission of the author.

JOHN PATRICK GROGAN, *Dieppe and Beyond*. Used by permission of Juniper Books Limited.

HUGH HALLIDAY, *No. 242 Squadron: The Canadian Years*, Canada's Wings, Inc.

DOUGLAS HARVEY, *Boys, Bombs and Brussel Sprouts*. Used by permission of the Canadian Publisher, McClelland and Stewart, Toronto.

JOYCE HIBBERT, *The War Brides* (© 1978 Joyce Hibbert). Reprinted by permission of Stoddart Publishing Co. Ltd, Toronto, Canada.

HAROLD HORWOOD and ED BUTTS, *Bandits and Privateers*. Copyright © 1987 by Harold Horwood and Ed Butts. Published by Doubleday Canada Limited. Reprinted by permission of Doubleday Canada Limited.

ROY ITO, *We Went to War*, Canada's Wings, Inc.

GREG KEILTY, *1837: Revolution in the Canadas* (1974). Used by permission of NC Press Limited.

HAL LAWRENCE, *A Bloody War: One Man's Memories of the Canadian Navy 1939-1945*, © Hal Lawrence. Used by permission of the author and the Canadian Publisher, McClelland and Stewart, Toronto.

RAYMOND MASSEY, *When I Was Young*. Used by permission of the Canadian Publishers, McClelland and Stewart, Toronto.

JOHN MELADY, *Korea: Canada's Forgotten War*. Reprinted by permission of Macmillan of Canada, A Division of Canada Publishing Corporation.

FARLEY MOWAT, *The Regiment*. Used by permission of the author.

BILL OLMSTED, *Blue Skies*. Reprinted by permission of Stoddart Publishing Co. Ltd, Toronto, Canada.

GORDON REID, *Poor Bloody Murder*. Reprinted by permission of Mosaic Press.

REGINALD H. ROY, *The Journal of Private Fraser*. Used by permission of Reginald H. Roy.

Salty Dips, Vol. I, published by the Ottawa Branch, Naval Officers' Association of Canada, 1983. Used by permission.

ELINOR KYTE SENIOR, *Redcoats and Patriotes: The Rebellions in Lower Canada 1837-38*, Canada's Wings, Inc.

GORDON W. STEAD, *A Leaf Upon the Sea: A Small Ship in the Mediterranean, 1941-1943*. Copyright © 1988 by The University of British Columbia Press. Reprinted by permission of the publisher.

SAMUEL B. STEELE, *Forty Years in Canada*. Reprinted by permission of McGraw-Hill Ryerson Limited.

JEFFERY WILLIAMS, *The Long Left Flank* (Leo Cooper).

Every effort has been made to determine and contact copyright owners. In the case of any omissions, the publisher will be pleased to make suitable acknowledgements in future editions.

INTRODUCTION

The experience of war is a subject at once of fascination and abhorrence. For those who have not participated actively in its waging or been the victims of its violence and disruption, the effort to understand fully the reality of this most human activity is difficult. This may in part spring from the natural desire of the civilized mind to 'make sense' of war, to make it rational. But for the soldier or civilian who has experienced it, the recurrent memory—beyond the ordered preparations of tactics and logistics, the willing acceptance of subordination, the logic of training and planning—is in fact the illogical, impressionistic side of war: the emotion and warmth of battle-formed friendships; the sudden anguish of loss, whether of loved ones or of comrades—or, as often, the kind of numbness that seems to admit no grief; the disorder and staggering wastefulness of heavy-weapon action; the confusion and comic-opera chaos of small-arms 'fire fights' rendered humourless by the bloody wreckage of blood and bone that such weapons can make of young bodies. Equally vivid may be the fighter pilot's memory of exaltation in his winging mastery of the air and the sweaty-palmed, neck-turning tumult of the dogfight, with death only a rudder-flick away; or the sailor's memory of the numbing strain, the cold, the despairing seasickness of ocean-escort life upon an endless and malevolent Atlantic, and his fierce joy at seeing the shells punch into the dark conning towers. Other memories too can be crystal-clear: the urgent embraces of wartime love, bittersweet and transient, heightened in intensity by hovering death or imminent departure; the heady, strengthening impact of rum's illusion on exhausted bodies; the smells of Brasso, Blanco, wet wool, oil, diesel fumes, cordite, aircraft dope, and blood; the cold knot of fear in the gut before a crippled aircraft lands, and the flooding relief of the touchdown after a mission; the pounding piano and beer-fueled singing in messes and clubs; the drizzle of a rainsoaked day in a Nissen hut, with boredom the companion and the war far away.

It is kind of the human mind to allow itself to remember the good and warm far longer than the horrible; as a result, many of those who have experienced war can say with truth that they remember it as the time when they felt most alive.

Canadians have fought as troops of France, of Britain, and, finally, of their own nation. They have fought with a ferocious capability that has given them, a markedly unmilitaristic people, a military reputation far more respected than those of many nations who play more dramatically at the parade-ground chauvinism and *machismo* of overt militarism. Canadians maintain dedicated armed forces of minimal size, and get on with the peace, order, and good government of a highly civilized and self-disciplined people. Forced to take up arms, they have done so to put an end to war or fighting; having matched and beaten armed bullies, they put weapons away with little ostentatious crowing and get on with the nation's life. They do not, ever, play at war, nor do they see the gun as a solution to social injustice or personal failure. They are as close to the classical concept of the true citizen soldier as may be possible in a democratic society without being armed to the teeth, like the Swiss: men and women of a peacable nature, able to live without war precisely because they can be so fearfully good at it, without a shred of romance.

The roots to the military paradox of this peaceful kingdom may lie in the collective inheritance of the people, for virtually all Canadians spring from nations and peoples who have known the bitter reality of war far better than its glories. War to the native peoples of Canada was a ruthless affair of personal prowess ending, if lost, in ritual torture or slavery. The people of New France survived the holocaust of the Iroquois wars only to fight with heroic effort against a far more powerful enemy, the British: they lost, and Wolfe's rangers burned and pillaged pitilessly along the Saint Lawrence before the *habitants* knew the final bitterness of being abandoned, by their mother country and by their own upper class, to the mercy of the enemy. The Loyalists fought with unquenchable valour in the American Revolution, better troops by far than the Continentals they opposed, only to be trusted too little and too late by the Britain to whom they remained loyal. They lost everything, trekking north in poverty to New Brunswick and Upper Canada with little to show for their courage and loyalty but a meagre 'King's Bounty' and the far more important memory of the mistreatment and persecution they had suffered at the hands of their victorious enemies. In 1812, troops of the burgeoning Republic crossed into Canada and visited war on the peaceful farms of Upper Canada, the worst atrocities coming, ironically, at the hands of renegade Canadian marauders. The same grim landscapes of burned-out homes before which sobbing women and uncomprehending children huddled over the dead bodies of their men were repeated a few years later in 1837-38, when British troops and English-speaking Canadian militia marched through the countryside around Montreal to crush the desperate rebellion there and leave a hatred of uniforms and soldiery that remained strong almost a hundred years later. Then the Irish came to North America in their woeful, suffering thousands, ascribing a malevolence to government and authoritarian power that fuelled their hatred of force. And that hatred led them, ironically, into the use of force, and the peace of the Canadian countryside was threatened with the hate-and-whisky-inflamed gunmen of Fenianism, and again Canadians had to take up arms, to drive away and put an end to killing, rather than to begin it.

The development of the Canadian west brought with it no parallel to the bloody lawlessness and genocide that characterized the American frontier. There was an unwillingness to let loose on the open lands to the west the same kind of uncontrolled expansion that was taking place in the United States, and that unwillingness was firmly rooted in the Canadian fear of the republican mob, the unbridled passions of limitless democracy, and the gratification of personal appetite—because such excesses had in the past led not to greater happiness, but to disaster. The willingly adopted British inheritance of enforced order and propriety—couched in the phrase 'peace, order, and good government'—was a complement to the inherited Canadian fear of excess and produced an orderly, peaceful, but rather inhibited society. There would have been peace on the Canadian frontier had the Plains tribes and the Métis acquiesced quietly in the imposition of dour order from the east; but they chose to rise up in arms against the going of the buffalo and the coming of the land surveyor, and repeated again the Canadian tragedy: the rebellion lost, the recourse to arms bringing loss, defeat, prison, and disinheritance. The English Canada that succeeded against Riel's followers could feel reassured that the evil of armed resistance to authority had been put down; for French Canada the hanging of Riel and the aftermath of linguistic and cultural intolerance and bitterness reaffirmed the sense of oppression. The Northwest Rebellion of 1885 showed the capacity of the young country to put down, bumblingly but with eventual effect, a serious challenge to its authority. But it also displayed the exasperating divisions within the country that frustrated any sense of national unity. English Canadians basked in the late Victorian glow of Empire, an Empire not strictly of their own making, and one in which they were far less welcome than they imagined themselves to be. French Canadians largely withdrew and nursed their hurts, while their leaders argued over whether to shun the alien other half of this illogical country or risk absorption and disappearance by trying to work within it. The outbreak of the South African War served to highlight this dichotomy between English Canadians, or more particularly those of British stock, who saw virtually any fight of Queen Victoria's armies as their own, and French Canadians, who saw nothing at all applicable to Canada in Britain's imperialist adventures and if anything admired the Boers for standing up to the British in an embarrassingly effective way. The Canadian government attempted to resolve the unresolvable by pursuing a careful policy of refusing official participation but authorizing 'private' participation if it was welcomed by the British government. Those Canadians who did serve as infantry or mounted scouts at Paardeberg, Leliefontein, and elsewhere clearly demonstrated the Canadian ability to fight—almost to the surprise of the British, who had routinely tut-tutted over the flamboyance and disorder of the colonial troops. The South African experience was a foreshadowing of the Great War that loomed ahead, in which the turbulent colonials, the Canadians and their cousins the Australians and New Zealanders, would be looked on by the British with condescension and in some instances distaste, even as they proved to be the most effective fighting arm of the British forces.

The outbreak of the First World War was greeted with flag-waving fervour by the British Empire, including English-born Canadians, no one suspecting the appalling carnage about to take place in the mud of the European trenches. The common picture of war at the time was very much a romantic notion fostered by the novels of G.A. Henty or the *Boys' Own Annual*: derring-do tales of sturdy British lads winning through with pluck, playing-field sportsmanship, and low casualties. Few could have been prepared for the obscene and fruitless slaughter of millions of young men that went on for four years as baffled generals, unable to think of any other means to win, sought to achieve an attractive ratio between the volume of death inflicted on the enemy and their own losses. The war shattered the social underpinnings of Western Europe, although the forms of society that had rested on them continued for some decades. It marked the end of European primacy in the world, although it would take the war of 1939-45 to complete the humiliation of Europe and consummate its dominance by the huge proletarian superstates of the United States and the Soviet Union. The war of 1914-18 started Great Britain on its decline from the pinnacle of world power to the role of a small European nation trying to co-operate with its neighbours, rather like a titled dowager out of cash having to get along with the 'help' on the basis of equality. Eventually, this decline would leave English-speaking Canada without a cultural coattail to cling to, but the rush to the flag in 1914 had already set in motion a series of events and pressures in Canada that would push the country towards nationhood whether it wanted to go or not. Those events and pressures were in large part an outgrowth of the extraordinary performances of the 'unmilitary' Canadians on the most horrific battlefield the world had seen to that time.

The entry of Canada into the Great War was greeted by a Great Britain that, although hungry for raw manpower, was not inclined to listen to upstart colonies demanding equality. Much of the first part of the war was spent attempting to ensure that the Canadian troops were kept together rather than broken up piecemeal to fill the holes made in British Army ranks by German artillery and machine guns. The masses of Canadians who arrived in Europe were raw but enthusiastic, capable country lads for the most part, haphazardly gathered together by the bizarre Minister of Militia, Sam Hughes, who ignored the existing militia system and instead sent a partly trained, partly equipped horde off across the Atlantic armed with the accurate but disastrously unreliable Ross rifle and sure of nothing other than their eagerness to get at the Kaiser's troops in this 'grand adventure'.

Gradually the needed training was given, the equipment found, the organization imposed—the hated Ross rifle was even disposed of, over Hughes's lunatic objections, by 1916—and the Canadians soon exhibited the same strengths in the horror of the trenches that characterized them as a people: dogged endurance; physical toughness; a willingness to organize and plan with common sense; enthusiasm and scepticism at the same moment. In addition, an inner reservoir of fighting fury and impatience with pretention and unexplained demands for denigrating obedience made the Canadians less docile than the British and gave them an impetuousness and initiative that made them, with the Australians and New Zealanders, crack assault troops. At Vimy Ridge, in 1917, the Canadian Corps took an objective that had defeated the best efforts of the French and other British formations, and in virtually every other engagement of the war in which they were involved until the gunfire ceased on 11 November 1918, the 'unmilitary' men of Canada performed with matchless ability and valour. Some sixty thousand Canadians were killed in the First World War, and thousands more incapacitated. More than one author has wondered what the early twentieth century might have held for Canada had the nation not lost sixty thousand of its best citizens.

The performance of the Dominion troops in the British war effort earned Canada the right to insist on a separate identity at the post-war international bargaining table. As much as the exhaustion

of Britain, it was this new voice earned in blood and bodies that
moved the country dramatically closer to a sense of independent
identity. The price of recognition had been agonizingly dear, and not
all had been willing to pay it. In mid-war the dreadful toll of the
trench killing had led to the imposition of conscription in Canada.
Resentment at being forced to fight in what was seen, however
narrowly, as a foreign war between imperialist powers boiled over,
particularly in Quebec. In a way, the two sides in the conscription
battle were displaying two intensely Canadian characteristics: a
willingness to accept anything if convinced of its rightness—including the quiet surrender of rights and liberties for a time—and an
equally strong rebellion at being forced to do something felt to be
stupid, or simply wrong.

In the grim inter-war years, after the artificial prosperity of the
1920s had collapsed into the Depression of the 1930s, Canadian
veterans could have been forgiven a certain bitterness at what their
sacrifice had not brought as reward. Worldwide dismay over the
seeming bankruptcy of the European way of doing things—and the
real bankruptcy of the economies that operated on that system—left
the great mass of people in confusion: either hanging grimly on to
old ways and faiths, or drawn to political extremism in an effort to
make things somehow 'right' once more. Unaware of the cruelty and
misery of Stalinist Russia, thousands embraced Marxism with a
religious certainty that it held the cure to the baffling illness within
capitalist society. For similar reasons, others followed leaders who
claimed that only weakness and the traitorous underminings of
outsiders were to blame for social ills. Fascism and the worship of
force rose to freely elected power in a resentful, confused Germany.
It was but a matter of time before the weakened democracies, a far
cry from the wealthy, self-confident nations that had marched into
war in 1914, were dragged in gloomy foreboding into the horror of
another war. Canada waited a cautious week before declaring its
own war against the threat of Hitler and Fascist Germany. But the
recruiting lines were filled almost as quickly as in 1914, perhaps less
out of flag-waving patriotism than out of the need to have a job and
a decent meal. It was clear that an evil was afoot in the world, but
the true depth of that evil was not yet fully apparent.

The world war that these Canadian men and women experienced
was a different one from the first. In the latter there had still existed
a last glimmer of chivalrous thought, which tried to keep the war
from civilians, and which treated prisoners—at least in Western
Europe—with a certain decency. Very rapidly it became clear that
the new war would have none of that feeling. It was total war, in
which the Nazi military machine and, later, Imperial Japan made

deliberate efforts to terrorize and kill the civilian population of the enemy, and in which racist hatred and the dehumanizing of the enemy led to so appalling a level of murder, mistreatment, and deliberate imposition of suffering that this new struggle—far more than the First World War, with its pumped-up nonsense about the 'beastly Hun'—became literally a death struggle between the sorely tried decency of Western civilization and the unspeakable evil that had risen from within it.

This new and bewildering war left the stalemated butchery of the trenches and moved into the hulls of Valentine and Sherman tanks, the cockpits of Hurricanes, Halifaxes, and Spitfires, and the gun mounts and pilotages of the newly burgeoning Royal Canadian Navy. Movement and technology were the key now. There was still an infantryman's war, as Canadians found in the slow battles through Sicily and Italy, and after D-Day in Europe; there was still slaughter, as the Canadians at Dieppe and Hong Kong found out, aggravated by racist mistreatment and fascist brutality. But there was now a broader, more breathtaking scope to the epic struggle, and it became in true geographical terms a world war. When in 1914 a Canadian enlisted for service, he almost certainly knew that it meant an infantryman's life—and possibly death—in the relatively close confines of southern England, the Channel ports, and the trench lines in France (so close that on certain days the thunder of the guns was audible in England). But the Canadian enlisting in 1939 came from the grim world of the Depression into a military world that offered him a bewildering variety of ways to fight. Within months, a Saskatchewan farm lad with a single pair of shoes, raised on potatoes in a sod house, could find himself not only fed and clothed, brought together in camaraderie with other young men in what seemed to be a grand adventure, but vaulting miles above the earth in a fighter aircraft behind a thundering thousand-horsepower engine responding to his every whim. Canadians served as pilots and aircrew all over the world, from Burma to Europe, the Aleutians to the South Atlantic. With the Royal Canadian Navy or the Royal Navy they served at sea in virtually every ocean, in work ranging from the grim endurance of convoy escort in a North Atlantic winter to the wild, shirtsleeve heroics of motor gunboat action in the midsummer heat of the Mediterranean. At first the Canadian infantryman chafed with inaction in Britain as two regiments of Canadians were lost under a Japanese assault on Hong Kong and thousands died or were taken prisoner at Dieppe. When the larger action finally came, it was an undermanned, overextended war of movement and automatic weapons. And at the end of the fighting the Canadian soldiers discovered both delight and horror: the happy

wonderment of the liberation of the Netherlands and the outpouring
of affection from the Dutch; and the ultimate horror of the death
camps, where humanity destroyed itself without pity or remorse.

The final events of the Second World War divided the world, for
all practical purposes, into the armed camps dominated by the
United States and the Soviet Union respectively, with the members
of the former colonial world struggling to make their own way or
being drawn into one or other of the two camps. Canada in 1945 had
emerged as a nation of considerable power, and would retain this
enhanced stature until the rebuilt European nations and Japan, the
phoenix of the Eastern world, rose again to claim their places. The
advent of nuclear weapons, beginning with the United States, indicated clearly that war was at last capable of destroying all of
humanity, and not just a part. Canada had the ability to arm itself
with nuclear weapons, but chose not to; its foreign policy was
anchored instead on two major rocks: a commitment to collective
security through the North Atlantic Treaty Organization and the
North American Air Defence agreement, in partnership with European allies and under the leadership of the United States; and an
equal commitment to participation in the world peacekeeping
process through strong support of the United Nations. The first
commitment reflected practicality and realism in Canadian thinking, for the lessons of world disunity in the face of the fascist threat
were still fresh. The second reflected the strong Canadian desire to
see war vanish as a phenomenon, and allowed the national capacity
for compromise, discussion, and peaceful resolution of problems to
come to the fore.

When, in 1950, the polarity between East and West came into stark
relief with the North Korean invasion of South Korea, the Canadian
government supported the United Nations' 'police action' against
the North Koreans and Chinese through the raising of special
infantry battalions to serve in the Commonwealth Brigade, and the
rotation of RCN ships and RCAF transport aircraft in Korean-theatre
service. The Korean conflict cost Canada several hundred lives, and
demonstrated again the steady professionalism without flamboyance that is the hallmark of the Canadian military. A scant three
years after the Korean peace, the equal commitment to prevention
of war led to the Canadian proposal for the first of the United
Nations peacekeeping forces, intended for the Middle East. Through
the perilous Nuclear Age the nation has chosen to maintain a steady,
if cautious, adherence to the NATO and NORAD agreements. But it is
in the field of peacekeeping that our small, superb armed forces
carry out with patience and skill those most Canadian of pursuits:
the calm defusing of tensions and animosities, the putting down of

weapons, and the search for less destructive ways to resolve argument. In the courage of a Canadian Forces peacekeeper, quietly and without arms facing down two armed formations of Middle Eastern belligerents and leading both away from bloody confrontation, there is a mirror of the courage that held against the attacks at Kapyong, in Korea; that fought and defeated the ss in the wetlands of Holland; that held at Ypres and took Vimy Ridge; and that turned back a vast American army at Châteauguay more than a hundred years before. It is the courage of peaceful men and women.

Not all Canadian regiments, ships, or squadrons will find mention in this book of anecdotes. There has been no effort to provide an even chronological coverage of Canadian military history, nor to achieve a balance between air, land, and naval experience. Rather, the goal has been to provide, in glimpses of experience, a feeling for what the realities of war were for Canadians caught up in it. The selections have been made solely with that aim in mind: to be with ordinary Canadians in moments of war's experience, to gain a basis for sympathy, for pity if necessary, and finally for respect. Above all, however, I hope that these selections will be a source of ringing pride in the human beings that Canada has produced. The peaceful kingdom is such because of these people. Their lives have been gifts of a value beyond simple praise.

I am indebted to the kind patience and guidance of Richard Teleky and his staff at Oxford University Press in the preparation of this book, and to Captain Mark A. Reid and Daniel Glenney for their assistance in locating and selecting key items.

1

THE EARLY DAYS

The North American continent that the first Europeans came to was not a land without war. As a human phenomenon, war was already present in the societies of the people native to the Americas. As the Europeans gazed in awe at the dark, shadowed wall of forest laced with silver rivers and lakes, they were soon to meet peoples of cultures wherein war was an integral activity, in most cases, of tribal society; an accepted activity based as often on questions of honour and reputation as upon harder issues of hunting-land rights or territoriality.

Moreover, the native peoples were physically awesome, particularly in the north, where the Iroquoian men towered in muscular, robust strength over the pale, short-statured Europeans. The introduction of Europeans into the North American scene, and the struggle between native nations for control of the fur trade that arose to meet the European hunger for furs, generated savage wars of extermination that built on earlier tribal hostilities. The first contact between the Iroquois and Samuel de Champlain in the early seventeenth century heralded a century of nightmarish war between native and native, and native and European.

The warriors of the Long House, who had nothing but contempt for their northern foes, came out to do battle with taunting laughter. Champlain estimated their number at two hundred and he was surprised, and perhaps a little dismayed, at their physical magnificence. Tall, lithe, splendidly thewed, they were superior in every respect to the braves from the North. Their voices rang high through the woods, proclaiming their victory in advance. Three chiefs, their heads topped with snowy plumes, strode boldly in the lead, their eyes fierce, their stone hatchets held aloft. The allies, whose response to the exultant howling of the Iroquois had become somewhat forced and reedy, now proceeded in great haste to carry out the plan which Champlain himself had prepared. Their ranks parted and he stepped forward slowly into the breach thus made in the line.

Seeing a white man for the first time, the Ongue Honwe fell into a startled silence. Their eyes lost for a moment the glitter of tribal hate and became filled with a sense of awe. This, clearly, was a white god who had come down from the sky to fight on the side of the despised Hurons. The stone hatchets, no longer brandished in the air, hung at their sides.

Although Champlain advanced with no sign of haste, he knew that the Iroquois pause was a momentary one, that they would recover their spirit immediately. It was clear to him also that the Huron braves lacked the fighting pitch to sustain a charge from their hereditary enemies, who outnumbered them several times over. The balance between life and death hung tautly in the air. In no more than a second of time it would be settled. Everything depended on him, the steadiness of his hand, the sureness of his aim.

His arquebus had been loaded with four bullets. Taking aim at the three chiefs, who stood together like a group carved by some Greek master, he discharged the contents of the carbine. His eye had not failed him. The spray of bullets stretched all three chiefs on the ground, two of them killed instantly.

The explosion jarred the senses of the Iroquois, but at the same time it had the effect of releasing them from the spell. Although an unfriendly god had brought down thunder and lightning against them, they must fight for their lives and their tribal honor. They reached for their bows and sent a downpour of arrows into the Huron ranks.

At this critical moment one of Champlain's men showed himself on the flank and fired point-blank at the aroused Iroquois. This was more than they could stand. Another god, another roar like thunder in the clouds! They turned and fled with a consternation which never before had been felt in an Iroquois heart. The Ongue Honwe had been surpassed at last.

The allies now came to life. With hatchet and scalping knife they sprang in pursuit of the stunned and disorganized foe. Many of the beaten tribesmen were killed and a dozen or more were captured. The fleeing Iroquois took to the shelter of the trees and so everything they had brought with them, even their canoes (which the allied destroyed scornfully), became the spoils of the victors.

Thomas B. Costain, The White and the Gold (1954), pp. 68-9

The grim conflict between the Europeans and the native North Americans that Champlain's arquebus had begun would last for two centuries. But very soon the Europeans began to fight among

*themselves for control of North America. The Spanish had claimed
the tropical regions to the south; the English had established themselves on the eastern seaboard and in Hudson Bay; and the French
had claimed a vast, crescent-shaped empire in the interior, anchored on Quebec and stretching to the Gulf of Mexico. Finally, in
1759, the British army under James Wolfe arrived at Quebec, and
the long story of France in America was about to come to an end.
But Wolfe's red-coated soldiery were facing a formidable enemy in
the Marquis de Montcalm's troops, and an initial attempt to gain a
foothold on the Beauport shore below fortified Quebec was bloodily
repulsed.*

In the middle of the morning when the tide was at full flood, the
Centurion, a sixty-four-gun frigate commanded by Captain Mantle,
sailed slowly into the north channel towards the Beauport coast and
anchored near the gorge of the Montmorency River. As the anchor
settled down on to the rocky bed of the St Lawrence, the ship's guns
opened up in a furious cannonade on the redoubts at the edge of the
strand, beneath the overhanging cliffs.

It was the signal for an intense bombardment. The *Centurion*'s
guns rolled and boomed at the French entrenchments, and the two
catamarans, each with fourteen guns, tacked in as close as they
could get to the redoubt nearest the Montmorency River and soon
their guns too were flashing and smoking in the warm sunlight. As
the ships in the river fired continuously at the redoubts on the
strand, a battery of nearly fifty heavy pieces in the camp at Montmorency bombarded the French positions along the clifftop, while
the battery at Pointe de Lévy cannonaded them from across the St
Lawrence basin. For two hours the thunderous bombardment continued while the troops who had been in the landing-craft since ten
o'clock waited, hot, cramped, and sweating, for the attack to begin.

About two o'clock some of the landing-craft moved out into
midstream and the sailors rowed them up and down in front of the
Beauport coast in an attempt to mislead the French commanders as
to their landing-place.

Montcalm and Lévis, however, were not in any doubt as to where
the attack was intended. Already the Canadians on the threatened
heights, standing up well under the heavy fire from which they were
partly protected by well-constructed traverses, had been reinforced
by three regular French battalions and some heavy pieces of artillery
which had been moved east from the village of Beauport. By five
o'clock more than eleven thousand men were concentrated along
the three and a half miles of cliff-top between Beauport church and

the waterfall, while along the Montmorency River, in case of a secondary attack in their rear, five hundred more men were posted in the woods.

The day was still excessively hot, but the sun was now hidden behind low, dark clouds and the air was sultry and heavy. The tide was ebbing, and the catamarans stranded by the falling water were stuck securely in the silt as they kept up their fire against the redoubts.

In the early afternoon, when the tide was running low and the long stretch of dark mud along the river's edge was almost a quarter of a mile wide, Wolfe gave the order to attack.

The sailors rowed the unwieldy landing-craft across the narrowing channel towards the French redoubts. Wolfe, standing, cane in hand, in one of the leading boats, peered ahead at the landing-place as the sailors struggled to keep the boats from being washed too far down-stream in the rushing currents. All the boats in the first wave, containing three companies of grenadiers and a detachment of Royal Americans, were swept too far downstream and grounded on ridges of mud, where, as the sailors struggled to release them, they made an easy target for French and Canadian sharpshooters on the cliffs above.

Some boats got free and slipped into deeper channels as others became more securely embedded in the silt. The *Centurion* and the two catamarans increased their rate of fire as the French batteries opened up with telling effect on the tightly packed men in the stranded boats.

Wolfe, shouting orders from his boat, was three times struck by splinters and had his cane knocked out of his hand by a round shot. Deciding that it was impossible to get the boats in any closer to the dry sand, he told Captain Hervey Smith, his aide-de-camp, to go to Townshend and tell him to halt his men as the landing of the first troops had been delayed. He realized now that he must wait until the tide was at its lowest before he could get his men ashore. Some of them had now been nearly eight hours in the crowded boats, and they waited impatiently for the order to get out.

While they were waiting a Captain David Ochterlony, who was in command of the detachment of the 60th and who had been wounded the day before in a duel with a German officer, Captain Wetterstroom of the grenadiers, saw Wetterstroom in a nearby boat. Standing up he shouted at him, 'Though my men are not grenadiers, you will see we shall be first at the redoubt.' The grenadiers roared back their defiance, and a moment or two later Wolfe gave the order for the boats to get in as close as they could to the strand and for the men to disembark.

The men of the 60th and the grenadiers, cheered by the sailors in the landing craft, raced each other across the slippery mud, in wild disorder, excited and uncontrollable, towards the redoubt at the edge of the dry sand. The French defenders of it, seeing their fierce, lumbering advance of nearly a thousand men, abandoned it; and a minute or two later the British were in possession.

No sooner, however, had their own troops got out of range than the French on the heights above rained down a furious fire of musket shot on the heads of the disorderly British soldiers, who could not with any hope of success reply to it.

Behind them the scene was chaotic. Monckton was already landing the second wave of troops, Amherst's Regiment and Fraser's Highlanders, a thousand men in all; while Townshend's two thousand men were already across the ford. No one knew what was expected of him. Now that the French were obviously not coming down to fight, what was to be done? Nobody knew. The orders previously given to the grenadiers, to form up in four sections and await the arrival of the second wave of troops and Townshend's brigade, were now plainly unworkable. But no other instructions were given them. As the officers waited indecisively for orders the rain began to drizzle down.

In those few minutes of doubt the grenadiers decided for themselves what the next step should be. They had had enough hanging about for one day. Eight hours cramped up in a boat in the sweltering heat was enough to try anyone's patience. They knew where the enemy were so they thought they might as well get at them. Without waiting for orders from the General, or it seems from their own officers, they dashed across the strand, shouting at the top of their voices, and began to clamber up the steep and slippery cliff, encouraged by a solitary drummer who stood below them wildly beating his drum. The ascent was extremely difficult. The boots of the grenadiers slipped and slithered on the loose stones and shale and on the wet earth. Here and there, there was a bush to cling to or a root of a stunted cedar or hazel tree, but most of the surface of the brown cliff was bare and smooth; and higher up it was made more difficult to climb by the easily dislodged trunks of barkless trees which the enemy had put across the small ravines where the going would otherwise have been easier.

The soldiers struggled up, some with their muskets slung across their backs, others grimly holding them in one hand as they clawed at the earth with the other; but none of them able to return the fire of the French from the crest of the hill above them. Their officers, forced into the mad assault by the enthusiasm of their men and wondering what else, in any case, the General could have intended them to do, were now determined to make it successful. They encouraged the men with shouts and gestures to get to the top of the cliff while their desperate energy lasted.

The French and Canadians, delighted to have so perfect a target, and having suffered very few losses during the day's bombardment thanks to their well-made defences, shot carefully aimed volleys of musket balls down the slope and tilted up the breeches of their cannon to such an angle that the barrels were pointing sharply down the line of the cliff.

Despite the storm of shot and ball, lead and splinters, the grenadiers and Royal Americans struggled on, more slowly now as they became short of breath and their arms and legs grew weak with exhaustion. Soldier after soldier stumbled and fell in the smoke and then rolled down the cliff face until stopped by a ledge of earth, a tree trunk, or another soldier still clambering breathlessly upwards.

And then the black clouds, which all that sultry afternoon had been growing more heavy, suddenly broke and the rain poured blindingly down. Within a few minutes the cliff face became a morass. The grenadiers, soaked to the skin, could no longer see the top of the cliff through the sheets of slanting rain; their powder became sodden, their muskets unusable. They were forced back at last, and in a slithering, tumbling mass they slipped and slid down the cliff like ants washed down the slopes of an ant-hill. Behind them hundreds of sprawled bodies, their red-and-white uniforms coated with mud, could be seen through the storm. Some of the wounded, too weak to hold on any longer or losing their footholds in the now slushy earth, rolled over and over in agony to the bottom of the cliff.

The French, until then shouting 'Vive le Roi!' in triumphant excitement, fell silent as they looked down at the havoc which they and the storm had wrought. It was a piteous and subduing sight; and as if to emphasize its horror the rain then stopped as abruptly as it had begun, and the cliff face, littered with sodden corpses, steamed in the sudden silence.

Christopher Hibbert, *Wolfe at Quebec* (1959), pp. 91-5

Despite the valour and courage with which Quebec was defended, James Wolfe and his brigadiers eventually found a way to put their army on a battlefield outside the walls, there to challenge Montcalm's French regulars and Canadian troops to a final contest. A flotilla of boats had crept quietly along the river to a small cove just above Quebec, and it had let the redcoats ashore to scramble in the darkness up a steep, rocky path to the heights above. At dawn the French had looked out from the walls of the city and seen the motionless red line waiting in the open fields to the west. Montcalm pulled his troops from now-useless entrenchments and moved out to array them against the waiting line of Wolfe's men. The artillery began its long-range murder, and the two armies waited like actors for one side or the other to cue them for the most dramatic and decisive moment in Canadian history.

The rain had stopped, the clouds had gone, and the sun shone warmly down. The British soldiers, lying full-length in the deep prairie grass and bracken, to escape the exploding shells as much as to deceive the enemy, felt grateful for the warmth and the rest after the long, cold night in the boats and the hard climb. Occasionally a shell from Ramezay's guns burst amongst them, but the line was very long and the chances of getting hit seemed small. Only on the left, where some French field-guns, dragged over the St Charles River, were now firing on Townshend's brigade, were the casualties more than slight.

A brass six-pounder pulled up the heights after dawn by the artillery was returning the fire under the skilful and animated direction of Captain York; and a second one which had been damaged as it was tugged up from the river was repaired by the gunners soon after ten and then it too fired against the regiments of Béarn and La Guienne in the French centre. Unlike the other regiments which stretched out in line from the St Foye Road to the river at Anse des Mères, these two stood in column on either side of the Sillery Road, where the ground did not permit them to deploy. And the sick and wounded French soldiers looking across the plain from the windows of the General Hospital could see the plumes of smoke puffing up from the ground and the bodies jump and fall as the shells exploded in the clear morning light.

The long nights of duty in the entrenchments and the months without leave had made it as difficult for the French as for the British soldiers to look their best. Their pale grey coats and breeches were crumpled and soiled, their queues more black than white; but their tricornes trimmed with yellow, and their black stocks fastened behind their necks with buckles and decorated with red and yellow buttons gave at least an illusion of smartness. And on the right wing, next to the colony troops, the regiment of La Sarre looked as neat as it always did. Here the straight lines of soldiers, with their wide blue collars and their red waistcoats with white facings and yellow buttons, stood proud and still as if on parade at Versailles.

Each side watched the other waiting for the attack.

Montcalm rode up and down the French line, showing himself to his soldiers and stopping constantly to watch the English, trying to see how many there were. 'He looked sad', a French officer remembered, 'and very tired.'

Wolfe too looked tired but far from sad. A soldier who afterwards proudly wrote that he 'was standing at this precise moment of time within four feet of the General' described how happy he looked. 'I shall never forget his look,' he said. 'He was surveying the enemy with a countenance radiant and joyful beyond description.'

Nothing mattered to Wolfe now but victory. In his disguised excitement and near-hysterical fervour he seemed unable to feel fear or to recognize danger. He walked quickly back along the line from the left where the bullet had cut into his wrist, towards the river. As he passed in front of the 43rd Regiment a shell exploded in front of him and a small piece of metal tore into his belly just below his navel. He stumbled and almost fell, but he walked on and when he took his position on the right wing between the 28th Regiment and the grenadiers no one appeared to notice that he was hurt.

Bleeding from his wrist and with a severe internal haemorrhage, he kept on his feet waiting restlessly for the French attack. He did not now have long to wait.

At about ten o'clock a party of light infantry made a feint of attacking the French centre along the Sillery Road, and as soon as they had drawn the enemy's fire retired in apparent disorder with shouts of affected panic. So realistic was their display that Wolfe was obliged to turn round and assure the men behind him that it was only a ruse to draw the French on to attack.

And the trick came off. A minute later the grenadiers saw the whole French army come towards them.

At first the advance was slow. The line of grey, white, and blue figures approached in three main groups with fixed bayonets. In most places they were six deep, but in the centre where the ground was more constricted the line was deeper. The soldiers walked with almost phlegmatic deliberation across the five hundred yards of open ground which separated the two armies. The line was more than half a mile long, and the soldiers in the front rank of each regiment were not much more than four feet apart. It seemed a solid, unbreakable phalanx. Although the going was rough and the ground uneven and broken up by clumps of bushes and scrub, the army approached in ominous silence and order. In spite of the constant cannonade from the batteries on Pointe de Lévy and from the guns in Quebec, it was possible to hear from the British lines the sharp, regular, disconcerting, hollow-sounding drum-beats and to feel the rhythm of the tramping boots on the damp earth. The British soldiers, standing up now, watched quietly, their muskets loaded with an extra ball, murmuring softly. The sun shone cheerfully down.

The Canadian troops on the wings were the first to break the regular pattern of the advancing line. As soon as the British ranks were in range they let off a scattering fire and then, following their usual custom, threw themselves to the ground behind cover before reloading. If no cover was available immediately around them they ran across the front of the French regiments, and the soldiers shouted at them to get out of the way.

As the advance continued it was possible for the French to see the full length of the enemy line and the battalions on the flanks threatening to get behind the sides of their own more constricted columns. To avert this the regiments in the centre inclined outwards in a late effort to extend the front of the advancing army, and as they did so large gaps began to appear on either side of the Sillery Road.

The armies were now less than a hundred and fifty yards apart, and the French pace quickened. The order to open fire was given and a hail of musket shots tore into the steady British line. A few men fell and the ranks closed. The officers shouted to warn the men to hold their fire.

At sight of the falling British soldiers the French let out, in curious unison, a shout of triumph and hurried forward. As they came on they loaded again, and again they fired, and once more the thin red line in front of them shook like a ripple and several more gaps formed and were immediately filled again.

'Hold your fire! Hold your fire!' The shouts of the British officers and sergeants restrained the men, who waited in angry impatience for the chance to shoot. Every man had his finger on his trigger; the French were so near now that 'you could count the buttons on their coats'; but along the whole line not a shot was fired. The magnificently disciplined troops in the straight and motionless ranks stood their ground, praying for the order to fire, cursing under their breath, watching the shouting enemy getting closer and closer and firing as they liked. The whole of the excited front rank of the French army was shooting now, and the crackle of fire was incessant. The Canadians, who did not care for these parade-ground tactics, decided that they had got quite close enough to the enemy and allowed the regulars to pass through them. The French ranks became more untidy and more confused as they pushed by the colony troops and militia, but they came on with loud shouts, firing constantly still, despite the unevenness of their line. The seventy yards of ground between the armies narrowed to sixty and then to fifty. A volunteer in the 47th Regiment remembered afterwards how sick he felt. His friend who had been standing next to him had been shot in the stomach and lay groaning on the ground, and he could not help him. Would the officer never give the order to fire? The French were less than fifty yards away now and he was sure he could not miss.

'Fire!'

It was Wolfe who gave the order and all down the line it was repeated and immediately obeyed.

The shattering volley of the hundreds of steady, waiting muskets as each regiment fired was so instantaneous that a French officer subsequently described it as being like the shots from six cannon. For their weeks of boring, constant practice the soldiers were at last rewarded.

Through the thick smoke which now hid the enemy from them they could hear the screams of pain, the shouts of alarm, and the urgent commands of the French officers. Into the smoke they fired again, and so well trained were they that this time also the crack of their guns was like a short, tremendous, barking roll of thunder. Quickly and calmly they reloaded, advanced twenty paces in accordance with the instructions of the drill book, and fired again. For several minutes the crackle and clatter of musket fire continued, and the bullets flew into the smoke and thudded into the French bodies behind it. After six minutes—some of those who were there thought it was nearer ten—the rate of fire lessened, and the clouds of white smoke slowly lifted. And through the drifting whorls the British soldiers could see for the first time the havoc that their murderous fire had caused. All down the French line as far as the eye could stretch, the bodies of soldiers, some struggling in screaming agony, some kneeling or sitting and groaning softly, many quite still, were revealed behind the gauze-like screen of smoke-filled air. Beyond them the remains of their companies stood in shocked helplessness. Already some men had turned their backs and were running helter-skelter from the walls of the town. For a few seconds the British ranks stood still, firing spasmodically but with an obvious lack of spirit. And then from the right wing Wolfe gave the order to charge, and the stolid, patient line came into sudden life. Like dogs unleashed, the soldiers rushed forward, shouting excitedly, at last within reach of those 'dastardly God-damned Frogs'.

Seeing them racing across the ground, with their bayonets flashing in the sunlight, the French soldiers ran for their lives. The only regiment which made an effort to hold its ground was the Royal Rousillon, which still stood, battered but as yet unbroken, on a shallow ridge to the south of the Sillery Road. But they were able to hold their ground here for less than two minutes, and when they too joined in the retreat all but three of their officers were either dead or wounded.

Despite the ragged line of squirming bodies which they had to stumble through, several of the hunters caught up with the hunted and cut them to the ground. The Highlanders were soon out in front, their kilts swishing around their knees, swinging their swords in the air and screaming like savages. Most of them had dropped their muskets so that they could swing their broadswords with more effect, and they rushed after the enemy, the glinting blades held high in the air, waiting the opportunity to bring them down on the back of a Frenchman. One long-legged Highlander caught up with a party of stragglers and swinging his sword in a wide circle cut two heads clean off before he fell, shot through the neck by a sharpshooter hiding in the bushes in front of him.

For although the army was in wild and disorderly flight, these brave Canadian snipers covered the retreat as best they could. Everywhere that there was cover a Canadian was likely to be hiding. And on the right flank, where Wolfe was leading the grenadiers and the 28th Regiment, there was cover in plenty. Also here was an English sergeant who had been reduced to the ranks by Wolfe and had deserted to the enemy before the demotion could take effect. He had sworn revenge, and his request to serve with a party of Canadian sharpshooters so that he might have an opportunity of shooting the General in the battle had been granted.

In that bright, gay uniform it could not be long before Wolfe was picked out and hit. Indeed, not long after he had given the order to charge and had started to lead the men on, waving his cane despite his blood-soaked wrist and the agonizing pain in his stomach, he had been shot again. And the English sergeant afterwards claimed that it was he who had shot him. This time Wolfe was hit in the chest, and the bullet cut through his lung. He sank to his knees, and the lieutenant in the grenadiers who rushed to his help thought that he was already dead. The blood was coming out of his mouth. But he found the strength to ask the lieutenant to help him get back on his feet so that the soldiers should not see him fall.

So many men afterwards claimed that they had helped to carry the hero back to die in their arms that the next few minutes are clouded in confusion. It seems most likely, however, that he was carried out of danger by Lieutenant Brown of the grenadiers, an officer of artillery, and two soldiers, one of whom was James Henderson, a young volunteer. Brown sent for a surgeon, but Wolfe protested, 'There's no need now. It's all over with me.' And when a surgeon's mate came up he said, 'Lay me down, I am suffocating.'

They laid him down on the ground. He was scarcely conscious and his eyes were glazed in delirium. Henderson supported his shoulders and undid the buttons of his coat.

> Then I opened his Breast, [Henderson later wrote home] And found his Shirt full of Blood At Which he Smiled And when he Seen the Distress I Was In, My Dear, Said he, Dont Grive for me, I Shall Be Happy In a Few Minutes. take Care of Your Self As I see your Wounded. but Tell me O tell me How Goes the Battle their, Just then Came some Officers Who told him that the Freinch had civen Ground and our Troops was pursuin Them to the Walls of the Town, he Was then Lyin in my Arms Just Expirin That Great Man Whose Sole Ambition Was his Country Glory Raised himself up on the News And Smiled in my Face.

After a few seconds, with an effort of pathetic determination, Wolfe raised himself again. 'Go to Colonel Burton,one of you lads,' he said with a concentration that was painful to watch. 'Tell him to march Webb's Regiment with all speed to Charles River to cut off retreat of the fugitives from the bridge.'

Then he turned away from them and closed his eyes for the last time. 'Now, God be praised,' they heard him murmur. 'Since I have conquered, I will die in peace.'

Meanwhile the rout of the enemy continued. In front of the St Charles River two hundred Canadians kept four times their number at bay while the French withdrew across the bridge of boats, until a concerted attack by the 58th, the 2nd Battalion of the 60th, and the Highlanders drove them back to the river line. Here they held their ground again until the Highlanders rushed at them across the open meadow and cut them apart with their swords. The Canadians were massacred, but when the brief and furious encounter was over, many of the pursuers also lay dead.

On the right Bragg's and Kennedy's regiments were also held up by a company of Canadians in a coppice to their front and a solitary gun firing from Quebec. But within half an hour the coppice had been cleared and the pursuit continued.

It was not yet eleven o'clock.

                                                        Ibid., pp. 149-57

With the collapse of New France, Britain stood astride virtually all of North America: the prospects of Empire seemed endless. But the departure of France brought into focus the widening gap that existed between Britain and her American colonists. A little more than fifteen years after the fall of Quebec, the American colonies revolted and began the war that would divide North America in half and send the Loyalists north to swell the population of Canada. The conflict was bitter, and more like a civil war. American armies marched to Quebec and were driven southward again; British armies marched south from Montreal and were defeated in turn. Pitched battles took place around Montreal and Quebec. But war came as well to Nova Scotia, that 'fourteenth colony' which had refused to join the rebellion of its Yankee cousins.

In 1782 Lunenberg was defended on the east, toward the sea, by a blockhouse and on the west by two forts overlooking the town, with shore batteries that should have been able to defend it from any attack by sea. There were also picket lines for defending musketmen and barracks for troops. As at Annapolis Royal all these defences were empty when the Americans arrived at dawn, having landed just before daylight at Blue Rock Cove near Red Head, three miles east of the town.

Five privateer ships, manned by crews of 150, armed with forty-four cannon, and accompanied by a 'rowing galley' (possibly a large landing craft), had put ninety men ashore at Red Head. Magdalena Schwartz, out to milk her cow, discovered them marching towards the town and ran to warn her husband, who ran in turn to alert the defenders. The Americans fired at him, but he escaped unhurt, and the noise of musket fire awakened the slumbering inhabitants. John Creighton, formerly a British army officer, was colonel of militia, his house close by the eastern blockhouse. Hastily summoning five neighbours with muskets, he took command of the blockhouse and began firing at the approaching raiders.

Meanwhile the ships had left their anchorage and sailed around East Head to the inner harbour, where they landed another party of men with four ships' guns. This party then rushed up the hill behind the town, took over the forts, spiked the twenty-four-pounder shore batteries that could have sunk their ships on approach, and rolled the guns off their mountings, downhill almost to sea level.

Other crewmen had hauled their ships' cannon up to the deserted forts and trained them on the town. They now controlled both Lunenburg and the approaches to it by sea. Colonel Creighton and the other defenders in the eastern blockhouse were outflanked and under the attackers' cannon. Their musket fire had wounded three or four of the invaders but to no purpose. They had no choice but to surrender. The Americans clapped Creighton into irons and placed him prisoner on board their flagship, the *Scammel*, commanded by Captain Noah Stoddard of Boston. Stoddard apparently planned and directed the whole operation, and like the raiders who sacked Annapolis Royal, he obviously had detailed information concerning the exact state of the town's defences.

The privateers now proceeded to sack the town, or as the Boston *Gazette* gleefully expressed it, they 'fell to plundering with a natural and pleasing vivacity'. Indeed there was an element of playfulness in their actions, but there was serious purpose too: they confiscated guns and ammunition wherever they found them. Barrels of gunpowder and tubs of cannon balls intended to supply the forts were removed to the ships' holds. They looted the stores of everything. They seemed to be especially fond of the scarlet uniforms supplied for the militia. Soon they formed a parade, some dressed in the scarlet uniforms, others in bows, laces, and plumed bonnets. The 'vivacious' visitors tossed all kinds of merchandise about the streets and looted the shops of supplies of cakes, raisins, and figs, which they generously distributed to barefoot boys who gleefully followed them as though they were a gang of Pied Pipers.

The carnival atmosphere lasted most of the day, helped along once again by the vast supplies of rum discovered in the merchants' storehouses: no fewer then twenty puncheons—not mere casks, mind you, a puncheon was an oversized barrel made of oak, holding as much as a hundred imperial gallons, not of the watered stuff sold today but of proof spirit. The war had made good rum a scarce commodity in the rebel colonies, and this was the world's best, straight from the British Caribbean.

The privateersmen trussed up a local Protestant clergyman, the Reverend Johann Gottlob Schmeissar, who made a nuisance of himself trying to stop the looting, and left him lying in the street, but apart from that and the arrest of the militia leaders, they behaved rather well: nobody was shot, beaten, or raped. Even the black slaves, who surely might have been confiscated as valuable property, were allowed to go free.

Harold Horwood and Ed Butts, *Bandits & Privateers* (1987), pp. 42-4

Gradually the resistance of the native peoples to the European incursion crumbled, and they were forced to choose sides as the Europeans battled among themselves for control of the continent.

Britain's loss of the American colonies in 1783 had sent the Mo-hawk, a nation of the Iroquois Confederacy, to Canada from New York state as punishment for their loyalty to Britain. When American troops crossed the Canadian border in 1812, the Mohawk rallied to the British cause, displaying again the mercurial courage and the arresting combination of song, paint, and oratory that had characterized the 'Indian' warriors of the eighteenth century. This tradition was embodied in a remarkable warrior and orator named John Norton.

John Norton, or Teyoninhokarawen, was of half Cherokee, half Scottish descent. Because of his friendship with Joseph Brant, he was adopted as a Mohawk. Following Brant's death in 1807, Norton became the principal war chief of the Iroquois and led detachments of warriors in nearly every battle of the War of 1812 as allies of the British. A devout Christian, Norton was more literate than most Europeans of the period.

The following narration was taken from his journal, where he described the battle of Queenston Heights. The Iroquois arrived shortly after General Brock's death, when most British resistance had temporarily ceased. The Americans were crossing the Niagara in great numbers to secure their position. The outnumbered Iroquois hesitated to attack such a superior force, whereupon Norton addressed them. . . .

> 'Comrades and Brothers—be Men;—remember the fame of ancient War-riors, whose Breasts were never daunted by odds of number;—you have run from your Encampments to this place to meet the Enemy,—We have found what we came for. Let no anxieties distract your minds:—there they are,—it only remains to fight. . . .
>
> My heart strongly forbodes that before the Sun shall have sunk behind the Western Hills these invading foes shall have fallen before you, or have owed their Lives to your Mercy.'

Norton and his warriors went on to attack the Americans, harassing them until British reinforcements arrived later that day. One reason the British final charge was so successful was that the Americans had spent their time chasing warriors instead of digging in. In addition, almost half of the American force remained on the New York side of the Niagara, and refused to cross. One reason for this was their dread of the Iroquois. General Sheaffe acknowledged the valuable role played by his Iroquois allies in his official dispatches.

Carl F. Klinck and James Talman, *The Journal of Major John Norton* (1970), p. 305

The battles of the War of 1812 were tightly-fought struggles that reproduced on Canadian soil the vast conflicts of musket-armed columns that had characterized European war until the advent of rifled muskets and deadlier artillery. Even surrounded by dense forests, the key struggles for Canada, from the Plains of Abraham to the Battle of Crysler's Farm, were fought in the linear style, more often than not on tilled or logged-over fields. And more often than not it was a confusing business, in which the participants had very little grasp of what was happening until after it was all over.

W. Woodruff, a young private in the Lincoln Militia, fought at the battle of Queenston Heights, October 13, 1812. He wrote down his memories of the battle in 1840, offering a rare glimpse of war at the level of the common foot soldier. The narrative that follows begins late in the afternoon, a few hours after General Brock's death. Woodruff and his company had just arrived at Queenston as reinforcements from Niagara/Fort George.

> We was then ordered to advance; our little field pieces commenced firing. It was returned by the Americans with a six-pounder masked in the brush. A rapid advance was ordered, without firing a musket shot on our part, until within a small distance of the enemy under cover of the woods and underbrush. We was then ordered to halt and fire, which was done. About this time the company of 41st joined us on the extreme right. We stood but a short time until, I suppose, we was ordered to advance with double quick time. The musketry made such a noise I heard no order, but as others moved we all followed. The object I suppose was to dislodge them from their cover, and, if possible, to take the field-pieces, for without knowing or seeing (for the smoke was very dense) we, our company, came smack upon their field-piece which, when we advanced, I suppose they had abandoned. The General and his aid, no doubt, as they ought to, had a position that all was clear to them, but as the wind blew from the enemy we had their smoke and ours in our faces.

> Col. E. Cruikshank, ed., *Documentary History of the Campaign Upon the Niagara Frontier in 1812*, part IV (1908), pp. 77-9

To be wounded in such a battle, whether by lead musket ball or bayonet blade, was to risk almost certain death. A British private named Shadrach Byfield tells of his wound, received in action in what is now Michigan in January 1813.

It being now light, I saw a man come from the fence when I said to my comrade, 'There is a man, I'll have a shot at him.' Just as I said these words and pulled my trigger, I received a ball under my left ear and fell immediately; in falling I cut my comrade's leg with my bayonet. He exclaimed, 'Byfield is dead.' To which I replied, 'I believe I be,' and I thought to myself, is this death, or how men do die? As soon as I had recovered so as to raise my head from the ground, I crept away upon my hands and knees, and saw a sergeant in the rear, who said, 'Byfield, shall I take you to the doctor?' I said, 'Never mind me, go and help the men.' I got to the place where the doctor was, who when it came to my turn to be dressed, put a plaister to my neck and ordered me to go to a barn which was appointed for the reception of the wounded.

Recollections of the War of 1812 (1964), p. 17

Byfield was fortunate on that occasion. But at last, in the summer of 1814, he received a far more serious wound at Black Rock, New York. His fortitude, calmly related, is awesome.

About this time, I received a musket ball though my left arm, below the elbow. I went into the rear. One of my comrades, seeing that I was badly wounded, cut my belts for me and let them drop. I walked to the doctor, and desired him to take my arm off. He said it might be cured without it. . . .

After a few days, our doctor informed me that my arm must be taken off, as mortification had taken place. I consented, and asked one of my comrades, who had lately gone through a like operation, 'Bill, how is it to have the arm taken off?' He replied, 'Thee woo't know, when it's done.' They prepared to blind me, and had men to hold me; but I told them there was no need of that. The operation was tedious and painful, but I was enabled to bear it pretty well. I had it dressed, and went to bed. They brought me some mulled wine, and I drank it. I was then informed that the orderly had thrown my hand to the dung-heap. I arose, went to him, and felt a disposition to strike him. My hand was taken up and a few boards nailed together for a coffin, my hand was put into it and buried on the ramparts. The stump of my arm soon healed, and three days after I was able to play a game of fives, for a quart of rum.

Ibid., pp. 40-1

The bones of Shadrach Byfield's hand may still lie within the
ramparts of Fort Niagara, across the Niagara River from Niagara-
on-the-Lake, Ontario. The remarkable strength of spirit evident in
a man like Byfield appears to have been by no means rare. And such
spirit sometimes brought to the fratricidal tragedy of 1812 incidents
of cocky courage. A fine example is the well-documented 'Battle of
the Songs', which took place at sea in the last year of the war.

In May 1814, the crew of a captured American privateer, the *Prince*
de Neuchatel, was taken by HMS *Leander* and put in her cable tier.
Here they sang patriotic songs, celebrating their victories, to pass
the time and keep up their spirits. To combat this a choir of British
seamen was assembled round the hatch and the musical contest was
joined. But the Americans had more voices and more songs, so the
British began to sing of their victories over the French. A dreadful
din followed. A British officer forbade the Americans to continue,
but an outburst of Indian whoops followed this order. The prisoners
were then warned that if the noise did not cease marines would fire
into them. This provoked jeers and cries of 'Hurrah for Old Iron-
sides' and 'three cheers for the gallant Perry' so that the marines
withdrew. The following night the prisoners began again, but the
British officers, whose wardroom was above them and who had
suffered the most from the noise, arranged for forty-two pound shot
to be rolled along the decks, which caused a terrible noise and
effectually stopped the singing.
    E.S. Maclay, *History of the American Privateers* (1899), pp. 388-90

The War of 1812 had seen Canadians—both French and English—
fight sturdily in support of British Canada. The very resistance
against the 'republican' enemy, however, made evolution towards
democratic government in Canada difficult. By 1837, a desperate
land shortage and strangulation of government by a self-serving
clique in Lower Canada (Quebec) , and similar withholding of
rights and self-government in Upper Canada (Ontario), led to
armed rebellion. In Upper Canada the rebellion amounted to a
series of pathetic skirmishes.

About midnight our numbers increased, and towards morning I proposed
to many persons to march to Toronto, join such of the reformers there as
were ready, and endeavour to make ourselves master of the garrison and
musquets.
    To this it was objected, that I was uninformed of the strength of the

fortress, that the other townships had not yet joined the men from the upper country, that we were ignorant of the state of the city, and that gentlemen who had advised and urged on the movements, and even the executive who had ordered this premature Monday rising, stood aloof, and had neither joined us nor communicated with us.

Next day (Tuesday) we increased in number to 800, of whom very many had no arms, others had rifles, old fowling pieces, Indian guns, pikes, etc. Vast numbers came and went off again, when they found we had neither musquets or bayonets. . . .

About noon we obtained correct intelligence that with all his exertions, and including the college boys, Sir Francis [Bond Head] could hardly raise 150 supporters in town and country; and by one P.M. a flag of truce reached our camp near the city, the messengers being the Honourables Messrs. Rolph and (*Robert*, ed.) Baldwin, deputed by Sir Francis to ask what would satisfy us, I replied, 'Independence'; but sent a verbal message that we had no confidence in Sir F's word, he would have to send his messages in writing, and within one hour. I then turned round to Colonel Lount and advised him to march the men under his command at once into the city, and take a position near the Lawyer's Hall, and rode westward to Col. Baldwin's where the bulk of the rebels were, and advised an instant march to Toronto. We had advanced as far as the college avenue when another flag of truce arrived . . .

At a quarter to six the whole of our forces were near the toll bar, on Yonge-street (*at Bloor St today*, ed.) on our way to the city. I told them that I was certain there could be no difficulty in taking Toronto; that both in town and country the people had stood aloof from Sir Francis; that not 150 men and boys could be got to defend him; that he was alarmed, and had got his family on board a steamer, that 600 reformers were ready waiting to join us in the city, and that all we had to do was to be firm, and with the city would at once go down every vestige of foreign government in U.C.

It was dark, and there might be an ambush of some sort, I therefore told six riflemen to go ahead of us a quarter of a mile on the one side of the street, inside the fences, and as many more on the other side, and to fire in the direction in which they might see any of our opponents stationed. When within half a mile of the town, we took prisoners the Captain of their Artillery, a Lawyer, and the Sheriff's horse. Our riflemen ahead saw some 20 or 30 of the enemy in the road and fired at them, the 20 or 30, or some of them, fired at us, and instantly took to their heels and ran towards the town.

Unfortunately for the cause of Canadian liberation, the Patriots now reaped the fruit of Mackenzie's earlier folly in causing Colonel Anthony Anderson to be killed.

Our riflemen were in front, after them the pikemen, then those who had old guns of various kinds, and lastly those who carried only clubs and walkingsticks. Colonel Lount was at the head of the riflemen, and he and those in the front rank fired, . . . and fell flat on their faces, the next rank fired and did the same thing.

The patriots had drilled all fall as separate units. Lount's riflemen from Holland Landing had chosen a method of fighting that imitated in a rough fashion the normal army firing procedures of the time, firing in tiers with the front rows dropping to their knees after firing, to reload.

However, with the military commander, and commander of the pikemen, Anderson, dead, no one had co-ordinated the activities of the men from the different areas. When the Lloydtown pikemen and the others behind the riflemen saw their entire force drop in the dark, with the clamour and smoke of 100 or more rifles and muskets being discharged at once, they were sure they had walked into an ambush.

They beat an undisciplined retreat to the toll gate. They had taken only a couple of casualties but they refused to regroup for another march that night.

1837: Revolution in the Canadas, as told by William Lyon Mackenzie, edited by Greg Keilty (1974), pp. 175-7

Some of the little battles, however, were grim enough. This short but deadly fight took place on ice-bound Pelee Island in Lake Erie.

By March 3, there were 1000 men gathered on this 11,000 acre island. Once again their strategy was to march into Canada and establish a liberated zone.

Before they could move, the British army from Fort Malden was mobilized. There were four companies of the 32nd regiment and one of the 83rd along with twenty-one men from the St Thomas Cavalry, a few other volunteers and artillery.

They came upon the island at daybreak March 3. Above the camp flew 'a large tri-coloured flag with two stars and the word "Liberty" worked upon it'. The sentry sounded an alarm and the Patriots withdrew to the interior of the island to form up.

This time the British strategy of encirclement almost worked. Two companies of the 32nd Regiment were loaded on sleighs and took up a position behind them. The Patriot commander was Henry Van Rensselaer, a relative of the Navy Island general. He ordered a retreat but when they got to the south of the island the British were already drawn up in battle line.

Meanwhile, the St Thomas Cavalry were having a rough time alone and decided to join the 32nd on the south side of the island. This is how one of the troopers described the scene.

'As we proceeded we saw the sleighs retreat, and the soldiers were strung out in a long line across the ice like fence posts. The enemy were approaching them at a quick march. We could not see them just at first. They approached Captain Browne's force in a solid column, and then spread out in a line about the same length as that of the British infantry. There were about 500 of the enemy. Captain Browne had ninety men, and our troops then numbered but twenty-one. Both sides fired simultaneously. We got none of this volley. We were approaching at a gallop. We heard the enemy call out, "There comes the cavalry! Fire on them!" They did so and the bullets whistled around us. We were coming on their flank. We halted and fired. The infantry charged with fixed bayonets at that moment, in the face of a heavy fire from the enemy. When the infantry were within about six rods of the enemy the latter retreated in disorder . . . staining the snow for a quarter of a mile in width with blood.'

Thirty of the British were cut down but only four or five died. The Patriots were not so fortunate. Major Hoadley and Captain Van Rensselaer were killed along with 11 others. Eighteen were wounded.

Ibid., pp. 200-1

It was in Lower Canada that the rebellion had all the horror and tragedy of a bloody civil war. Any Canadian can take a sad pride in the sturdy resistance of a rag-tag force of French and English rebels against the British at Saint-Denis in 1837. Desperate men, taking up arms because they could think of no other solution, they confronted the regulars of Lieutenant-Colonel George Wetherall on the banks of the Richelieu River.

The brigade that was to move on St Denis from the north started on its way at three o'clock on Wednesday afternoon, November 22nd, from Montreal. Embarking on the steamer *St George* under the command of the quartermaster general, Colonel Sir Charles Gore, were the flank companies of the 24th Regiment, the light company of the 32nd, a detachment of Royal Artillery with a twelve-pounder howitzer, and a party of the Royal Montreal Cavalry under Cornet Campbell Sweeney. Deputy Sheriff Edouard-Louis-Antoine Juchereau-Duchesnay and Magistrate Pierre Leclère accompanied the troops, carrying warrants for the arrest of the *Patriotes* charged with high treason.

Having disembarked at Sorel at six o'clock in the evening, the brigade was joined by a company of the 66th Regiment. Now numbering about 300, it moved off at about ten o'clock toward St Denis, a village on the Richelieu of about 100 houses. Gore's instructions were to 'proceed . . . to St Denis . . . which I was directed to carry, and then move on rapidly to assist Lieutenant Colonel Wetherall, of the Royal Regiment, in his attack on St Charles'. Instead of following the direct route to St Denis, Gore, on learning that the village of St Ours was occupied by insurgents, determined to avoid the village by taking a back concession road. Mud reached to the knees of the soldiers as they tramped through the freezing rain. After eight hours of marching, Gore's force reached St Denis, exhausted, wet, and cold.

Word of the troop movement had already reached St Denis. The parish priest at Sorel, Curé Cayley, had sent a courier to the loyalist priest, Curé François-Xavier Demers at St Denis, alerting him of the movement of the regulars. It is unlikely that Demers would have told Papineau and Nelson this news, unless he did so in the attempt to frighten the chiefs out of the village. Yet by nightfall of November 22nd the chiefs in St Denis knew that troops would move in on them from Sorel. They had not expected this. The military headquarters was at St Charles and all its defences faced southwards in anticipation of an attack from Chambly or St Johns.

Nelson's hurried moves that night reflected his awareness of the troop movement from Montreal to Sorel. He pressed the village blacksmith, Jean-Baptiste Mignault, into the job of repairing muskets and supervising the casting of bullets. The blacksmith's helpers were Nelson's twenty-year-old son, Horace, and his medical student, Charles Dansereau. While Mignault was busy in St Denis, Nelson took ten men, including another blacksmith, Modeste Roy, across the river to St Antoine where he secured some lead and a sabre at Perrin's store. He probably inspected the supply of ammunition and powder in the store at the same time, for he decided to leave his men there to guard the store overnight.

As soon as Nelson returned to St Denis, he conferred hurriedly with the *Patriote* chiefs, Papineau and O'Callaghan, back from their day-long visit to St Charles. Others attending this crucial war council included Kimber, Perrault, and Bourdages. The decision was to fight. Those at the meeting urged Papineau to leave the village temporarily so that he would be out of the area of immediate military action. Whether they lost or won, the chiefs argued, he would then be in a better position to act as spokesman in negotiating a settlement with the civil and military authorities of the Crown. Papineau resisted these overtures, stubbornly refusing to budge. 'I have never preached armed revolt,' he insisted, 'only constitutional agitation, but since today the wine is poured, it is fitting that I drink it.' The chiefs gave up trying to persuade him to leave. Instead, they concentrated on defensive measures. Emissaries were sent to neighbouring parishes with the news of the imminent approach of the regulars and a summons to the *Patriotes* to hasten to St Denis with their arms and weapons. Like other villages under *Patriote* control, St Denis had elected its own captains from former militia men. These included François Jalbert, the old veteran of 1812, Jean-Baptiste Maillet, a former militia sergeant, François Mignault, an innkeeper, Charles Ollivier, and Jean-Baptiste Lussier. Nelson named Joseph-Edouard Mignault, a local notary, as his quartermaster.

At nearby St Ours, another group of about fifteen armed *Patriotes*, headed by Notary Calme Lenoblet Duplessis and *Patriote* Captain Joseph Duval, set out to imprison an elderly loyalist, baron Augustus de Diemar. Their plan was to send him to the *Patriote* prison at St Charles. Unlike Brown, Nelson did not imprison loyalists prior to November 22nd and he had no temporary jail arrangements. Nelson's lack of prison facilities was to create a problem for him shortly.

Colborne's despatch bearer, Lieutenant George Weir of the 32nd Regiment, reached Sorel after the brigade of regulars had moved off for St Denis. With some difficulty Weir hired a calèche and ordered the driver to head for St Denis with all possible speed. Following the direct route, the calèche reached St Denis about three A.M. Charles Dansereau described the excitement as the calèche rattled into St Denis at top speed only to be halted by one of Nelson's armed patrols. The town was experiencing bizarre scenes, but none topped the arrival of a British officer, in mufti, in advance of the troops. Nelson's astonishment was no less than that of the young officer when he discovered that Gore's brigade had not arrived and that he was alone in the heart of the insurgent territory. His calèche was soon surrounded by excited habitants and it was with some difficulty that Nelson got through to withdraw him from the crowd. Nelson brought Weir to his home, where he was immediately recognized by Ovide Perrault who knew him socially in Montreal. The young officer was put in a private room beside a stove to thaw out, for the long trip had been a cold one. If there had been any doubt that the troops were on their way toward St Denis, it was dispelled by Weir's arrival. Nelson's first move was to send a courier off to Brown at St Charles to alert him of Weir's capture and to say that he would send the prisoner to him for safe-keeping as 'the excitement was too great at St Denis'.

By five o'clock on the morning of Thursday, November 23rd, Nelson was mounted and ready to reconnoitre the roads and bridges leading into the town of Sorel. As he rode toward St Ours before dawn broke, he found himself almost face to face with the advancing British force. Quickly he withdrew and ordered his pickets to break up the bridges over the small streams that flowed into the Richelieu on the outskirts of St Denis. He then hastened back to the village to make what preparations he could to engage the Crown forces.

Contingents of *Patriotes* from neighbouring parishes were already beginning to arrive, prepared for battle, their officers soon supplanting those elected earlier in the fall by the men of St Denis. There was Bonaventure Viger of Boucherville, the hero of the Longueuil exploit against the Royal Montreal Cavalry, George-Etienne Cartier of St Antoine who had been joint corresponding secretary of the Permanent and Central Committee in the city, and Dr Napoléon-Eugène Duchénois of Varennes who had greeted most of the chiefs as they converged on his village from Montreal. Dr Thomas Bouthillier and Augustin Papineau of St Hyacinthe arrived with thirty or forty men. From St Charles a small party arrived that included the spy Michel-Jacques Vilbon. They had been about to set out on a raiding party to the store of William Chaffers in St Césaire when Brown countermanded the order and told them to hurry to St Denis by a back road.

The arrival of the latter group indicated the excellent communications maintained between Nelson and Brown, even on such a stormy and dramatic night. Nelson's first message to Brown alerting him that the captured British officer would be sent to the St Charles prison reached Brown by four o'clock that morning. His second message asking for reinforcements arrived about nine o'clock.

As the *Patriote* irregulars arrived, women, children, and non-combatants fled to the third and fourth concessions to the east of St Denis for safety. Nelson's family stayed in one of their farmhouses a mile and a half away from the fortified area. Walter Nelson, who was only seven at the time, watched the troops manoeuvring. He recalled that, as 'it was snowing some of the time and the ground freezing, the poor soldiers had a hard time of it'. As the regulars neared, Nelson ordered Captain Jean-Baptiste Maillet to transport Lieutenant Weir to St Charles. It was about 8:45 A.M. when Maillet, with his reluctant driver François-Toussaint Mignault, and another armed guard, Pierre Guertin, arrived at Nelson's home to fetch Weir. Weir had been invited to share breakfast with Papineau, O'Callaghan, Kimber, Charles Dansereau, and others in the house, but he refused either to eat or to have a glass of whiskey with them. When Maillet arrived, the British officer was in the dining room, guarded by two men. Weir had a presentiment that he would be killed; 'in spite of all our protestations that we made as well as we could in the English language,' Charles Dansereau said, 'we could not convince him otherwise.'

Weir's hands were tied as he took his place beside the driver, Mignault. Captain Maillet, armed with a sword, sat with Guertin in the rear. Maillet secured Weir by passing a leather strap around his waist and holding it. As the guards and prisoner left Nelson's home, they were met by young Horace Nelson, who cautioned them to be careful. Weir asked Horace to untie him, promising that he would go quietly. It is unlikely that young Nelson interfered with the security arrangements of the armed guard. As they travelled through the village, the driver, Mignault, noticed that Weir's hands were turning blue from the cold. He gave him his gloves, and soon after Captain Maillet undid the strap around his body, but Weir was unaware that a leather strap was still attached to his back and held by Maillet. As the road became more treacherous with the frozen ice, Mignault suggested that the third guard, Pierre Guertin, could leave as two men were sufficient to guard the officer. Captain Maillet agreed and Guertin got out. The wagon made its way past the St Denis church. The constant clanging of the church bell added to the urgency of the moment. Curé François-Xavier Demers had ordered the beadle to stop sounding the alarm, but the excited beadle continued to tug the bell rope.

Once Weir was on the way to St Charles, Nelson remained at his house just long enough to take Louis-Antoine Dessaulles upstairs to see Papineau and O'Callaghan. Dessaulles had travelled from St Hyacinthe with urgent despatches concerning the summons that Nelson's emissary had brought to St Hyacinthe during the night. This summons had put the men of St Hyacinthe in a quandary. They had been expecting to go to the defence of St Charles. When they got Nelson's appeal for aid, they sent Dessaulles to St Denis with a particular injunction to ask Papineau himself whether they should march to St Denis or to St Charles.

It was during this meeting that Nelson again strongly urged Papineau to leave the village. 'I beg you to leave,' Nelson said. 'You ought not to expose yourself needlessly. It is not here that you are needed. We shall have need of you later. We are your arms. You are the head.' Nelson asked Papineau to be reasonable. 'One man more or less will not change anything. Go to St Hyacinthe and await the results. If they turn against us, then it will be up to you to begin again.' Papineau turned to O'Callaghan and asked, 'What do you think, doctor?' O'Callaghan's reply was laconic. 'It's a matter of indifference to me. If you remain, I shall remain. If you leave, then I shall part with you.' O'Callaghan was the man upon whom Papineau leaned almost to excess after his rupture with his other English-speaking colleague, John Neilson. His preference for O'Callaghan's company and advice had already caused jealousy within the party. O'Callaghan may have been an able propagandist, but when the war of words gave way to one of bullets, he proved to be something of a handicap. On that fateful morning, Papineau made his own decision. He remained at St Denis.

Nelson wasted no more time. He hurried back to the fortified house to complete his arrangements for deploying his irregulars as effectively as possible. The northeastern approach to the village had certain advantages as far as defensive fortifications were concerned. The massively constructed stone building owned by Madame Georges Saint-Germain was situated on the main road for Sorel. Facing it across the street were five other smaller houses that the insurgents loopholed and occupied. Nelson's distillery, on the waterfront just behind the Saint-Germain building, provided another natural defensive site. Along the road leading into the village, Nelson's forces occupied some thirteen houses.

A barricade was hastily erected across the road in front of the Saint-Germain building. About 100 armed men took up positions inside, some on the second and third storeys, and others in the attic and on the ground floor. Among Nelson's sharpshooters was the wealthy St Denis merchant, Louis Pagé, whose wife that morning had made him a breastplate of layers and layers of paper. There was also David Bourdages, who calmly smoked his pipe while he waited to fire. Augustin Laflèche recited the rosary just before he saw the advance guard of the regulars and picked one off. Beside him was Captain Louis-Renault Blanchard of St Hyacinthe, one of Salaberry's old Voltigeurs, and George-Etienne Cartier, with his cousin, Henri. At Louis Pagé's house was Dr Joseph Allaire of St Antoine, who was the first to fire on the advance scouts.

Outside the stone house other sharpshooters were posted in ditches or behind the houses and barns occupied by insurgents. Thirty men were stationed near Nelson's distillery under the command of a professional hunter named Courtmanche. Another forty, commanded by André Beauregard, were waiting in ambush along the rear road. In all, some 800 men answered the alarm bell and placed themselves at Nelson's disposal, though at the start of the battle 'only a part of the insurgents took their places for fighting, and the others retired'. In his account of the battle, Nelson speaks of ninety or a hundred men rushing to his succour at first. At the start of the battle, then, there were about 200 armed men all told. But this was not the whole story. Unarmed men stood by ready to take the muskets of those who fell. In addition, the one field piece possessed by the insurgents, a parade cannon belonging to the militia, was charged with chain and scrap iron and placed in front of the fortified building to sweep the road clear of advancing troops. As long as ammunition lasted and the firearms worked, the battle could go on.

Gore expected little resistance at St Denis—he would occupy the village within an hour and then move on to St Charles. He was soon disabused of this idea. As soon as his troops safely crossed the first bridge above St Ours, he observed an armed party leaving the lower bridge to flank his line of march. Gore ignored this party, moving on 'to my point, which was now frequently impeded by the breaking up of the bridges'. Cornet Campbell Sweeney of the Royal Montreal Cavalry was sent ahead to disperse the *Patriote* skirmishers who were breaking up the bridges. As the troops neared, a body of armed men skirted their left flank in a wood. 'All the houses along the road were deserted,' Gore said, 'and on nearing St Denis, I was attacked by skirmishers occupying houses and barns on the road and along the banks of the Richelieu.' These skirmishers were rapidly dispersed by the advance guard under Captain Frederick Markham.

Instead of entering a sleepy village on the Richelieu, Gore quickly realized that he faced a fortified area, occupied, he thought, by at least 1500 determined men. Gore divided his force into three columns. One followed the river, the centre approached St Denis by way of the main road, and the third moved to the left in an attempt to surround the village from the rear. The latter move was the one most feared by the insurgents, for this was their weakest point.

As Gore's advance guard moved up, two of the men were immediately slain by sharpshooters from within the St Germain building. Gore quickly sent forward three companies under Captains William Joshua Crompton of the 66th and F.T. Maitland and Henry William Harris of the 24th to reinforce the advance. The Howitzer was brought up and positioned to the right of the road, some 350 yards from the fortified building. Each time one of the Artillerymen tried to sight the field piece and prepare it for firing, he was picked off by one of Nelson's men. Three regulars went down in quick succession before a fourth soldier succeeded in lighting the linstock. Off went the cannon ball straight through the second-floor window of the fortified house, smashing against an interior wall and killing three insurgents outright. At the same time another *Patriote*, Pierre Minet, was struck by a bullet as he neared the windows.

One of the insurgents, Modeste Roy, who was on the second floor when the ball came smashing through, panicked, 'Fear seized me,' he admitted candidly, 'and I hid myself in the cellar.' The blacksmith was not the only one to panic. A number of Nelson's men took off, some to hide in the chimney, others out rear windows. Nelson rose to the occasion. He threatened to cut the throat of any other man who tried to retreat. Then he ordered most of his men to the first floor where they would be less exposed.

Outside, the *Patriote* cannon stood silent. Its gunner, Pierre Bourgeois, seeing how easily the exposed British Artillerymen were cut down by the *Patriote* forces, prudently kept out of sight. The British hauled their cannon to a safer but less effective position to the left of the road. From here, the Artillerymen kept pounding away at the stone house for about five hours without any appreciable dint being made on it or its occupants. When the cannonading first began, Joseph Sicard, the Dessaulles family servant who had brought Louis-Antoine Dessaulles from St Hyacinthe, was busily getting the horse harnessed to the carriage, ready to get out of the village before the battle. As he did so, the wagon carrying Lieutenant Weir drove past. An instant later he heard a shout, 'My God! My God!' and glanced round to see what was happening. At the sound of the cannon, Weir had leaped off the wagon, shouting, 'Let me see the soldiers!' Unknown to Weir, a leather strap was still fastened at his back. As he jumped, the strap caught, dragging him to his knees while the wagon continued to move forward. Captain Maillet, startled by Weir's sudden move, jumped down from the wagon and began to strike the British officer with a sword. Before he had hit him three of four blows, the sword broke. Weir then began to move in the direction of the cannon fire, at which Maillet cried out for help and a crowd suddenly converged on them. By the time the driver, Mignault, had stopped the horse and wagon and returned to where the officer was, he could scarcely get through the crowd. When he did so, he found a villager, Joseph Pratte, viciously attacking the prisoner with a dragoon sword. Weir, now mortally wounded in several places, was still standing with his hands over his head to ward off the blows. Several in the crowd shouted to Mignault, 'Finish him! Finish him!' but the driver refused to shoot the officer. Just then Captain François Jalbert rode up, a sabre at his side and a pistol in his saddle. Seeing the condition of Weir, he, too, shouted, 'Finish him! Finish him!' Louis Lussier then aimed his musket at the dying officer. Three times it misfired before the *coup de grâce* was administered. Maillet and Mignault quickly picked up Weir's body and threw it into the nearby streamlet. Stones were thrown over the body to cover it. Dessaulles's servant watched in horror. Then he hurried with the harnessing of the carriage, fetched his master, and sped out of the village toward St Hyacinthe.

When Captain Maillet and Mignault returned to the fortified building to confess to Nelson what had happened, Nelson angrily shouted, 'Three armed men could control one unarmed man.' They replied simply that they had been too excited. Nelson retorted that they were 'cursed beasts who had done an evil deed'. While Nelson was receiving the news of Weir's death, Papineau and O'Callaghan were receiving a hurried visit from Edouard-Raymond Fabre, the bookseller whose shop in Montreal had been the headquarters of the *Patriotes*. Fabre, who had made his way out of Montreal the previous week in company with his brother-in-law, Charles-Ovide Perrault, had come from St Antoine at about 9:30 that morning. His news was probably that troops were on the move not only from Sorel but also from Chambly against St Charles. It was likely this news which stimulated Papineau to action. Immediately after the brief visit from Fabre, Papineau and O'Callaghan exchanged their city attire for country dress. Papineau donned a tuque and hooded cloak of coarse cloth. Horses were brought for them; Jean-Baptiste Masse handed them two pistols, and off they went. Aware that Nelson had sent an appeal to Brown for reinforcements, Papineau and O'Callaghan rode off to try to intercept these troops. Had Papineau and O'Callaghan intended to go to St Hyacinthe, there would have been no need for a disguise. They could, like Dessaulles earlier, have taken a carriage and galloped away by the rear of the village. This route was still open, for *Patriotes* continued to move toward St Denis all day by the rear concession. Instead, Papineau and O'Callaghan remained at the rear of St Denis most of the day. They questioned habitants as they approached St Denis, asking whether they came from St Charles and if the troops had arrived there yet. One habitant asked Papineau why he was away from St Denis. Papineau replied that he was going to St Charles for reinforcements and would return to St Denis later. Eventually Papineau found what he was looking for. The St Charles contingent under Dr Henri-Alphonse Gauvin appeared on the out-skirts of St Denis. Addressing Gauvin, whom he knew well, Papineau spoke only in English. When Gauvin assured him that there were no regulars at St Charles and no threat of attack expected there, Papineau told Gauvin that he feared 'The Canadians are at a disadvantage at St Denis.' He ordered Gauvin and his party to muster all the troops they could find along the way and to take them to St Denis.

Reassured about St Charles, Papineau and O'Callaghan then set out to do just what Nelson and the other chiefs had been urging them to do: to remain in the outer concessions until the battle was decided one way or the other. This was easier said than done. It turned bitterly cold and they were without food. Several times they met contingents of *Patriotes* who, not recognizing Papineau in his *étoffe du pays* costume, treated him with suspicion. Several times they lost their way as the late November day darkened early. They eventually stumbled on a route to St Hyacinthe and made their way, cold, wet, and hungry, to the home of Papineau's brother, Augustin Papineau.

When Gauvin's contingent from St Charles reached St Denis, the battle was far from decided. Gauvin was immediately detailed to go to the La Miotte River at the rear of the village to post sentries there and weaken the bridge so as to make it dangerous should the regulars attempt to cross it to surround the village. By noon, the redcoats were becoming less conspicuous as they began to take cover behind fences and wood piles. In an attempt to penetrate the fortified building, Captain Frederick Markham with Lieutenant John Inglis and some men of the Light Company of the 32nd darted toward the house just across from it. They drove the insurgents out of the house at the point of the bayonet, but Markham was wounded severely in three places. At this time, there was some defection within Nelson's ranks. Among those who furtively quit the village was Nelson's medical student, Charles Dansereau, who headed for the American border.

As Nelson's supply of ammunition and powder was running low by two o'clock, he sent George-Etienne Cartier with some men to St Antoine to replenish it. Not only did Cartier get across the Richelieu and back safely with the much-needed munitions, but other barges carrying reinforcements from Contrecoeur, St Ours, and Verchères sailed past the regulars unharmed, the *Patriote* soldiers defiantly singing their national songs. Gore was careful to explain to Colborne how these reinforcements got through to the *Patriotes*. 'During [our] operations, the rebels were crossing the Richelieu in large bateaux, from St Antoine, but I could not spare shot from the fortified house to obstruct their passage.' According to the insurgents, he did spare at least one shot. The charge came crashing near their boat, broke the oar of the ferryman, and tore away part of the ferry, but the ferryman ordered the twenty *Patriotes* to lie down while he continued to row toward the landing near Nelson's distillery. Had Gore kept his howitzer trained on the barges bringing over the reinforcements from St Antoine, the outcome of the battle might have been different. These reinforcements were the men who turned the tide of battle in favour of the *Patriotes*. They were at the rear of the village when Gore, in a last attempt to crash the *Patriote* defence cordon, sent 140 men on the double across the fields to the left. As the regulars made an encircling movement, they were met and forced back by the reinforcements from St Antoine and by a group of sharpshooters under Captain André Beauregard.

As the afternoon wore on, both sides reserved their fire for sure targets. When Ovide Perrault saw some *Patriote* pickets unwittingly expose themselves, he drew Nelson's attention to it, saying he would warn them of their danger. Nelson shouted, 'No, no, Perrault. Don't go; I forbid you.' Perrault protested that he would run, but Nelson replied, 'Don't go. You are a dead man if you do it.' Unheeding, Perrault dashed out the door and before he had darted many steps, he was mortally wounded, the only *Patriote* chief to be killed south of the St Lawrence.

By mid-afternoon, Gore concluded that 'the whole country was in arms'. No impression had been made on the fortified house by the cannonading, and as the soldiers' sixty rounds of ammunition were almost expended, he was faced with a decision. Either he had to assault the house 'so well defended and flanked by others loopholed, or to fall back before the bridge in my rear could be broken down.' Reluctantly Gore admitted, 'The hazard of a failure under such circumstances, and the jaded condition of the men, frost having succeeded the rain and snow, and their clothes freezing on them, determined me to fall back.' It was a hard decision for the officers and men, many of whom wore decorations from the Peninsular War.

As the *Patriotes* watched the regulars retreating, their astonishment turned to elation. Dr Joseph Allaire found the battle worth it all, even though his brother received a bullet through the cheek. 'I never had so much fun in all my life,' Allaire exclaimed after the battle. A comrade shared his sentiments. Philippe-Napoléon Pacaud commented drily, 'I don't know how many I killed, but I fired without remorse. It was not so much from a sentiment of insults and injustices, but the old instinct of traditional hatred of the races that awoke in us; we were fighting despotism, but it was above all the English that we loved to aim at,' a somewhat surprising admission, considering that his immediate military commander was an Englishman.

Elinor Kyte Senior, *Redcoats and Patriotes: The Rebellions in Lower Canada 1837-38* (1985), pp. 78-87

However brave the rebels may have been, the British army was a formidable adversary. A few days later, at Saint-Charles, not far from Saint-Denis, the redcoats reasserted the authority of the colonial government. The horror of the killing still lies somewhere in the collective memory of Quebecers. War had come to them again, and they had fought with a valour all the more heart-rending for its futility.

Not having received a reply from his request for a parley with Brown, Wetherall commenced action. He ordered the regulars to advance to a second position about 100 yards from the breastworks. The insurgents under their local leaders, Siméon Marchessault and Eusèbe Durocher, kept up such an effective fire that the first line of infantry had to lie down to avoid the barrage. Wetherall spotted the weakness of the insurgents' abatis. Its height of four feet tended to throw the elevation of their muskets off so that their firing passed over the regulars as long as the latter kept their heads well down. More of a problem for Wetherall's forces was the severe strafing from Desrivières's squad in the woods on the right. When the regulars attempted to storm Desrivières's position, the attack became so uncertain that the Grenadier Company of the Royals was sent to reinforce it. Once or twice the position of the regulars was so dubious that the officers considered a withdrawal. Wetherall's horse was shot from under him. So, too, were the chargers of Major Henry Warde of the Royals and of Captain Eleazar David of the Royal Montreal Cavalry.

After about two hours of indecisive action, Wetherall took the offensive. He ordered his three centre companies to fix bayonets and charge, with himself in the lead. Once the order to charge was given, the Royal Scots rose with a roar. Even this did not unnerve the insurgents. They redoubled their efforts with a galling fire that raked the earth in every direction. Some dwellings to the right of the breastworks were quickly taken by the regulars, but the other barns and outbuildings were so well fortified and so obstinately defended, that it took twenty minutes of sharp fighting to reduce them. The breastworks were easy to scale because the insurgents had made the mistake of filling the earth between the tree trunks from outside the abatis. As the insurgents saw the naked steel glinting in the sun, most withdrew hastily from the breastworks, for none had bayonets for hand-to-hand fighting. Marchessault galloped to the village to gather up his papers from his home and free his animals. Once he gained the outer concessions, he tried, unsuccessfully, to rally some of the insurgents. Bonaventure Viger was one of several men who jumped over the bank of the river into the icy Richelieu and managed to swim across to St Marc.

After the breastworks were taken and most of the insurgents were in retreat, some fifty appeared on bended knees with their arms reversed as though in an act of surrender. As the regulars approached expecting to make the men prisoners, the insurgents suddenly assumed an attitude of attack, killing one sergeant and wounding a number of soldiers. Lord Beauclerk reported that 'this act of treachery caused . . . a general massacre which, whilst it lasted, was indeed dreadful'. Boucher-Belleville gave a different account of the last moments of the battle. He said that some of the *Patriotes*, believing that Brown had fled before the battle started, were disheartened and fled or fought slackly. Then when the charge came, they laid down their arms and asked for quarter, but the troops 'massacred them with a barbarity worthy of the ancient savages of America'.

Wetherall's report of the battle stated tersely, 'The slaughter of the rebels was great; only sixteen prisoners were made. I have counted 56 bodies, and many more were killed in the buildings and their bodies burnt.' The action had lasted almost two hours. Unlike the action at St Denis, where soldier and insurgent agreed on the vigour and bravery of both sides and all testified to the kind treatment shown to the wounded troops left behind, the action at St Charles has had mixed reports.

Brown's account of the battle belittles the insurgents, minimizes the number who remained to fight, and gives the impression of chaos, unpreparedness, and even cowardice. Boucher-Belleville's account is not that different. On the other hand, the victors of St Charles praised the determination and bravery of the insurgents. A sergeant of the Grenadier Company of the Royals reported that 'every building was loop-holed and obstinately defended . . . the men had to fire through loopholes to dislodge the rebels.' Reports of the battle carried to Upper Canada dispelled a notion held by some there 'that the Canadians are cowards'. A captain of the Royals assured the grand master of the Orange lodges, Ogle Robert Gowan, that the Canadians 'fought like devils at St Charles'. Making every allowance for the victors' exaggeration of the resistance they had met at St Charles, the fact remains that irregular local troops withstood for two hours a seige by some 406 regulars and twenty Royal Montreal Cavalrymen, and dispersed only after a bayonet charge led by one of the top line regiments, the Royal Scots.

Ibid., pp. 96-8

Courage and the ability to perform well in a military situation were characteristic of Canadians under arms. If the men were shaky in battle, it was usually because of bad leadership or misunderstand-

ing of the situation, as at Ridgeway, Ontario, in 1866, when Canadian militia ran unnecessarily from a Fenian force of armed Irish veterans of the American Civil War.

For the Fenians, the battle was not going according to plan. The Canadian militiamen had not taken to their heels. Instead, they came on at what seemed a determined pace. It was the Fenians who began to flee, drifting back in ones and twos. The chief problem was that the woods, orchards and undergrowth made it impossible to catch more than glimpses of the advancing troops. Suddenly, it began to occur to some Fenians that these were not militiamen at all but seasoned British regulars. For all that Starr and other Fenian officers could do, the panic in the front ranks became general. With the contagion spreading to the main body, a furious John O'Neill, accompanied by other mounted officers, galloped forward to rally the men. If they failed, the battle would be over in a few minutes and all of them would be helpless fugitives.

A quarter of a mile away, Booker had dismounted from his awkward perch on horseback and found himself standing by Gillmor and Otter. Suddenly, from the road ahead, came shouts of 'Cavalry! Look out for the Cavalry!' A few men of the 13th came pelting down the track, driven by the glimpse of horses in the bush ahead. 'Cavalry,' shouted a red-faced Booker, 'Prepare for Cavalry!'

For that order, there was only one response. The Queen's Own had practised the manoeuvre only a week before at the great sham battle. Gillmor snapped out the orders, bugles blared and the five companies of riflemen in the centre doubled forward to form a square, a tightly packed clump of men, standing and kneeling, the sun glinting off their fixed bayonets. A few redcoats from the 13th mingled in the mass. The astonished Fenians could hardly believe it. It was their first real target all morning. After a few seconds to clear their minds of thoughts of retreat, they began pumping bullet after bullet into the dense cluster of men.

Almost as quickly, Booker realized his mistake. 'Extend!' he shouted, 'Reform column.' Two of the companies, Nos. 1 and 2, did so. The others stood where they were. At once Gillmor realized that they must be moved back out of the line of fire. 'Sound the retire,' he commanded his bugler. The notes blared out, to be repeated by other buglers in earshot. Then, when the order was apparently ignored by the two extended companies, the call was repeated.

All at once, a shiver of apprehension spread through the militia force. Why retire? For most of the troops within sound of the bugles, the battle had been going beautifully. Still, the order was plain. The three companies which had formed the centre of the square turned about and, with their backs to the Fenians, began to march. Through the woods to their rear, they could see scarlet tunics. 'Reinforcements,' someone shouted. The cry was repeated, spreading along the line as parched throats gave vent to their excitement.

They were not reinforcement but the three remaining companies of the 13th. So far, they had seen little of the battle. Through the smoke which hung over the windless field, they had glimpsed the square forming and then, inexplicably, disintegrating. Now the Queen's Own men were marching back at them, shouting. By God, the battle was lost. The bugle sounds proved it. For the raw youngsters of the 13th, it was enough. The ranks disintegrated as men fled for their lives.

As the red-coated militiamen broke and ran, the contagion of panic spread to the three companies of Queen's Own. Behind them, almost invisible through the trees and smoke, they could hear the gasping and pounding feet of running men. It was the sound of forward companies of the 13th, racing back to join the main body. For the men of the Queen's Own, it meant something else. Everyone was running away. Suddenly, they too broke ranks and fled down the hill toward Ridgeway.

A few seconds of miscalculation and inexperience had utterly transformed the battle. For Gillmor, Otter and, especially, for Booker, it was utterly bewildering. In utter dismay, they turned and followed the terrified throng down the hill.

Desmond Morton, *The Canadian General Sir William Otter*
(1974), pp. 33-5

Later Fenian incursions were dealt with successfully for the most part. The next serious threat to the authority of the Canadian government would be the Northwest Rebellion of 1885, and the militia army that struggled west under General Middleton to deal with the Métis and their Indian allies did creditably enough. Here Sam Steele, a stalwart member of the Northwest Mounted Police who had become the commander of scouts and cavalry of the Alberta Field Force under General Strange, tells how the Force set out to rescue captives held by rebels and capture those responsible for the murder of several people at Frog Lake on 2 April.

On the 20th the first column, under General Strange, pulled out from Calgary. I was in command of the advance guard, and my force was small for the work. There were 175 teams and the rest of the force to protect. Nothing that caution could dictate was neglected. The start in the morning was like a circus. The horses, with few exceptions, had seldom been ridden, and bucked whenever mounted, until two or three days had gentled them. This little performance interested the men from Montreal as they gazed at the gyrations of the cow-puncher soldiers and Mounted Police.

The scouting of the men the whole way and at all times was excellent and the discipline the very best. The cowboy has no superior in the world, and in spite of his free life he takes to the order of military experience as if he were born to it. The Mounted Police and the scouts were, of course, British subjects, but there were in the ranks several American cow-punchers and broncho busters, first-class men, ready for hard work, good-tempered and obedient.

On the 25th we reached the Red Deer, 90 miles from Calgary. The stream was much swollen and rising rapidly. The following day the 65th was sent across the river to scout the dense woods and to cover the passage. The ford was so deep that the waggon boxes of the transport had to be raised on the bolsters to prevent the supplies from getting wet, and several carts were swept away and recovered with difficulty.

At the Blind Man's River, 8 miles further on, General Strange received a dispatch from the Rev. John McDougall, who had arrived at Edmonton with his scouts, to the effect that the pace was safe. He approved the general's projected movement to the eastward along the North Saskatchewan to restore the settlers to their homes. Many of them had taken to the woods for refuge from the Indians, and were likely to die of starvation. This movement had already been thought out, and it had been ascertained that scows could be built to transport the gun, infantry, and supplies down the river. As I had been over that part of the country before and knew the trails and the settlements, he called me to his tent to discuss the route. After further consideration he sent orders to Mr McDougall to construct the scows and boats to transport the troops and supplies to Fort Pitt.

On the evening before we arrived at the Battle River the Rev. George Mackay, a brother of Mr Thomas Mackay, of Prince Albert, came into camp, having ridden 200 miles from Fort Macleod to join the column and offer his services in any capacity. Brave as a lion, an excellent horseman, a good shot and speaking Cree fluently, he was just the man for the cavalry, to whom the general very kindly attached him as chaplain!

At the Battle River we were joined by Fathers Lacombe and Scollen, well known to many of us, who had been busy with the

Indians to induce them to keep the peace. We also had confirmation of the report that the Indians of Bobtail's and Ermine Skin's bands had plundered the Hudson's Bay Company's stores. Those chiefs were with the priests, but the general refused to shake hands with them; they had had for years an unsavoury reputation, and he warned them that on the conduct of themselves and their bands their future treatment would depend. They were a most forbidding pair, and their bands the most depraved in the north west. Even in the days when the buffalo were plentiful the majority of them preferred to loiter about the posts on the frontier rather than make an honest livelihood. They were 'coffeecoolers' of the worst type.

We arrived at Edmonton on May 1 and were met by Major Griesbach, my old comrade, who was in command at Fort Saskatchewan, where he had under his protection the whole of the Beaver Lake refugees. My three brothers, Richard, Godfrey, and James, were at Edmonton, and were sworn in as scouts. The Home Guard there did much to calm the fears of the people from the settlement who, on hearing of the massacres and murders, had taken refuge in Edmonton, which at that time was a very small place but of great promise. The company was disbanded the day after the arrival of General Strange's column and the men returned to work on their farms in the vicinity.

On the morning of the 6th I moved east by the old Edmonton-Pitt-Carlton trail, with 110 Steele's Scouts under Captain Oswald, 25 Mounted Police under Lieut. J.A. Coryell, two companies of the 65th under Captain Prevost, and a large waggon train of supplies in charge of Mr John Colman, late of the NWMP. We were the advance and flank guards of the river column which was to be moved by scow down the Saskatchewan.

Before the general left Edmonton he was given a great deal of unnecessary trouble which caused delay to the advance. Objections were made to him by a senior officer to the effect that the construction of the boats was faulty, that the power of resistance of the flour sacks, the only means available for the protection of the men in the boats, should be tested, and finally a request was made to condemn a large proportion of the ammunition issued to the troops. This sort of thing was straight obstruction, and was met by General Strange in a characteristic manner. He ordered a board to assemble and take the evidence of experienced Hudson's Bay Company navigators and boat builders, the penetration of the flour sacks was left to hostile bullets, and those who objected to the quality of the ammunition were advised to reserve their fire for short ranges. The boats were reported fit for service, and the troops held in readiness to embark.

One night the 65th, according to orders, had tied up their scows for the night and were resting, when one of their sentries gave the alarm of Indians! No more was necessary for the corps. They were under arms in a moment and, led by their gallant commander, charged up the heights with loud cheers and swept the prairie with a shower of bullets. Five of my scouts who were out had to lie down in a deep hollow, where there was cover for themselves and their horses, until it was discovered that the sentry's Indians were young poplars waving in the wind!

The first news of the rising had been received by Inspector Dickens from Mr Rae, the Indian agent at Battleford, 90 miles east of Pitt. It was to the effect that the country was in a state of rebellion, and that the Indians were much excited, but that he had hopes that Dickens and sub-agent Quinn would endeavour to prevent Big Bear and his people from going to Battleford. On receipt of the report Dickens at once advised Quinn to come in if he considered that there was serious danger, and offered to reinforce him if he could not leave. Quinn replied at once that the Indians at Frog Lake were perfectly quiet, and that he was confident that he could keep them there by feeding them well and treating them kindly; but, as the presence of the detachment of Mounted Police might excite them, he would send Corporal Sleigh and party to the fort.

The corporal and his men arrived on April 2 and reported to Dickens that the white people at Frog Lake had at first decided that they would go to Fort Pitt, but Quinn and Farm-Instructor Delaney were determined to remain at their posts, and the others had made up their minds to stay with them. Corporal Sleigh at first refused to leave without the white women, but Quinn insisted that he should leave without them, and gave the corporal a letter to Dickens, explaining why the Mounted Police left and asserting that the Indians were quiet.

Sergeant Martin had been at Onion Lake the same day and found the Indians excited, firing their rifles and yelling, and they told him that they had been informed that 2000 soldiers were coming to kill them, but the sergeant told them to keep quiet as there was no danger whatever. This had the effect of calming them for a time. On the 2nd Sergeant Roby, who had been at Onion Lake, reported to Inspector Dickens that the Indians were talking of something which had taken place at Frog Lake, and that Mr Simpson, of the Hudson's Bay Company, on his way there with freight, had hurried on there hoping to be in time to prevent mischief. Inspector Dickens had redoubled his guard but, although he had the letter of the agent at Battleford, he had little faith in the rumours of Indian war talk. Mr Quinn had promised to send a messenger in the event of anything serious, but in the afternoon Mr and Mrs Mann with their children came in from Onion Lake, the Indians there having informed them that all the white people at Frog Lake had been murdered and that they must fly for their lives, as the Indians had risen and were going to kill all the whites in the country.

On receipt of this news preparations were made at Fort Pitt to receive an attack, the windows and doors of the dwellings and store-houses were barricaded and loop-holes made in the walls. It would have been impossible, however, to have held the post in the night time, for it covered so much ground and had so many combustibles, such as hay and firewood, that it could have been set on fire at any time. It would have required at least 200 well-armed men to defend it, but Dickens prepared to hold out to the last. On April 4 Henry Quinn, a relative of the agent, arrived at the fort and reported that he and the remainder of the white people at Frog Lake had been made prisoners by the Indians and were being taken to camp when he broke away on hearing them say that all the white men would be killed.

He was hotly pursued for a considerable distance, and had with difficulty succeeded in making his escape. The same day the Rev. Mr and Mrs Quinney were escorted into Fort Pitt by four of the Onion Lake Indians, and later, John Saskatchewan, a well-known plain-hunter and guide, arrived there with a letter to Dickens, advising him to proceed to Battleford by the north trail. This he refused to do as he had not enough transport and the Indians could easily overtake them travelling slowly, as they would have to do with the women and children, and if attacked in the open they would have to protect them and would be worse off than if they were in the Hudson's Bay post. The civilians were of the same opinion, and, as matters were getting very serious, Dickens wrote to Battleford, asking for 50 men, as under the present circumstances it was impossible to move.

No reply was received to this letter, the bearer having been intercepted, but for all that there was no excuse for leaving the people in Fort Pitt in such a terrible plight. Battleford was perfectly safe and could not only have defended itself but have spared more than 50 men to assist those in distress. It was reported later that 50 NCOs and men had volunteered to proceed to the relief of Fort Pitt, but were not permitted to go.

In the meantime Dickens continued to strengthen the post, and a scow was being built by the carpenters of the Hudson's Bay Company, when on April 12 a large body of Indians appeared on the rising ground to the north of the post. They had with them as prisoner Cameron, Halpin, and Dufresne, of the Hudson's Bay Company. The latter was sent to the fort with a flag of truce. He brought letters from Mr Halpin, in which he stated that Big Bear demanded the surrender of the arms and ammunition. This offer was, of course, contemptuously refused, and shortly after this Mr W.J. McLean, believing the Indians to be a peace party, went out to interview the chief, and the latter agreed to keep them quiet that night. But next morning he sent a demand that the Mounted Police leave the place at once. Dickens refused all overtures and would not permit the Indians to approach the fort.

Later on in the day Mr McLean went out again and was taken prisoner, and constables Cowan and Loasby and Special Constable Quinn, who had been out to ascertain what had occurred at Frog Lake, came upon the Indians, who lay between them and the fort. Young Cowan, a fiery, hot-headed lad, in charge of the party, decided to ride through them. Quinn would not agree to this, and turned back to find his way round. Cowan and his horse were shot, and the Indians rushed forward and drove muskrat spears into the poor fellow's body, tearing them out again to increase his torture. Loasby's horse was shot under him, but he got up and ran towards the fort, the Indians pursuing him for a considerable distance, until he was struck down wounded, and feigned death, while the redskins took his belt, bandolier, and ammunition. By that time the men in the fort had opened fire, compelling them to retreat, while Loasby, under the cover of their rifles, staggered into the fort.

Shortly after this incident darkness came on, and with it a message from Mr McLean directing his family to join him. The remainder of the civilians prepared to depart with them and surrender to Big Bear, whereupon Dickens, finding that their minds were made up, decided that it was now his duty to see to the safety of his men, who had remained at their post for the protection of the people. He caused the spare arms to be destroyed, collected the food and ammunition and, under cover of darkness, embarked his detachment on the scow. Mrs McLean did not leave the post until the last man was on board, knowing that it was unlikely that any of the Indians would come to the fort until she went to the camp. The party eventually arrived safely at Battleford.

While these events were transpiring Quinn had gone round to the Saskatchewan, moved along the shelter of the cut bank until the fort was between him and the Indians, and galloped into it to find to his horror that it was in their possession. He was seized and would have been put to death, had he not said that he was a friend of Mr McLean, who had done a good turn to the leader when he was in a scrape some years previously. This saved his life, and he was conducted to the camp and placed with the prisoners, amongst whom were Interpreter Pritchard, of the Frog Lake reserve, and the two white ladies from there, Mrs Gowanlock and Mrs Delaney, whose husbands had been put to death. They owed their lives to Mr Pritchard, who, seeing them in the possession of one of the Indians, gave him a couple of horses for them. This purchase of the ladies is explained by the custom of the Indians in war, which gives them the right to the captive, to dispose of him or her as he pleases.

The day after our arrival before the ruins of Fort Pitt, I sent scouts across the river and to the north and east of our bivouac. Whitford found a heavy trail in the direction of Onion Lake, but there was only the trace of a cart and the print of a white woman's shoe, which had no doubt been picked up by some squaw and appropriated to her use. In the forenoon, when looking round for traces of the direction taken by the hostiles, I found Miss Amelia McLean's first letter to her mother from St John's Ladies' College at Winnipeg. Mrs McLean had shown it to me in 1880, and I recognized it at once.

On the afternoon of the 26th Big Bear's trail to the north was found, and I was directed to proceed in pursuit to locate the whereabouts of the enemy. I was ready to start when the general told me that the scouts at headquarters and several gentlemen who were attached to the force were of the opinion that the hostiles had crossed the Saskatchewan and gone south to join Poundmaker, the prominent Cree chief, who had been on the warpath near Battleford early in the spring. I assured him that the south side had been carefully scouted by my best men and a cart trail and the track of a woman's shoe were all that was to be found there, and there was no sign of a large number of the enemy except to the north, where there was a heavy trail going east. The general agreed, and I trekked north, taking with me 2 officers and 90 mounted men. About midnight a Chippeway scout, named Beatty, was brought to me, saying, 'Beatty smells Indians and has cold feet!'

Soon afterwards I halted on the high bank of the Saskatchewan, and to the westward, about 3 miles away, I saw the camp fires of General Strange's column. As it was time to halt, I passed the word to Coryell to keep a sharp look out, and went down the hill with Sergeant Butlin and Corporal McLelland to find a place where I could bivouac without danger of the horses being stampeded. Captains Oswald and Wright followed, and I had just found a suitable bivouac and remarked, 'This is just the thing!' when an Indian, lying in the grass to my right front, sprang to his feet, fired two shots at us in rapid succession, and ran across my front towards a horse tied to a tree to the left. I turned to fire, but Corporal McLelland, close on my left, was between us, and at 60 yards dropped the red man. When the Indian fired at me I saw another sitting on his horse about 30 yards off, and the moment the Indian discharged his rifle we were in the midst of a yelling, whooping band; rifles and pistols cracked, while the lurid remarks of Butlin and McLelland could be heard a mile away. The hot flashes of the Winchesters of the Indians almost singed our faces, and several times we had to pause lest we should shoot one another. This lasted a minute, when the Indians departed with headlong speed to the eastward, exchanging shots with my rear party as they passed by. As no more Indians were to be seen, we concluded that this was a party that had been watching the first of the column with the intention of stampeding the horses as soon as the camp was in darkness.

Soon after daylight I continued east along the Indian trail. At one of their bivouacs I counted where 187 camp fires had quite recently been.

Whitford went to the front, and I had not long to wait for intelligence. He had not been gone more than half an hour when I heard Indian yells and saw him, at the head of his scouts, riding for dear life, followed by a large band of yelling braves, and more could be seen in the hills behind him. I pushed forward some men to cover his retreat, and extended the remainder, dismounted, ready to receive them if necessary, but as soon as the savages caught sight of us they halted at a respectful distance and galloped away. Whitford explained that the scouts had kept together to a place at the hills, where they intended to extend, when he heard a horse stamp as if annoyed by mosquitoes, and his attention was further attracted by hearing an Indian say, 'Wait, wait, let them come a little further.' Whitford halted and then said in a low tone, 'Shall we fight or fall back?' and the answer was 'Let us draw them; to fight is no good. We were not sent here for that.' Whitford turned at once and came back at the fastest pace until he got to us, followed by the band of yelling Crees.

Shortly afterwards General Strange appeared with the infantry, a small party of Hatton's corps and the 9-pounder gun. The infantry had been placed in waggons to save time, and the 65th Rifles went down the river on the flat boats so as to be ready to land when required. A company of the regiment had been left to fortify and protect what remained of Fort Pitt, and guard the large quantity of stores and camp equipment left there. On reaching me the waggons were formed into a corral under Captain Wright; the drivers, being armed, were able to take care of the transport. When that was arranged the march was resumed. About 2 miles further on the scouts reported the enemy to be holding the wooded hills in front, and the general extended the force and advanced to the attack. No sooner was the movement begun than a fine-looking band of Indians appeared on the summit of a large round butte, about 1500 years distant. They were galloping in a circle to warn their camp, their excellent horsemanship and wild appearance making a remarkable picture as they were silhouetted against the blue sky. Directly they were sighted General Strange gave them a shot from the 9-pounder; the first fell short, the next swept the butte, the shrapnel tearing up the grass and gravel a second after the wild horsemen disappeared from the summit. The advance was continued and the position carried. The 65th, on hearing the firing, left their boats and dinners behind them and joined us. Owing to the density of the woods the gun had to keep on the Indian trail. The scouts were far to the front before dark and could be seen moving up the slopes of Frenchman's Knoll, which had changed since I last saw it in 1876 from bare prairie to fairly thick woods. Scout Patton, one of the Edmonton men, was very far forward and obtained a good view of the ridge behind which the Indians were posted. The force was corralled for the night, and great precautions were taken. My scouts were out to the front about a mile; the advanced post, under Patton, could see the glow of some fires amongst the trees along the ridge.

At daybreak next morning the woods were again reconnoitred and the force advanced, the Mounted Police and scouts in front on foot. About half-past six the enemy's position was located on a thickly-wooded ridge about 600 yards distant across the valley of the Red Deer. The general ordered me to turn the enemy's right. The gun came into action with shrapnel, but soon after I was informed that the force was to retire out of the woods and I was to cover the movement. The gun had kept up a rapid fire and no doubt had a good effect, but no Indians were seen on the ridge. The reason for our retirement was that a report came in from Hatton's corps to the effect that the hostiles were turning that flank, and there appeared to be nothing for it but to get clear of the woods. The correctness of the report was doubtful. When the force was clear of the woods it was halted and the situation was discussed. The general decided that the proper thing to do was to attack the rifle pits on the right and drive the Indians out, but before giving any orders he had a talk with two senior officers, and later summoned me. It was clear that his plan was not received as cheerfully as it merited, and the force retired to Fort Pitt.

Samuel B. Steele, *Forty Years in Canada*, pp. 213-23

Just over fourteen years later the South African war against the sturdy Boer marksmen revealed how competent Canadian soldiers could be with proper training and leadership. They remained, in the best sense, civilians under arms, without the plodding docility of European conscripts. Never comfortable with the rigidity and restriction of military existence, they reacted to the military environment in illuminating ways. The experience of the military life, as much as the experience of war—for the two are not the same—began to reveal as much about Canadian national character as it did about the professional military as an institution.

2

LIVING AND LEARNING
IN THE MILITARY SETTING

The peculiarities of military life and 'service' thinking, not to mention the bare realities of communal life in barracks situations, came as a shock to many young Canadians.

The Nissen hut was nothing more than a concrete pad over which corrugated iron sheets were bolted in a continuous arch from one side to the other. The end walls were made of wood. A door and two tiny windows were located at one of the ends. It was large enough to house a row of six iron cots on either side of a centre aisle, which was the only spot where you could stand fully erect. Heat was supposedly supplied by a tiny iron stove, erected in and blocking the centre aisle. A short length of stove pipe ran through the tin roof to allow the choking clouds of smoke to escape. It wasn't very effective since the soft, oily lumps of coal that were allocated, seven lumps per day, were rain soaked and unburnable. It didn't matter how much coal you stole from the closely guarded coal pile, or how many lumps you rammed into the tiny stove. It was perfectly heat proof.

'Why doesn't somebody light the stove?' a voice would cry out from under its blankets.

'For God's sake,' came the answer, 'it is lit.'

'Well put some more coal on the fire.'

'I can't get any more into the damn thing.'

'Pour some paint dope on the coals.'

'I have, and it still won't burn.'

But the Nissen hut was very cleverly designed to hold maximum moisture. The tin acted as a conductor that made the inside of the hut damper than the outside. Putting on clothes in the morning, if you had had the courage to remove them the night before, was like putting on a wet bathing suit, only much colder.

J. Douglas Harvey, *Boys, Bombs and Brussels Sprouts*, p. 33

It was not an environment for the gentle, the tender, or the seeker of sympathy.

As soon as we were out in the Channel all went below and the deck was battened down. The sea often washed right over the craft. We had to strap all our equipment to anything solid we could find and lie down, as the wind tossing would throw you violently. In an hour nearly everyone was sick and casting up all that had been eaten before getting on board. The passageway to the boiler room below had a ledge about twenty inches wide on the right of the stair, with an iron rail running three inches high. I lay on the ledge and gripped the rail. The fumes from below were as nothing compared with those around me. At midnight I was sick for five minutes, taking care to be well away from my ledge. Then I returned and slept till morning.

When we docked at Le Havre the deck was a fearsome sight, the men trying to clean their uniforms. The stench was deadly. I got my equipment and edged close to the exit. Then we were allowed up. The gangplank was already down. I raced to the wharf and never stopped. There were some buildings beyond and I shot into the first alleyway. The others yelled laughingly after me, but an officer halted them. Then he and another came and picked out twenty of the men looking fittest and took them back to clean the boat with mops and buckets. The task took an hour. The rest of us stayed in the sunshine while they laboured.

As soon as we marched away from the dock, French women and kids were alongside trying to sell 'Apoo, Choc'lay, Orange'. We gave them no heed and after quite a march arrived at a camp that was three inches of mud no matter where you turned. We were shown tents on a slope. The floor boards had the same list as the hill, and the unfortunate who slept on the downward side might slide out in the night. At mealtime we waded through the slime to the door of a long dirty hut. Inside the entrance, a trio of unwashed characters broke up loaves of bread and tossed a chunk to each man, the size of your chunk depending on your luck. Another pair poured each man a tin of cold, greasy tea and you received a piece of stringy meat in your messtin top. You went to long tables and ate your food from your fingers. Everything was dirty. Presently an officer and sergeant entered the front of the hut and walked rapidly between the tables, not looking right or left. At the rear door they paused just long enough to shout: 'Any complaints?' They vanished before anyone could reply.

Will R. Bird, *Ghosts Have Warm Hands* (1968), pp. 9-10

It was the group existence, as opposed to the civilian experience of life largely as an individual, that was perhaps the most significant adjustment to military life (the term being used, to the admitted disgust of some historians, to refer to life in all three armed forces).

I don't think a man has *really* lived unless he has been in the services during the war. For the horrors of war I am, of course, truly sorry. But for the experiences, the broadening, the complete understanding of what makes my fellow man tick, I have to thank the war. I am positive that every veteran in civvy street today has a broader and more tolerant outlook on the foibles and weaknesses of mankind than a non-veteran could possibly possess.

I could draw upon hundreds of experiences that typify how men are bonded together through comradeship, whether it be in the navy, the army or the air force. The methods may differ but the pattern emerges the same.

It is difficult to cite one phase of service life that is common to all three branches. However, all of you who signed on the dotted line for the King's Shilling will remember the troop trains, be ye navy blue, air force blue or just plain khaki.

Troop trains were undoubtedly the most boring and uncomfortable form of travel available. Yet, bless 'em, when you look back they were a lot of fun. A heck of a lot more fun than you enjoy today trying to squeeze through traffic or board a crowded bus.

Nobody loved a serviceman aboard a troop train. The despatching officers shoved you aboard with a sign of relief—glad to be rid of you. The porters tolerated you. The waiters gave you the bored treatment as you tendered your pasteboard meal ticket. A troop train to them was a tipless nuisance . . . and so were you.

But mingled in with that there was always an air of excitement. Especially on that final trip. The one to the East Coast. You had travelled plenty before, but this was the Big One. Somewhere along the end of the line there was a big ship waiting. And somewhere in the hold of that big ship there was a hammock just for you. And somewhere on that big broad ocean was a German U-boat waiting, so it seemed, just for you!

You weren't exactly scared. It was as yet too remote. And besides it always happened to the other fellow. Never to you. Yet the prospect gave you room for thought. But you didn't show it as you laughed, sang and kidded with the rest of that boisterous gang.

Somewhere along the line the train was always picking up old chums—guys who had been in training with you. I remember one trip East starting from Regina. We picked up a bunch at Winnipeg. Last leave stuff.

You kidded the pants off the fellows who were kissing their gals goodbye. Nothing or nobody was sacred. One chap in particular was moon-sick over the sweetie-pie he had just left behind. It was pure suicide to let the gang see you wearing you heart on your sleeve. Immediately the mob would break into melody, 'I wonder who's kissing her now, I wonder who's teaching her how'—with the emphasis on the HOW. Whereupon the poor unfortunate would either blow his top or else become glummer still.

Then there was one Lothario whose chick bid him farewell on the platform in no uncertain fashion. Man, she was chesty! If my memory serves me correctly, that gal made Jane Russell look like two badly bent pin-pong balls. The boys just about went wild as she threw her final clinch. For the rest of the trip the refrain kept up, to the poor guy's torment, 'For I'm dancing with . . . in my eyes'. No conscience, no conscience at all in that bunch!

Usually after the first day the train was dry. Anything in liquid form that came aboard with you unfailingly died a quick death. Then there would be feverish councils of war. The planning and the strategies for the next stop on the time table!

Was there a liquor store there?

How far was it from the station?

How long would it take by taxi? If not possible, did the taxi driver know of a bootlegger? How much?

Then the hurried forking-up, 'Here's my two bucks.'

Or, 'Lend me five 'til pay-day, willya? I'm broke.'

Not that the trip was one mad, exciting event. It wasn't. You spent hours just staring out the window—hours listlessly reading a bunch of words in a magazine that had little meaning for you. Hours more of just plain dozing or staring straight into space.

Truth known, most of the guys' thoughts centred on home. You secretly wondered if you would ever see home again. You couldn't get out of your mind the strained look on your mother's face as she said goodbye.

You were grateful to the Old Man who hadn't said much but who had slipped a ten-spot in your hand with a mumbled apology, 'I wish it could be more.'

You didn't want to think it, but you couldn't help wondering about your girl. Will she wait for me? You had told her to go ahead and have other dates, but secretly you hoped that she wouldn't have them.

Photographs were produced by the score. A photograph seemed the only remaining link you had with your loved ones. You showed the gang pictures of your girl. They showed you theirs. Whether the lass was comely or homely, the polite thing to do was to give an appreciative whistle. You made some comment like, 'You lucky dog, how come you rate such a luscious dish?' The guy then put the picture back in his wallet feeling mighty good. And so it went all around.

Somewhere along the aisle of the train would come the click, click, click of the rattling bones. With them were the famous quotes in tones of eternal optimism.

'Come on baby, natch.'

'Eighter from Decatur.'

'Shoot the works!'

'I'm bust, anyone want to buy a good wrist-watch?'

Welcome breaks were the leg-stretching periods at the stations. Mad dash for the lunch counter where you begged to be served scalding hot coffee dregs along with the privilege of paying two bits for a stale cheese sandwich dying of old age.

Above the magazine counter would be scads of flashy silk cushion covers, all bearing endearing captions, 'To My Sweetheart' . . . 'Dearest Mother Mine', and so on. These you could have for a mere four bucks, or nearly three days' pay.

Gad, what a racket! The slushier and more tear-jerking the verse, the greater the sales. They tell me that certain jokers in Montreal and Toronto retired after the war filthy rich.

I can well believe it. They got eight bucks belonging to me. I now have two moth-eaten cushion covers around the house that I'd love to trade back for half price. Only I haven't the nerve. The good woman would scalp me!

Most troop trains wound up either in Debert or near Halifax. There, after you were bedded down, you began to wonder.

You began to wonder what the blazes all the rush, hustle and bustle had been about getting you aboard that troop train.

At the time of departure from your military depot you were shoved aboard like mad fiends.

The Hun was astride the Channel!

England needed every man! You were the one who was needed—not tomorrow, but right now, right away!

Then you arrived at Debert and sat on your fanny for three or more weeks doing blister-all but stare at the gumbo mud.

Horrible, boring days, weren't they? I wouldn't particularly care to go through them again. But then again I wouldn't have missed them for anything. Would you?

Doug Smith, *Memoirs of An Old Sweat* (1961), pp. 115-17

The friendships that arose from the military experience were often unique to their setting: intense or detached depending upon the sense of danger—or the need to protect oneself against loss.

It has always been my fortune to fall in with 'characters'. Then, of course, as the Little Woman always says, 'Birds of a feather flock together'. Anyhow, I like characters. They make life interesting.

Every 'character' who didn't fit in with the 'solid' citizens of other units seemed to drift into our outfit. The funny part about it was that, being birds of a feather, they understood each other. In any other company they would be labelled as screwballs. In our gang nobody paid any attention to them. So they went along and did their jobs the way they saw fit and the end result was usually good.

The only one who lost weight and hair was the adjutant. A decent, sensible type, he had to clean up the paper mess afterwards. 'Adj' was always bemoaning his fate and praying for a transfer.

One day he tried to be a good guy and go along with the boys for a ride. They took him in a Bren carrier to see the Big Show up ahead. They got lost. Worse, they got captured. Luckily the Boche turned out to be conscripted Balkanites with no special love for Der Fuhrer. They took one look at our compo rations, said, '*Schnitzlle on the Fritzlle*', and kameraded to get in on the Allied feed-bag. After that 'Adj' stuck to his paper work.

I had almost forgotten some of the characters when out of the blue came a Christmas card from 'Frenchy' MacDonald. 'Frenchy' was as Frenchy as they make them. He hailed from Outremont. In spite of his Scotch surname he didn't know a haggis from a plum pudding.

Frenchy rode through the last show like a tourist with a million bucks couldn't imitate. He was style all the while. And he treated the war as a Coney Island holiday. Don't get him wrong. He was no slacker. He landed at Courseulles on D-Day. And he picked up a sound stripe plus a MID. But to him life was a bowl of cherries just waiting for him to gorge on.

Frenchy and myself were standing outside the Abbey aux Hommes in Caen. The troops had broken through across the Orne. The Trun-Chambois sector was a shambles. Where the front line was nobody knew. Headquarters moved several times in one day. Bewildered commanders were saying, 'Where's Brigade?' Brigade was saying, 'Where's Div?' Div. didn't even know where Corps was.

Says Frenchy, 'Hey, Smeety, what t'hell we 'ang aroun' for. Let us go.' So away we went after the pack. We finally came to a halt in Lisieux.

Lisieux as I remember it was a pretty town with green, sloping hills all around. On the top of a hill was a beautiful structure—a shrine called St Theresa's. It reminded me a lot of Brother André's shrine in Montreal.

However, just as we were admiring the view, the Jerries zeroed in with their 88's. We decided to scram and leave what was left of the town to the British 51st Division who were mopping up patches in the nearby woods.

On the way back the motor conked out. Frenchy volunteered to mosey down the lane to a farming village to clean out the carburetor. An hour passed and no sign of Frenchy. Throwing my last Woodbine in the ditch I cursed him and jogged down the dusty lane.

Was Frenchy cleaning out the carburetor? No sir. He was cleaning out the last of a bottle of vin rouge! He was happy as a pig in clover. The French villagers off the beaten path had been by-passed by the troops. They wanted to celebrate their liberation, only they didn't have a guest of honour. And what better guest could they have than a compatriot who not only spoke French but whose grandmother (he said) had come from Normandy?

My French was strictly of the vooley-voo type. But it didn't matter. All they wanted was someone to wine and dine. We figured it was our patriotic duty to fill in for the unavoidable absence of His Majesty, Winston Churchill, General Montgomery and anybody else they cared to toast.

Hours later, stuffed with rare steaks, huge buttered beans washed down with cider, cognac, calvados and champagne, we left the cheering villagers enroute for Caen. A good Norman mechanic had fixed the carburetor and put it on.

We didn't make Caen that night. We ended up by bivouacking in an orchard. A mobile ack-ack battery set up shop in the next field. The boys banged away for several hours that night. We didn't hear a thing.

A few days later we ended up in Rouen. The British had taken over. In the meantime the Essex Scottish, the RHLIs and the Royal Regiment of Canada were hightailing towards Dieppe, prepared to pay off an old debt.

We Cooks-toured the lovely city of Rouen. We said a prayer in the magnificent Rouen cathedral. Later, in a café, we bought some 'feelthy pictures'. Such is the Jekyll and Hyde in us all.

Rouen was in a stage where one mode of law and order had ceased and no new one was established. However, a strict curfew was established at night for obvious reasons.

At two ack emma we left our hosts and felt our way along in the blacked-out streets. We were lost. And not a soul was in sight. We knocked on doors but we knocked in vain. After four years of listening to Gestapo bangings after midnight, the good people of Rouen weren't answering any doorbells.

I lost Frenchy somewhere along the darkened streets and was prepared to curl up in a doorway for the night. Suddenly my hair stood on end and I nearly jumped out of my tunic when the silence was shattered by a rapid burst of gunfire.

Doors flew open. Windows flew up. FFIs scrambled out, tucking in their shirts, guns at the alert and trigger-itchy. I followed the sound of the guns. There, in the middle of a huge square, was Frenchy. High over his head was his Sten gun rat-tat-tatting to the heavens.

By this time a crowd has milled around. They wanted to know where the sal Boche were. Frenchy was all smiles. There were no Boche, he explained. He merely wanted to know where his quarters were on la rue Rheims.

An excited crowd escorted him back jabbering away in French. I tagged along shaking my head at his method of direction-finding.

It seems that Frenchy did OK for himself after the war. His Christmas card was postmarked from Brussels. He had returned and married Mademoiselle Yvette Therien. Yvette's papa owns a big café near the place Bruchère. But papa has retired to Deauville, and guess who runs the show?

Frenchy's message was typical, 'Come on over, sucker, and quit working. I give you a good job. You can handle my upstairs department.'

Blessings on you, Frenchy.

Ibid., pp. 67-9

There came, too, the inevitable moment of disillusionment, when the initial wonder and pride in being in uniform, in the service of one's country, would vanish as the dark side of the military environment became evident.

The worst punishment was the lack of food. Old bully Simms had his tent at the entrance to the Farm, and each night at six a cook delivered an entire roasted chicken with all the accompaniments to his table. The prisoners had been reduced to three and we slept in the first tent inside the farm. So I concocted a plan. At a few minutes to six we would take our water pails and apply to the guard to be taken to the pump, which was within ten feet of Simms' tent. We watched. The chicken arrived but Simms was not in sight. The guard was a nervous type and when we came with our pails he told us to hurry. I filled mine, while the other two bumped against each other. There were hot words and they came to blows. The guard tried to break it up and was twisted about so that his back was to me. The chicken was dropped in my pail of water. Then I begged the chaps to ease up. They did, and a thankful guard got us back into the Farm.

There were six tents in a row reaching back from the entrance. I went through them to the last one, unrolled the tent flaps, put the chicken in it and rolled it up again. I was just back in our tent when Simms arrived, had a quick look around and began shouting.

The guard was grilled without mercy. Simms yelled at him until he scarcely knew what he was saying. A sergeant was called. Soon he and Simms came into our tent and searched where we slept, looked around to see if we had dug a hole anywhere to bury the lost one. No luck. They searched the other tents. Dire threats were made and after an hour another chicken arrived. We had no light of any sort and had to turn in at dark. At ten Simms sneaked into the gate and came to our tent with a flashlight, but we were lying there and looking hungry. He tried it twice later, so we made no move until two A.M. Nothing ever tasted sweeter than that chicken.

That turn in the Fox Farm changed me from a soldier proud to be in uniform to one knowing there was no justice whatever in the army. I was determined to buck every Simms and Fordley I met, to outwit all their type if possible.

Will R. Bird, *Ghosts Have Warm Hands* (1968) p. 5

But it was also possible to retain the pride and commitment—if not for the regiment, or ship, or squadron, or aircrew, or gun's crew, then at the highest level: in the bonding of comrades against all and any odds, in the almost mystic thing the Australians call 'mateship'.

He was bitter about some of the discipline handed out, so I told him about the day we had seen 'Old Sunshine', the regimental sergeant-major of the RCRs, have a man spreadeagled to the wheel of a cart. We went up the hill and cut the fellow loose, and along came Old Sunshine roaring threats. None of us ran. We simply stayed and defied him. He was told that if the man, or any other, were tied to another wheel we would get him, sooner or later, tie him to a cartwheel and send the cart downhill. We were not drunkards or rowdies. He grew hoarse and went away, but all of us saw the fear in his eyes and never again did we see an RCR on a cartwheel.

Ibid., p. 35

An expression often repeated in the armed forces to the dismayed victim of unfairness or indifference was, 'If you can't take a joke, you shouldn't have joined!' Wit and a kind of humorous common sense were the weapons by which the wrongs of the system and the bullies or 'bad eggs' within it could be resisted.

My acquaintance with Baillie had begun back in Aldershot, Nova Scotia. We were not given many passes for late evenings, and as there was entertainment in plenty in the town a mile away, many men tried to slip back to their tents without being seen by the guard. Camped above us on the slope were the Cape Breton Highlanders. Their battalion sergeant-major was one of those men whose greatest joy in life is to make someone else miserable. He had nothing to do with us, but we would come down the transport road through their lines and slip into our tents from their camp corner. He got a flashlight and would station himself there, grab some of our lads if they did not spot him first, make them give him identification and send in their names to our officers. Such action naturally gave rise to many threats, but after he caught Baillie there was more than threats. Baillie was a big fellow and powerful. He went to town and bought a bottle of whiskey, came in late by the same route; when the BSM grabbed him, Baillie threw that individual on his back, knelt over him and by holding his nose forced him to swallow all the whiskey.

Someone found the BSM some hours later, making queer noises. He was rushed to hospital and recovered. He had glimpsed Baillie before being overpowered and sent in a report that might have committed a man to life imprisonment. But our officer did not like the manner in which the BSM carried on and Baillie was only given three days CB (Confined to Barracks). The conscientious military police thought he should be required to do something during the period and hunted jobs of whitewashing which were well performed until, just at noon time, he was taken to the company commander's tent. There was a neat flower bed ringed by stones, and the stones would look better whitewashed. The policeman got a call and was leaving, so Baillie asked what he was to do. 'Whitewash,' came the answer.

'Whitewash what?' asked Baillie. There were posts marking off the tent site, and they had not received attention. 'Everything,' yelled the police officer, by then almost out of hearing. 'Everything.' He felt Baillie ought to know what he had in mind.

An hour later an irate company commander found his tent and cot all covered with a heavy coat of whitewash, and the police officer found that five men, good and true comrades of Baillie, had heard the specific shouted directions. Baillie was acquitted.

Ibid., pp. 76-7

But there were occasions, too, when in their desire to be simply human, to ignore orders or regulations, men underestimated the need for those orders, with sad results.

There were strict orders when we moved into the trenches to stay low. The 22nd Battalion had been in the line just in front of Neuville Vitasse. Mercatel and Telegraph Hill were in the same front. They found things a little quiet around the support line, so they decided to get out and start a baseball game. There was a wonderful view because Neuville Vitasse was at quite a height. Other troops got out and became spectators until there was quite a crowd present. Then the Germans let them have it. There were lots of casualties. That was the French Canadians' nature. They were fed up with that slow motion stuff in the trenches. Our orders were no more playing baseball.

Gordon Reid, *Poor Bloody Murder* (1980), p. 167

The Canadian approach to military subordination and discipline tended to fall somewhere between the seemingly languid casualness of the Americans and the unquestioning observance of hierarchy among the British, under whose military structures and methods Canadians have most often fought. Face to face with the rigidity and ruthlessness of the European military mind, the Canadian was sometimes in for a rude awakening.

At the working party, we mingled daily with German and Polish workers. I talked to these people every chance I had. My ability to speak and understand the German language, improved to the extent that I was often used as a interpreter on the job, when the 'Meister' (the German civilian boss) wanted to issue special instructions so that everyone understood.

We walked two miles to our place of work by a warehouse with a spur line of track, running into the yard. Our job was unloading boxcars of loose wheat. We bagged the wheat inside the railway cars, then loaded it on trucks. There were prisoners of other countries also working in the area. Heavy set Ukrainian women and girls unloaded boxcars on another line. They often unloaded rubble, with bare hands.

There was a main railway line, within sight of where we worked. Frequently we would see boxcars crowded with Jews, in striped pajama-like uniforms. Teen-aged girls, all their hair shaved off, eyes, which appeared larger than life, staring out through the small, barbed wire covered opening. Painted in white letters on the outside of the boxcars was, 'Forty Men or Eight Horses'. A guard told me one time, that these Jews were being moved to a new modern camp where they would be treated well. The new camp was located outside a village called 'Auschwitz'.

One day, at work, the 'Meister' asked me to tell everyone that, as soon as the remaining two boxcars were unloaded we could return to camp. Everyone agreed, and at 2:30 in the afternoon we had finished. Then the Meister told us there had been a mix up and there were four more boxcars coming in on the siding.

Hennessey and O'Day were the first to complain, and a loud argument broke out. 'If we let them away with this,' said Hennessey 'it's hard to say what they may come up with next time. Let's refuse to work; we'll go on strike.' He looked angrily around to see how the rest of us were taking this.

'Good show' said Bill Bennett, an Australian. Then he promptly sat down on a ledge at the side of the building. One by one we sauntered over and sat down on the ledge. Hennessey became quite vocal about the rights of prisoners of war. The Meister and the guard were in quiet conversation, off from us. Then the guard came over and tried reasoning, smiling as he spoke. He then became angry, and began shouting.

Then he removed his rifle from his shoulder, and began threatening, 'Pay no attention to him chaps,' whispered Hennessey. 'When he gets tired shouting, he will have no choice but to take us back to camp.'

While the guard continued to threaten, the Meister had walked off to the office. Within twenty minutes the 'Unteroffizer' accompanied by a guard from camp, appeared on their bicycles. Then began shouts and threats from all. Rifles were pointed at us, safety catches released and bullets driven into the breech, all done with menacing show and noise. Bennett whispered, 'Don't let the bastards bluff you.' There was whispered conversation from people up the line from me. Across from us at the other siding the Ukrainian women had stopped work and were staring over at the disturbance. The civilian in charge soon had them working again with a few loud shouts.

The Unteroffizer decided. He walked quickly towards the office. 'He has gone to get permission to return us to camp,' said Hennessey. I felt sick.

A half hour went by, and the Unteroffizer had not returned. Then we could hear, from the direction of the main road, the heavy sound of marching feet. A company of regular German soldiers turned into the gateway of our work site. A young officer in a belted leather coat, brought the company to a halt in front of the office, where the Unteroffizer now stood. A few quiet words were exchanged. Then on a command from the young officer, the soldiers marched towards where we sat.

I could hear the man next to me breathing hard. The soldiers stopped, then formed a half circle around us. No one was speaking in our group.

The German officer walked over to us, removing as he did so, a pistol from a pouch which hung from his leather belt. He cocked it as he walked. He stopped in front of Hennessey. The pistol was pointed towards the ground.

'What is your name?' he asked in English. Hennessey went to stand up. 'Don't get up,' said the officer. All was quiet.

'Patrick Hennessey.'

The officer placed the pistol to the side of Hennessey's head and said. 'Meister Hennessey, will you work or will you not?'

'I will,' said Hennessey.

The officer pointed his pistol at the ground. Uncocked it. Put the safety catch on. Returned it to his belt. He then walked quickly over to the company of soldiers. On command they formed up. On a second command they marched down past the office, through the gate onto the road. Soon we heard, above the sound of feet hitting the pavement, 'One-two-three,' and the soldiers' voices in song. 'We are marching, against England.'

It was well after dark, before we were finished and returned to the camp. For sometime afterwards, we argued the pros and cons of the strike. The only thing that Hennessey said was. 'I might have ended up dead, and the rest of you would have gone back to work.'

'He was only bluffing,' said Bennett. 'But what the hell, you win some and lose some. Still,' he went on thoughtfully, 'I didn't like the look in his eye, when he cocked that pistol.'

'One thing, we had the old Unteroffizer and guard baffled for awhile,' laughed O'Day.

'But that officer with his company of soldiers had me scared. Cool efficient bastard, wasn't he?' mused Hennessey.

John Patrick Grogan, *Dieppe and Beyond* (1982) pp. 48-51

The fact that other troops had similar colonial backgrounds did not always mean good relations.

We never had anything to do with the Australians. The Canadians and Australians always fought like tigers when they would meet in pubs behind the line. It got so bad that eventually they never put the Australians or Canadians together in the same part of the line. They hated each others' guts. You couldn't meet a nicer crowd than the New Zealanders. They were splendid.

Gordon Reid, *Poor Bloody Murder* (1980), p. 150

Until recent times, in fact, it was difficult for Canadians to gain acceptance from their various allies, who tended to view them with varying degrees of condescension, suspicion, or uncertainty as much as admiration.

A few days later I found myself sitting on a barstool in the Union Club beside the SOO. We chatted amicably enough, but I suppose the recent frictions must have come up, for he suddenly announced that he was not afraid of me even if I was a VR and a Canadian. A light went on. I had negotiating power I had not realized. VRs had no career ambitions and could thus talk back, and Canadians were thought to get belligerent if crossed. However, I assured him I had not come overseas to get into rows with my own side, but I would not be pushed around. This seemed to clear the air.

Gordon W. Stead, *A Leaf Upon the Sea* (1988), pp. 133-4

And on occasion the Canadians had to establish their identity in unequivocal terms.

We were put through a sort of initial training at King Alfred and I think each course was two weeks. The first two weeks they asked us what we'd like to do. One of the courses you could do if you wanted was a special MTB course. I don't know why, but it was Astral Navigation. We were in two classes of twenty-five each to start with. I remember once when they were falling us out in the evening—they had some reason to speak to all the English people, it was about leave or something. So the young RNVR Lieutenant in

charge said, 'Fall out the Colonials.' The Canadians just stood fast.
So then he said 'Did you hear me?' And the senior Officer of one of
the classes said 'Yes, but we're not bloody Colonials!' That settled
it. There was no argument thereafter. The British were pretty good.
There was no argument about it. They realized they had made a
mistake, and we weren't Colonials any more, we were treated as
normal.

Ottawa branch, Naval Officers' Associations of Canada,
Salty Dips, vol. 1 (1983), pp. 15-16

*In both the First and Second World Wars, Canadians very soon
developed a reputation for quick practicality—and equally quick
tempers when faced with narrow stupidity from whatever quarter,
as indicated by this anecdote from the memoirs of the combative
Canadian naval officer Jeffry Brock.*

One night, when I was ordered to leave south Dock to proceed on
patrol, there occurred an incident that I was not permitted to forget.
I had notified the Bridge and Lock Masters of my time of departure
and had agreed the prearranged signals for my arrival off the railroad
bridge, which would swing open to permit my exit. It was a raw,
dirty, and windy night. After casting off and clawing my way toward
the bridge with a very strong and gusty wind abeam, I made the
appropriate single to the Bridge Master to open, and he did so.

A single-screw ship is difficult to handle in a crosswind at slow
speed, and I therefore increased engine revolutions on approaching
the gap to ensure good steerage way while getting through the
opening. Just at this moment, the air raid siren sounded and, to my
astonishment and dismay, the railroad bridge started to swing closed
just ahead of me.

'Full speed astern.'

'Full speed astern, sir. Engine full speed astern.'

'Hard-a-starboard.'

'Hard-a-starboard, sir. Wheel hard-a-starboard, sir.'

'Stop engine.'

'Engine stopped, sir.'

With some difficulty, because when going astern a single-screw
ship tends to twist its stern to port, I managed to place *Kirkella*
alongside the 'knuckle' of the bridge opening. It was not necessary
to secure the ship because by now the wind was gusting so hard that
it held us firmly against the concrete dockside.

In a blinding rage, I stepped ashore from my wheelhouse to the
raised portion of the lock basin and stormed over to the bridge

operator's control position. There I found that he had sought shelter and was hiding in a funk hole close to his control panel. I peered down at him and said:

'Did you see me coming?'

'Yus.'

'Why, then, did you close the bridge in my face?'

'Because, sor, I have as much right to find shelter as anyone in an air raid.'

'But there are no bombs falling. Did you hear any aircraft overhead?'

'No, sor.'

Infuriated, I reached in, grabbed him by the scruff of the neck, and hauled him out of his funk hole. Unconscionable action though it was, I must admit that I had so lost control of my temper that I struck him very hard with my other fist and dispatched him with a good hard kick in the arse back to his duties. He opened the bridge, and I managed to claw my way off the dockside and finally got through to the open sea without further trouble.

About a week or ten days later when I returned from that patrol, one of the first messages flashed to me by the Shore Signal Station was a rather peremptory summons from the Naval-Officer-in-Charge, Swansea. The message was not a polite request for me to call upon him at my convenience, but was couched in rather formidable language, which was a clear indication to any knowledgeable naval officer that he was on the carpet for certain. The message read: FROM NOIC TO KIRKELLA. U.C.M. ON ARRIVAL. There was a time of origin and the message ended. What this meant in simple language was, 'You see me as quickly as you bloody well can, dressed in your best bib and tucker.'

I quickly cleaned into my best uniform, took my gloves, buckled on my sword and sword belt, and raced ashore to see the Base Captain.

When I arrived at the office of the Naval-Office-in-Charge, Swansea, I was immediately shown into his presence. He looked balefully at me over the top of his glasses:

'Well, "Kirkella", I see you are safely back again.'

'Yes, sir, not too bad a trip. Nothing very special to report.'

'Now look here "Kirkella", I must ask you a serious question. A couple of weeks ago, did you or did you not deliberately attack the Bridge Master at South Dock and give him a bloody nose?'

'Yes, sir, I did.'

'Why?'

I explained to the Captain of the base the circumstances surrounding the incident and he listened carefully until I was finished.

'I don't know if you know it or not, but we had great difficulty in preventing the whole of the Great Western Railway from going on strike as a result of this incident. What do you think about that?"

'Bloody bunch of bolshie bastards, if you ask me, sir. I think I'd do the same thing again under the same circumstances.'

'Humph. Well, I have been ordered by Their Lordships to inquire into this, and, if you were found responsible, to administer a reprimand. Consider yourself reprimanded. Now come and have a gin with me. You know, my boy, I think it highly likely I'd have done the same thing myself.'

Jeffry V. Brock, The Dark Broad Seas, vol. 1 (1981), pp. 35-7

Neither were they unafraid to look substantially higher authorities in the eye and tell them what was on their minds, and in no uncertain terms. Arthur Currie, in command of the Canadian Corps, demonstrated this to Field Marshal Haig during the First World War.

But Currie was by no means intimidated by Haig either. His chauffeur, Sergeant-Major Lewis Reece, recalled the time that Haig outlined his plan on a map and then asked for Currie's opinion. 'Well, sir', he replied with typical frankness, 'I don't think it is worth a God damn.' The shocked expressions on the faces of Haig's aides told Reece that the commander-in-chief was not often addressed in such a manner.

Daniel G. Dancocks, Legacy of Valour (1986), pp. 93-4

What a Canadian had to say was rarely a matter of empty words or 'hot air'. Competent, forthright action based on common sense was characteristic of Canadians like Currie. Neither docile ploughhorses nor undisciplined solo performers, Canadians routinely earned the praise of allies wherever they fought, and won recognition for their unique personality, which seemed to combine acceptance of sufficient subordination to get a job done with prickly sensitivity when they were treated stupidly.

Soon afterwards, Sir Douglas Haig attended a conference at Canadian Corps headquarters at Ten Elms. Currie was uncharacteristically late, testing Haig's patience, for the field-marshal detested unpunctual people. When Currie finally did appear, he was covered in mud and seemed to General Macdonell to be ill or tired. Haig evidently had the same impression, for he asked, 'Everything all right, Currie?'

'No, Sir,' the Canadian replied. 'I was promised so many guns to cover our front and they are not there.'

'Careful, Currie—careful!' cautioned the commander-in-chief. 'If you make a positive statement you will be required to substantiate it and you could not do that unless you had counted the guns yourself.'

Currie's reply was measured and deliberate. 'I have just returned from counting the guns.'

'Some one will smoke for this,' Haig muttered and, turning to his artillery chief, Sir Noel Birch, said, 'Investigate. Someone will be dealt with.'

Whether heads rolled is not known. What is known—and is more important, anyway—is that Currie got his guns.

Ibid., p. 103

Getting into the military was not always a matter of sober reflection on the need to serve the nation: as often as not, the impulse to 'join up' was the result of the actions of friends or even social pressures, as in this First World War memory.

At that time all the girls were going around with white feathers. They'd stick one of those feathers on you if you were not in uniform. My brother and I went to enlist near the end of August 1916. The army took him, but they wouldn't take me. I went back to the recruiting office and complained to them, 'Gosh. You walk down the streets here and somebody sticks a feather on you.' The Lieutenant there said to me, 'Do you want to go that bad?' I said, 'Sure I do. My brother is going and I want to go with him.' He said, 'You be at the docks, take the boat to St Catherines, go to a certain hotel in St Catherines and I'll be there. I'll take you to a doctor that will pass you.' That's how I got in. On Friday, the 13th of September, 1916, we pulled out of Halifax harbour.

Gordon Reid, *Poor Bloody Murder* (1980), p. 15

Other nationalities may have approached the First World War in a spirit of jingoistic nationalism overlying long-smouldering ethnic hatreds. It was hard to find a similar feeling among Canadians, at least as the war began. Hate was not the fuel of the Canadian military engine.

Our training was somewhat similar to what we had previously, but we were getting more shooting practice and bayonet fighting experience. We had some instructors from the British Army. One day while practising bayonet fighting, jabbing dummy men, the instructor came up to me and said, 'Put more into it! Just imagine these dummies are German and you hate Germans don't you?' I said, 'No, I don't hate anybody.' He turned around to the men and said, 'Blimey. Some of these Canadians are funny blokes!' One day later he came over and said, 'I've been thinking about you said the other day. I guess none of us really hates anybody!'

Ibid., p. 27

The exasperation of other nationalities, particularly the British, with the Canadian refusal to be formed in a traditional military mode is expressed in this letter to his mother from the future Field-Marshal Montgomery.

'I saw Donald. I went over and lunched with his Brigade (sic). The Canadians are a queer crowd; they seem to think they are the best troops in France and that we have to get them to do our most difficult jobs. I reminded them that the Ypres Battle began on 31st July and the only part they have taken part in is the last 10 days. They forget that the whole art of war is to gain your objective with as little loss as possible.

'I was disappointed in them. At plain straightforward fighting they are magnificent, but they are narrow-minded and lack soldierly instincts.'

Jeffery Williams, The Long Left Flank
(n.d.), p. 19

Montgomery, it should be noted, later appreciated Canadians' 'soldierly instincts', although remaining critical of the quality of Canadian officers. And Canadian officers had to be prepared to put up with a lot more than their British cousins.

Our foremost future VIP was a lieutenant named Massey. Before my time with the battery it was in training for some months in the summer and autumn of 1915 at Niagara Camp. Among the officers was a supernumerary attached only for training. He did not go overseas with us but did follow us later with another battery. He is, however, well and favourably remembered by such of our boys as were at Niagara Camp.

His first name was Raymond. When you hear his name now you think of Abraham Lincoln and Dr Gillespie. That of course was long before he was known as anything but one of the Massey boys, the descendants of one of the founders of a great Canadian industry. I well remember the thrill we used to experience in France when we saw, as we often did, the name Massey-Harris on the side of a binder or mower.

Sanitary arrangements at Niagara Camp were rudimentary in those days, and when the battery needed a bath some officer marched the men over to Lake Ontario where they stripped off on the beach and had a good swim. One day late in October the wind was blowing across the lines towards the officers' quarters, the major sniffed the breeze, announced that the battery needed a bath and detailed the supernumerary to conduct a bathing parade.

Lieutenant Massey marched the boys over to Lake Ontario. It was a coldish October day and the swim was short but invigorating. As the bathers came out of the water Massey could not repress a chuckle at their shivering plight. Without waiting to dress they seized him and threw him into Lake Ontario, uniform and all. The fact that that was done without reprisals is, I think, the best evidence that he was a regular guy.

Ernest G. Black, *I Want One Volunteer* (1965), pp. 142-3

The Canadians had a way of getting what they wanted from their officers: the best of the latter worked with that knowledge, and earned the respect of their men.

Then it was announced that a prize would be given for the best-drilled platoon in the brigade, and at once McIntyre set to work. He did not trust any non-com drilling and took sole charge himself. In a short time we were performing like guardsmen, as we really took a pleasure in the work and we wanted to please the officer. Any good soldier liked being in a smart unit. One by one we met Thirteen, Fifteen and Sixteen Platoons and defeated them. Then came competition with winners of the other companies. We won our first go and at noon talked with a runner who informed us the losers were getting a day's leave as compensation, and the rest of our company was being taken to a good show in Auchel.

That decided the issue. We purposely made a few mistakes as the afternoon contest began, and lost our chance. We expected a verbal explosion but McIntyre only grinned. 'You blighters let me down,' he said. 'But I'm glad you did. I want to have a good time myself.' No officer ever met a difficult situation more diplomatically, and we loved him. He had come up from the ranks and knew the score.

Will R. Bird, *Ghosts Have Warm Hands* (1968), pp. 58-9

For the Canadian officers, the difficulties of putting egalitarian, tough-minded individualists 'into shape' were often compounded by the sheer lack of material support—a problem that the wealthier Americans and the basically but adequately equipped British rarely faced. Sending Canada off to war always seemed a matter of slapping things together on luck, good will, and a shoestring. This recollection of an officer in the RCNVR (Royal Canadian Naval Volunteer Reserve) in 1939 is a graphic illustration.

We had absolutely nothing, we started completely from scratch. We had no uniforms in stores, or any sort of equipment whatsoever, except for a few old Lee-Enfield rifles and the twelve-pounder gun. On the third of September, which was a week before Canada declared war, the prewar Division was drafted to Halifax, including most of the officers and the Supply Officer, Lieutenant Howland, who went down as Captain's Secretary in Stadacona.

I took over his job in Toronto, and was faced with many problems right at the outset. My first thing to deal with was making out warrants for the draft of the prewar Division to Halifax, and as a matter of fact we had no transportation warrants. It took a week to get these down from Ottawa.

We were inundated with people wanting to join up. The Army had opened up a camp at the Exhibition Grounds, and the various Toronto Militia units had started training. They all had the newly issued battledress, which had come out in the fall of 1938. The prewar Toronto Division, which consisted of 125 officers and men, half a destroyer company—a half-company it was called then—left for Halifax, and we immediately started taking in suitable people. At first we had quite a wealth of people who had some experience, who wished to join up. We were further inundated with a tremendous number of ex-RN people from across Canada, Royal Fleet Reserve, and even people who had come across from the Chinese Customs and so on, all Britishers who had received all-up notices, and who were told to report in to the nearest Naval Division and get transportation to the UK. Well, we had authorization to do this, and issued them transportation warrants recoverable on the British Admiralty.

The Division itself had absolutely nothing in the way of accommodation. There was an old gas stove in the basement, and the Captain, Lieutenant-Commander Shedden, thought it was essential that we have people living in, sentries posted, and a 24-hour-a-day duty watch. So I was elected to arrange accommodation. The only worry we had was that the recruits were entitled to their basic pay, which I remember was only about thirty dollars a month at that time, plus a dollar and a quarter per day, called lodge and comp. or, more properly, subsistence allowance.

I was desperate to find where I could get bunks and cooking facilities and all the rest of it. Having been with the T. Eaton Company in Toronto, I went to see John David Eaton, who very kindly gave me a charge account number and said: 'Charge whatever you want to that number, and if anybody gives you any trouble, just refer it to me.' So, I got bunk beds and lockers, and we set up accommodation for sixty seamen in the building.

Ottawa branch, NOAC, *Salty Dips* (1983), vol. 1, pp. 7-8

The new units, whether they were regiments, squadrons, troops, or ship's companies, soon devised unique ways of establishing special identities, as Farley Mowat, Canadian author and Second World War infantryman, relates.

The hunger for a mascot gained force, but it was to remain unsatisfied until the day before the regiment left Picton for the east.

That day was fast-approaching. In early December there were new and stricter medical examinations, and many of those who had grown into the Regiment so that they believed they had always been a part of it, were suddenly cast out to return to their civilian homes, and their lost jobs, and to face a bleak eternity of cold regrets. Theirs was a great tragedy, greater because it was so seldom recognized.

Those who passed the final tests were subjected to the endless assaults of hypodermic needles, and the stuff injected into their arms must have been the stuff of which rumours are made. December drew on and the Regiment seethed with speculation.

On Saturday night, December 16, George Ponsford, who was later to become a living legend in the Regiment, came to a personal decision on the mascot question. For days he had been eyeing a huge pewter statue of an Indian, probably Tecumseh himself, that stood in somewhat faded majesty on the roof of the tanning factory. On Saturday afternoon George laid his plans and procured a long ladder which he secreted behind the building. Close on midnight, he recovered his ladder and, with the help of another man, made his way up the roof.

The Indian was securely fixed in place, for he had stood at his post through three decades. It took much labour with a huge pipe wrench to free him, and when he was liberated at last, he slowly keeled over, almost crushing his kidnappers, and thoroughly drenching them in rain water which spilled out of a number of bullet holes, the legacies of many local Nimrods over the long years.

The kidnapping was further complicated by the unexpected arrival of a third soldier, very much the worse for wear, who stumbled against the ladder, and with proper Hastings spirit accepted the challenge and clawed his way up to the roof. He was very, very drunk, and the two men with their trophy were hard put to it to prevent first the Indian, then the drunk, from plunging over the parapet. They sweated blood as they lowered their two charges to the ground.

The possession of the Indian was one thing, his disposal quite another. But Ponsford was always a man of wit. Having bribed the sentry to look the other way, he and his companion dragged the Chief, complete with spear, to the doorway of the Sergeants' Mess, and there they set him up with a bottle of good whisky cradled in his arms. It was an enlistment credential that could not be denied.

In the morning the Indian was found, and the same morning the long-awaited word arrived from Ottawa. The Regiment was ordered to entrain that night. Its destination, Halifax—and after that, no man could say.

There was never any doubt about the Indian. That same day he was officially taken on strength, issued with his identification tags, and secreted in the battalion baggage. He was a fit emblem in a Regiment which boasted many original inhabitants of North America amongst its soldiers. They named him Little Chief, in defiance of his great stature and formidable weight, and he became much more than a mere mascot, for in the end the Regimental Indian became an institution.

Farley Mowat, *The Regiment* (1973), pp. 13-14

And soon enough came the Great Crossing overseas—for, thankful-ly, Canadians have done most of their fighting in other lands.

The crossing had been a trying one. The wet and piercing cold of northern seas had penetrated the crowded troop decks with their make-shift bunks and seamen's hammocks; for while *Ormande* possessed air-conditioning to guard against the equatorial sun, she had no heating arrangements whatsoever. Neither did she have an easy motion, and the seas had been unruly. Most of her passengers had become seasick the first day out from Canada, and had remained in that condition all the way across.

Such prolonged bodily discomfort had had its effects upon the new soldiers. There had been near-riots when the English cooks served herrings at each succeeding breakfast—herrings whose sunken eyes stared balefully up from the heaving tables of the mess decks. Frozen mutton and rabbit from Australia had been greeted with mutters of outrage and there were many men who drew the whole of their sustenance during that voyage from what confections could be purchased at the ship's meager canteen.

It was not a happy crossing. The new regiment was unprepared to accept these approximations to wartime conditions, for as yet the men had no real understanding of what war could be. Each new hardship imposed by the 'Limeys' who ran the ship was taken as a personal affront.

There was more to it. This was the first time that many of the men had ever been outside the confines of the two counties and in-dividually they were unprepared for new and inexplicable experien-ces.

There was a man, nick-named 'Toby Tanglefoot', who one morn-ing found he could not face the kippers, and made an urgent dash up the companionway. But Toby was met, head-on, by a large, cold sea on its way down. He was literally washed back into the mess deck, bellowing with the desperation of a man who sees the Lord ap-proaching.

'Take out, boys, take out! The son of a bitch has sunk!'

Ibid., pp. 15-16

Waiting across 'the pond' for the rough-edged Canadians was Eur-ope, and in particular Britain, the discovery of which almost always led to a deep and abiding affection.

We find it difficult to understand this enthusiasm and the emotion that is evident everywhere. None of us has yet struck a blow for England. Each time we have started out for the battle-front we have been turned back before firing a shot. Yet we are honoured like heroes. Much of the demonstration is, of course, a manifestation of the matchless spirit of English hospitality. Much of it is a response to the gesture of brotherhood implicit in our coming here to fight hand-in-hand with the British. But there is something new in this excitement, a new intensity, and something that is at once grim and boisterous. Perhaps this is the real fighting spirit of Britain, coming to the surface—the first result of Dunkirk.

But there is a reaction that comes of a grave feeling. It is plain also that these people are at last aware of the imminence of the danger to their homes. Tradition has taught them that Canada is a powerful force in war. They now receive us as the vanguard of Canada's offensive might.

We wish our battalions were divisions. However, they are over-joyed by what they see.

Whee! That was a young girl, her face tense with mixed determination and apprehension. At the risk of being sent spinning by our fender, she stood holding a package of cigarettes where I could catch it as the truck dashed by. Probably she could not afford the cigarettes any better than I can, but there could be no thought of failing to catch them. Her apprehension gave place to excited joy as she placed the package in my hands. In my hat I had a rose, one of many that have been thrown into the cab along the road. I plucked it out and threw it back. There was a cheer as elders scrambled to retrieve it for her.

At frequent intervals along the road men and women stand with jugs of tea or lemonade, girls of all ages and young boys with arms full of flowers for the troops. Cigarettes, and they cost a mighty price here, are bestowed in abundance.

Says my mate, 'If the people at home could see this . . .'

He didn't finish his sentence, for, as we rounded the bend, his eye was caught by three lovely young things using six hands to throw him kisses.

'Gosh!' says Jimmy. 'What a country!'

Howard Clegg, *A Canuck in England* (1942), pp. 110-11

3

WINNING IT AT SEA

Other anecdotes in this collection will document the horror and waste of war at sea: the numbing endurance of the North Atlantic convoys, the sick anger at the torpedoings and the dying in frigid water or flaming oil, the deaths of so many ships and so many men—and women and children. But there were moments when luck or bravery won out, when ships and men worked well, and victories were won, or lives saved, or simple duty carried out. Often these moments are recounted in matter-of-fact language that hides the drama beneath.

On one dark night, I actually caught three U-boats on the surface, maintaining contact with one of them on radar, illuminating another with starshell, and chasing the third until he submerged and we were able to attack. On another occasion, we were vainly trying to illuminate a surfaced U-boat we had as a radar contact but after firing a great many rounds of starshell in 'spreads,' we were unable to see our target.

'Cease firing,' I said.

'Cease firing, sir,' as the gongs rang at all gun quarters.

'Y gun reports one starshell "up the spout", sir.'

'Don't permit them to unload. Too dangerous. Tell them to get rid of it. Fire on bearing green six zero.'

'Y gun fire on bearing green zero, sir.'

There was one last resounding boom and the starshell burst over the dark waters, slowly descending toward the sea in its parachute.

'By God, sir, there she is. Surfaced U-boat bearing green six zero.'

'All guns with high explosive load, Coxswain, starboard twenty.'

'Starboard twenty, sir. Twenty degrees of starboard rudder on, sir.'

'Thank you, Coxswain. Gunnery Officer open fire when ready. Coxswain, midships.'

'Midships, sir. Wheel amidships.'

'Steady as you go.'

'Steady as she goes, sir. Course two seven seven.'

'Thank you, Coxswain. A/S Operator, sweep ahead twenty-twenty. You want to pick up this fellow when he dives. If he doesn't I intend to ram the bastard. First Lieutenant, ensure that damage control parties double check all weather-tight doors forward.'

'Aye aye, sir.'

The U-boat dived before we got there and we commenced our anti-submarine hunt. Within minutes, we were in contact and delivered a couple of thumping attacks. I suspected that this one had gone very deep and I decided to use our ahead throwing 'hedgehog equipment' instead of depth charges. We did and we sank him. There were no survivors.

Jeffry V. Brock, *The Dark Broad Seas*, vol. 1 (1981), pp. 121-2

And there are tales of derring-do worthy of any adventure anthology.

The urgent jangle of the action-station bells in *Oakville* jerked me from sleep. Swarming up the bridge ladder I got a heel in the face—some matelot in an equal hurry to get to *his* action station aft. We struggled past each other.

Three steps brought me to the asdic shack. Leading Seaman Hartman, our best man, shoved the cruising-watch operator out of the seat and, donning the headphones, pointed ahead. Four plumes of water from the aircraft's depth-bombs were subsiding into a misty haze and showing small, ethereal rainbows in the moonlight. Hartman knew his job and was swinging the transmitter around to the bearing of the depth-bombs' splashes. Ping, went the oscillator. The sound-wave searched outwards, reverberations coming back fainter and fainter. Carefully, Hartman trained his transmitter three degrees to the right. Ping, again; the reverberations died away. The aircraft circled in a continuous, tight bank, making S's in Morse code with its signal-light. Its engines were loud and I had to press the earphones against my head. A flare drifted down, its ghostly radiance matching the moon.

'Fire a five-charge pattern when we cross the spot where those depth-bombs landed,' rapped the Captain.

Lieutenant-Commander Clarence King had won a Distinguished Service Cross in the First World War for sinking one U-boat and getting two 'probables'. His score in this war was zero and he didn't like it.

He was quivering, but his excitement was controlled. *Oakville* trembled under the thrust of her screw at full speed. I pressed the fire-bell; out arched depth-charges, one either side from the throwers; three splashed from the stern. We tensed. Because of our relatively slow speed these things could damage us as well. With a rumble they exploded. Water erupted to mast-head height. *Oakville* bucked, shuddered, and resumed her eager trembling. Poor old girl; there was worse to come.

Hartman was still sweeping his arc; three degrees to the right; ping. Before the reverberations died out, there came a low drumming note in our earphones. Intuitively, Hartman swung the oscillator rapidly right. The low drumming changed to the clamour of fast engines and the unmistakable turbulence of a submarine blowing her ballast-tanks. She was surfacing.

'Submarine hydrophone dead ahead,' I reported to the Captain. After a few moments Hartman asked, 'Moving left?' I watched the instruments: yes, that submarine was moving left. 'Target moving left,' I responded. This report, which should have elicited from the Captain a quiet 'Very good', was answered by a dozen shouts, 'There's the bastard!'

A black snout reared out of the water. The conning tower burst through a swell and she surfaced completely. Water cascaded from her decks, white and foamy in the moonlight.

'Ho-ho,' cried the Captain, not very nautically.

The Captain altered course to ram. Two rockets, the submarine-sighted signal, hissed skyward and burst into white stars.

We had only about three hundred feet to manoeuvre in. The Captain couldn't make it and we missed. U-94 bumped down the port side. The Captain opened the range to get another run-in. This gave the gunners a chance.

Our 4-inch gun roared out again and again. Two splashes we saw and then a satisfying orange flash on the submarine's conning tower. The Oerlikon banged away, the red tracer flowing out and ricocheting at wild angles off the pressure-hull of U-94. Our bow swung on again.

Now the .5-inch machine-guns started their insane chatter. The port gunner, ignoring the Captain's ear just six inches from the muzzle, let go the first burst. Have you ever seen a standing side-jump of twelve feet? Captain King did one that night. Olympic standard, I thought, and him fiftyish too.

We bore in. The 4-inch flashed again and U-94's 88-mm gun rocked over. Four steams of lead spewed from the .5's, and down below I could hear the Lewis gun spitting. With precision and speed the German gunners poured out and made for their weapons. In that murderous fire none made it.

Ites was manoeuvering U-94 with skill and by now at good speed.

We hit with only a glancing blow; again U-94 passed down the port side, this time about twenty feet off. Now we unleashed a weapon hitherto untried in modern warfare.

Stationed on the fiddley abaft the funnel were six stokers not needed in the engine-room during action. Their job was to reload the depth-charge throwers. But we weren't firing the throwers and so these stokers had nothing to do. And yet here were German faces on the bridge of a U-boat just a few feet away. U-94 was so close our guns could not depress to fire. Also on the fiddley abaft the funnel, the canteen manager stowed his empty Coke bottles. To the stokers, ignorant engineers uninstructed in the art of war, the connection was obvious.

Imagine, if you can, six stokers pelting the enemy with Coke bottles at twenty feet, crying, 'Yah! Yah!' Ducking heads on U-94 testified to their accuracy. If Ites' courage ever forsook him, it must have been then.

Depth-charges were fired again. One exploded directly under her. She bucked, spray obscured her, then she slowed. *Oakville* opened the range. If destroyers are the 'greyhounds of the Fleet', corvettes are the tenacious terriers. We opened the range, swung round, and plunged in the third time. The two .5-inch sent a steady stream of fire and U-94 rolled under. Beneath our bottom we felt three distinct shocks and heard rending metal. U-94 wallowed astern, and stopped. But Father was just warming up.

'Away boarding-party,' he cried. 'Come on, Lawrence! Get cracking!'

Obediently I slid down the ladder to the boarding-party locker, piously hoping I'd brought the list of names up to date and posted it on the notice-board. To my relief all twelve hands were there, struggling into their gear.

This gear requires a word. Obviously you keep on the lifebelt we all wore at sea. You need a pistol. Hand grenades might be handy: I had two. A gas-mask is recommended—'in case of toxic fumes'. One fathom of chain bent into a fathom of rope is mandatory; you tie the rope to something on the U-boat bridge and lower the chain down the hatch so the wily Germans can't close hatches, submerge, and leave you foolishly treading water. A flashlight is secured around your neck with a lanyard. That makes two lanyards; the other secures the pistol. The signalman has a lamp to signal with. The engineer has a bag of tools for his own mysterious purposes. And so on. A forked stick for carrying messages is about the only thing not demanded by the Regulations.

'Never mind lowering the boat,' bellowed the Captain from the bridge above; 'I'll put you alongside.'

I thought sceptically of his two misses. Meanwhile, the guns hammered away.

'Port side,' yelled the Captain.

I noted as we mustered on the port side that the 4-inch gun was silent. It has misfired. Was the round truly misfired and completely dead or was the charge smoldering and would it go off in five seconds, say, or ten, or thirty? A ticklish point; but in action there's no time to ponder. Gordo, the Captain of the Gun, tenderly eased the breech open, gently slid the charge into his arms, took five lurching steps to the ship's side, and dropped the smoldering charge over. As you may imagine, the rest of the guns-crew watched this in silence and with interest.

Now with a whoop they loaded again. They were so intent they didn't notice my boarding-party. The muzzle swung. I was leaning over the rail gauging the narrowing distance to U-94 when I heard the reports given:

'Layer on.'

'Trainer on.'

One startled look over my shoulder and I scuttled for safety.

'Fire!'

Only fifteen feet from the muzzle, the blast was stunning and blew us all into an untidy heap in the break of the fo'c's'le a drop of ten feet. I came to in a few moments with Petty Officer Powell shaking me and slapping my face.

'Come on, sir, we're nearly alongside.'

A bump and the grating of metal brought me to my senses, although my nose was bleeding and my ears were buzzing. I sprang up. No time for the rest of the boarding-part, groping about, still confused.

'Well, come on then. Over we go,' I said.

Now, I was always a romantic youth, and from age ten onwards, stories of the Spanish Main were a large part of my literary diet. And so, as I dropped the eight-odd feet to U-94's deck I though incredulously, 'Mother of God!' I really am boarding an enemy ship on the Spanish Main.

A small calamity brought me back to earth. As I hit the deck of U-94 the belt of my tropical shorts snapped on impact. My pants slid down to my ankles. I stumbled, kicked them off, and rose. Clad only in a pistol, two grenades, a gas-mask, a length of chain, a flashlight, and a lifebelt, I lurched up the deck.

'The bridge,' I yelled to Powell, just as a wave washed me over the side. Powell helped me back but the chain was on a thousand-fathom journey to the bottom. 'The bridge!' We started forward again, swaying up the heaving deck.

The enemy were still below but they wouldn't stay there long. If we could gain the bridge first, we would be in control.

Oakville was stopped a half-mile away. Her after-gun opened up at us. Luckily it started at the other end of the U-94's hull and methodically worked its fire to our end. The bullets ricocheted off with nasty whinging sounds. 'There's always *someone* who doesn't get the word!' I thought resentfully. Over the side again; we were safer in the water.

I swam back on board with the next wave, throwing off the gas-mask. A sort of strip-tease had started: first my pants, then the chain, and now the gas-mask. Powell was there again.

'The bridge,' I said desperately. 'Damn it, this is becoming more like a swimming party than a capture.'

Despite casualties, there were still some thirty able-bodied Germans on board. We were two. We reached the forward gun, by now a tangled mess of steel. A German slid from behind it. With my pistol barrel I knocked him over the side. Twenty-nine to two.

Rounding the conning tower we saw two more. We rushed. Both took a long, horrified look at my uniform—or lack of it, and jumped into the water when we were within three feet. They must have been thinking along the lines of 'Blimey—he's come to bugger us all.'

Powell flushed another and kicked him over. Twenty-six to two.

'The bridge,' I urged again; 'we can't fight the whole bloody crew one by one. We've got to keep them below.'

Too late! As we reached the top of the ladder two were out. A third was emerging.

'Get below,' I ordered the leading one. It wasn't in German but a pistol three feet from one's face is international for 'stop'. He kept coming. I fired and he flipped backwards over the side under the awful power of .45 slug. Powell fired. The second sagged. Twenty-four to two. The third man, half-out, bobbed down.

A body lay crumpled behind the hatch; another hung by the after-gun, his arm swinging limply as U-94 rolled.

'Now keep them below,' I ordered Powell. 'Find out if they opened the sea-cocks or if they set scuttling charges. I want to look at that open hatch aft.'

I jumped down the ladder, hung on as a wave washed over, then tore for the open hatch. Made it! As the next wave swept the deck I hung on to the hatch with both hands. That's the secret, I thought. The brilliant moon showed the compartment flooded; no one would flank us from here. On a lifting deck I rushed back. Powell was sitting on the rail, his gun dangling casually, his eyes alert. The prisoners below were shouting.

'Better let them out if we're to salvage this boat,' Powell said.

I knelt by the hatch. 'Sprechen Sie Deutsch?' A clamour told me they all did. 'Ja, ja.'

'No, no, I mean, sprechen Sie Englisch?' Silence.

'How are you going to get them up?' Powell asked mildly.

Well, we had certainly been definite about their staying below. And, apart from 'Auf Wiedersehen', which did not seem to fit the situation, I had exhausted my German vocabulary.

I put the pistol on the deck, shone the flashlight on my face, and spoke in what I hoped was a reassuring voice.

'Come on up. It's all right. See—no gun.' I grinned, pleasantly. 'See—no gun.' I beckoned encouragingly.

A muscular arm shot. up. I leaned back, startled. Another arm followed and a body heaved out, and another, and another. Soon I found myself in a veritable mob, my pistol and flashlight trailing around my ankles. The pistol banged my shins painfully and the flashlight lanyard threatened to choke me. Someone was standing on the light. Such was the squeeze I couldn't bend to pick up either of them.

I had certainly lost command of the situation.

Powell hadn't. He shoved and kicked the submariners to the after gun-platform that abutted the bridge. Magically, I was unimpeded.

The bridge was pocked with bullet-holes, one section blown away completely. The forward end of the bridge was crumpled from the ramming and the hatch was stuck open at about fifty degrees. I slid over the body lying there, wriggled underneath the hatch, and dropped down.

Directly below the bridge was the conning tower.

It was black. From repeated wettings my flashlight was burning dull orange. Nothing here. Down the next ladder.

Now I was in the Control Room. Here it was blacker still, the water about chest height. In this compartment were the flooding valves I must close.

Now concentrate! Numbers one, three, and five were main-ballast tanks. Numbers two and four were trimming-tanks and unimportant. Number one was aft, three amidships, and five forward. The pressure gauges were all on the port side.

She rolled heavily. I slipped and went under. Coming up, I trod water. She rolled the other way. With a rush the water receded to my knees and I was standing again. But now, dammit, which side was port? I'd lost my bearings. Tortuously, I pulled myself from instrument to instrument, now floating, now standing, looking for the pressure gauges. The effective range of my flashlight was about a foot and getting dimmer.

A thump and a sudden list told me a water-tight bulkhead had given. Was it forward or aft? I didn't know.

At last I came on the pressure gauges. Before I could recall the correct procedure, there came a thump and a lurch and a particularly long roll to port. She lolled; there was little buoyancy now. Clearly, U-94 was mortally hurt.

'Come up, sir' yelled Powell, 'she's going!'

Murmuring a 'Hail Mary' I swam for the ladder. Water showered in from above. The sailor who had been slumped around the hatch had slewed around in the rushing water and stared sightlessly skyward.

Powell glanced at me with the question written on his face. The prisoners were huddled near his weaving .45.

'Get them over,' I said.

Powell jerked his thumb; the prisoners plunged over the side.

'You too.'

Powell stepped off.

Only a few moments left. A cloud obscured the moon. The black waves rolled toward us, white crests hissing gently. The water to leeward was ablaze with green phosphorescence. Off to the north the dark bulk of the convoy receded. Two 'whumps' of torpedoes striking home told me other U-boats were attacking. A pillar of flame erupted, mounted, and briefly took the shape of a crooked tree; star shell and flares blossomed. *Oakville* was a black silhouette about a mile away. The rollers crashed over our side. U-94 would never lift above them again; she would never be steamed into harbour flying the white ensign of a captured ship either. It's a sad thing to see a ship die, and to lose a prize of war.

I slid over, swam hard for a minute, and looked back. We hadn't abandoned U-94 too soon; she lifted her bow, and slid under.

Hal Lawrence, *A Bloody War* (1979), pp. 96-103

It was not only in the North Atlantic that Canadians fought their naval war, in corvettes and destroyers or DEMS *(defensively equipped merchant ships). They fought in the North Sea, the Mediterranean, and elsewhere, in the small 'coastal forces' family of motor launches, motor gun boats, and motor torpedo boats. And sometimes the action was equally furious.*

I remember one night. I was very friendly with a chap from New Zealand, MacDonald, who became quite a decorated officer. I used

to go out with him quite often. One night we went across the North
Sea.

We started our patrol and I was operating the radar. I detected
something at long range, about twelve thousand yards, normally
you couldn't detect anything at that range from sea level, so I said
to the bridge, 'They must be flying a balloon or something like that.'
Then on the radar I saw something coming right into the ground
wave. The thing seemed to go out the way it came in, and I thought:
'My God, they've done it! They've discovered the boomerang shell,
it's coming right at you, then goes back and maybe takes another
crack at you.' But of course it was going right through the primitive
radar beam and I was getting it on the back lobe as well. But it's
rather weird watching the radar while you're being bombarded and
see little things detach themselves and come right down the screen
at you and then go back out.

We went up to these things and intercepted them, but by this time
the Germans were ready. It was a nightly affair and they were very
alert, so our chances of getting at them were pretty slight. They
would run a convoy surrounded by flak trawlers which were just
trawlers, but loaded with every weapon you could think of. They
had one of these Hispano Suizas, I guess they were, and they just
never seemed to stop. You'd go up and see this stuff coming at you
like a fan. Oh, the streams of it! So we eventually decided that
discretion was the better part of valour and turned back. We had
chased them all night and couldn't get a shot at them. On the Dutch
coast there are streams of islands and there are gaps whenever you
go in between the islands to get into the ports. And they were
turning in there. MacDonald said, 'What do you think? Shall we go
in after them?' 'For my money I've had enough,' I said; 'I don't want
to go in.'

Anyway we turned around to come back. I was standing with
MacDonald on the bridge as the dawn was breaking, and we were
still only five or ten miles off the Dutch Coast, running roughly
parallel to it. Then the forward lookout pointed to the sky over the
horizon. We looked over, and couldn't see anything solid, only three
or four bow waves—you couldn't see the boats themselves but you
could see the bow waves. MacDonald took his glasses and looked
and said, 'They're German M-class.' This was a class about half-way
between a minesweeper and a destroyer. And there were four of
them! We were inside towards the Dutch Coast and they were
outside and coming towards us. I went down to get some ranges on
the radar and I heard MacDonald say on the RT to the other two or
three boats in the flotilla: 'Flag four.' That meant 'Attack with
torpedoes.' God, I was just about scared green because we were no

match for M-class boats, but they hadn't seen us yet. So I started to get ranges and he put forward the throttle to about forty knots and went tearing on. Then MacDonald fired both 21-inch torpedoes together, and our boat just stopped in its tracks. I'd never been in a boat before that fired both at once like this. We hit one of the M-class and the other boat behind hit him too and MacDonald said, 'Come up and have a look.' He was a mad guy and the guns were firing. When I went up, it was getting daylight. The range was only a hundred yards and there were guys diving off the German boats. They were on fire and they were shooting at us, and you know in the navy lately you never as a rule engage somebody at a hundred yards. There were big chunks flying off the boats. We were going about forty knots and they were going about thirty knots the other way. Oh my God! We had two Oerlikons and the guy in the back, our boy, never stopped firing. He was using tracer, and you could see the big chunks coming off the boats and they kept hitting the wheelhouse. Of course that's the name of the game, to sort of distract the bridge a bit. It all happened very quickly. And what they were shooting at us, I don't know. They were big shells that gave off black smoke when they hit.

It was all over in about two or three minutes. We sank one of them and left another burning. Of course we didn't bother hanging around very long, just tore back. We radioed C-in-C Nore what was happening as soon as we'd left them, and in about fifteen or twenty minutes the Beaufighters arrived. If one thing scared an MTB it was these Beaufighters. They weren't too hot on their recognition then, and they were murder because they carried a lot of cannons. I was on the bridge and scrambling around looking for the Verey pistol to fire a recognition flare. Anyway they knew we were there, and they went on and chewed those poor guys up some more. By this time it was full daylight and there we were still only about ten miles off the Dutch Coast. We just headed for home very quickly after that. It wasn't always like that, it was only a very odd night that you'd really get a lot of action.

Ottawa branch, NOAC, *Salty Dips* , vol. 1 (1983), pp. 112-13

Sometimes there was the happier occasion to save life rather than take it.

Shortly after daybreak, south of Pantelleria, a further air attack developed. By now long-range fighters from Malta were patrolling overhead, but they were less effective than they should have been owing to the lack of ship-borne direction to vector them onto their targets. In this action, one cargo ship blew up, a Stuka dive bomber crashed into the already damaged tanker *Ohio*, which was soon to take more punishment, one ship was set on fire, and another hit and stopped.

Meanwhile, our jaunty little force of four fleet minesweepers in box formation screened by the seven MLs came in sight of the shapeless flock of ships. The sea was flat calm, and the day was bright but with some scattered clouds. We could see planes diving and air combat overhead. Off to the northwards a fighter headed for the sea trailing smoke, and a parachute blossomed in the sky. Jerome told me off to pick up the pilot, and away we went home.

In time we sighted a yellow rubber dinghy with a man in it. I ordered the scrambling net put over the side and told John what I wanted done. As I brought *126* alongside the dinghy, I studied its occupant through binoculars. He was hatless and fair-haired, in the tan summer uniform common to all air forces in that climate, and he wore no identifying rank or other badges. All the operating instructions I could see on the dinghy were in foreign languages. I must assume the man was German.

When the dinghy was abreast the scrambling net, two stout seamen climbed down to help the airman up. He was not wounded, and on deck John jabbed a revolver in his ribs and hustled him up to the bridge. Not a word had yet been spoken. 'Sprechen sie Deutsch?' I demanded. 'Hell no,' he shot back. 'I'm from Regina.'

Gordon W. Stead, *A Leaf Upon the Sea* (1988), p. 97

Almost as a rule, the Canadian at sea was a tough customer, prepared to tackle any adversary with gusto, as in this experience of HMCS Haida, *a Tribal-Class destroyer, during the Korean War.*

We were going up the east coast, dead of night, bootin' along about 24 knots 'cause we were late. I was on watch when we picked up this radar contact. One big one in the centre and a whole ring of these bastards around her. And they're comin' south, fast, toward us. So we went to Action Stations and challenged them.

'This is King Cobra, identify yourself!' King Cobra was our call sign.

Not a word. We challenged them again.

'Identify yourself or we'll open fire.'

(Can't you just see it? Here is a large unidentified warship, accompanied by numerous escorts and there is *Haida*—playing David to an unknown Goliath—threatening to open fire. Typical.)

They're getting closer and closer.

Suddenly there are planes overhead, with great huge lights shinin' down on us. And the signal comes across; the voice of doom:

'King Cobra, this is Battle-axe.'

It was the American battleship *Missouri* and her screen. Well, as soon as the Old Man heard that he passes his hand across his eyes. I didn't catch what he said. Somethin' about 'Turn the light off, for chrissake!'

Speaking of the *Missouri*: We were offshore about three miles, shelling the coast. The *Los Angeles*, a cruiser, was about ten miles out, shelling the same spot. And the *Missouri* was another 22 miles farther out, hitting the same spot on the beach that we were. You couldn't even see her! From nowhere, it seemed, there'd be this whoomp! and you'd suddenly realize the power of those ships.

We were pretty close in; it was all being done by radar. The Old Man saw gun flashes from the mainland, and just as he did we were straddled, a shell on either side of us. But as soon as he got the stern around—wham!—the 3"/50 silenced that shore battery like nothin'! It's the only time the thing ever really worked!

Alan D. Butcher, *I Remember Haida* (1985), pp. 109-10

The Second World War saw Canadians make their first serious effort to come up fully to their capacities in modern sea warfare. It took time to become good at it, for they had no long national traditions upon which to build. But when at last they knew their job, the Canadians at sea knew no peer, and built their own tradition on the spot.

4

THE LAND WAR: LIVING AND FIGHTING

It was in the trenches of the First World War that many Canadians of that abstemious era were introduced to the mystic military substance, rum.

There was another single drink that I remember gratefully. It was just after we came out of Passchendaele. We had had six weeks of it and were out on rest at Verdrel, half-way up the ridge behind Barlin. As usual after a long time on a nasty front I had a reaction. While I was in the line I stood it I think as well as the next man. When I got out of the line there was a let-down. I would run a small temperature, have a bit of a headache and perhaps a digestive upset. It only lasted a day or two. When it came on after Passchendaele I reported sick and was put in charge of the sick parade. Our MO was on leave. He was replaced by Jack Maynard, the old Varsity football great. After the men had all been examined and disposed of he turned to me.

'What's your trouble, corporal?' he said.

I told him.

'I know just what you need,' he said. He reached into his hip pocket, brought out a large silver flask filled with Scotch whisky and then prescribed. 'Take all of that you can drink without choking.'

I had never drunk neat whisky before but my natural talents must have amazed him. I am proud of the fact that I did not parade sick again the next day just to get another dose of that perfect medicine.

Ernest G. Black, *I Want One Volunteer* (1965), pp. 126-7

It became a commodity deserving of some effort to find and keep.

One morning at the horse lines, after coming down the night before from the guns, I was roused by the sergeant-major long before reveille had blown with the news that it was my turn to take up the ration party. We saddled up and were away long before breakfast was ready. Before leaving we did get a mug of tea and a slice of bread. I always seemed to be starting with a slice of bread for breakfast. If we had known what was in store for us we would probably have taken some bully beef and cheese and biscuits to serve as a lunch.

We proceeded first to the depot near Ypres to draw rations for the battery. There was a long delay there and it was after lunchtime before we were on our way again. Remembering the kind of soldiers we were, I am at a loss to explain why we did not lunch on the rations we carried. We were not ready yet for raw bacon or beef, but there must have been at least one gunny sack full of month-old bread. It would have been no chore at all to rip one of those loaves loose from the sacking merged with its crust. Perhaps we were just in a hurry to get the job done. Even a soldier has times when he forgets his stomach.

Our progress was slow. We were now all dismounted and each leading two horses loaded with boxes and bags. There were delays in traffic and by the time we came in sight of the battery it was nearly four o'clock. At that point the Germans started to shell the plank-road. We unloaded our freight and piled it beside the road. I sent the drivers back with the horses to the Peggy Dump about a mile back to wait for me there. I kept one man with me to look after the pile while I walked into the battery position to get a carrying party to take in the rations. When that was done I sent Adam, the man I had kept as guard, back a couple of hundred yards to an old German pillbox to wait for me there while I got a receipt from the major for the rations. The carrying party dispersed to the guns and the cook and I stood on the plank-road while he checked my list and OK'd it for the major's signature.

As we stood there one lone packhorse came galloping down the plank-road from the front, riderless and unattended. Some ration party up front had been caught in the shelling and dispersed. Old Mac, the cook, was much more alert mentally than I was for he saw the opportunity and grasped it while I did not even guess what was going on. He got out into the middle of the plank-road and as the packhorse passed he grasped the flying bridle. Setting his feet hard and throwing his full weight back he swung the horse off the road and onto its side in the muck. In a moment he was on the horse, undoing the surcingle and allowing two long white boxes to fall into the mud. Each of the boxes contained two large earthenware jars bearing on the side the initials SRD, spirits of rum diluted. We had four gallons of rum.

We carried the jars to the mudhole that Mac called a cook-house.

I went to the major to get my ration receipt signed, intending to return to the cook-house for a bite to eat and a sandwich or two to take back to the drivers. What happened when I got back to the cook-house put all thought of food for myself or anyone else out of my mind. Part of the cook's equipment was a set of graduated granite mugs. Mac had the largest one, a pint, filled with rum for me. It was then after five o'clock and I had had nothing to eat since the night before except a mug of tea and a slice of bread before daybreak. I had been on my feet, walking or standing around. Even before I reached Adam at the pillbox the stuff had begun to work. I told Adam what had happened. I can still hear him wail, 'Oh, Ernie, what did you send me back for?' I remember that he had been pleased with the suggestion of the pillbox when I made it to him.

Away we went to join the drivers and the horses at Peggy Dump. Soon I was floating along, my feet scarcely touching the planks of the road. Presently a salvo of 5.9s came over. A 5.9 was a German shell approximately six inches in diameter and weighing about one hundred pounds. It dug a hole four or five feet deep and ten to twelve feet across depending on what kind of soil it landed in. Its burst, including black smoke and flying dirt, looked like a bush or small tree. Like a smart soldier, when he heard the express-train roar of the approaching salvo Adam went flat on the plank-road and was out of the way of flying splinters when the shells landed. Not me. Right after the bursts, which were close, with two on each side of the road, I took off my tin hat and made a sweeping bow to the black clouds blowing away from the shell holes. Adam did not approve. Most of his remarks I have forgotten but I do remember that he said something about a 'damn fool'. Away we went again. Presently we approached the Peggy Dump and the drivers. Tight as I was, before we got there I had made my plans.

'Look, Adam,' I shaid, no said. 'You tell the driversh to beat it back to the horshe linesh on their own and you shtay behind to help me get mounted.'

When the drivers were gone Adam helped me to get my left foot into the stirrup and then with great pushing and heaving managed to get me on my horse's back. Then he went around to the other side and put my right foot in its stirrup. Have you even ridden on a fluffy pink cloud right into a glorious sunset? Then you have no idea of the ride I had that November evening down the road through St Jean, Wieltj and Ypres to our horse lines near Vlamertinghe.

That incident had an unhappy sequel. Poor old Mac buried his four jars of rum near his cook-house. No one but he and I knew the secret and even I did not know the location of the cache. There was great speculation in the battery as to why Mac refused to take his reliefs and insisted on staying at the gun lines. On my trips to the guns I always got an extra ration but never again from the big granite mug. After eighteen days without a relief Mac was killed in his cook-house. I was then free to disclose the secret. We made a determined effort to find the rum. We probed all likely places but without success. Unless some Belgian plough has turned them out the remains of those four gallons of rum still lie buried near the Heights of Abraham in front of Passchendaele Ridge.

Ibid., pp. 129-32

The question of army food would always bring out the bad language in a soldier, so vital an element was it to men caught in the dull grind of routine or the discomfort of the front. It could also lead to displays of considerable ingenuity.

Another army meal that stands out in my memory was one we had at a gun position on the shores of Dickebusch Lake not far from the spot where we had our baptism of fire. Our gun-pits were built in the line of a hedge and there were hedges all about us dividing the pocket handkerchief fields. The hedges there were all berry bushes. I am unable to name them. Some called them blackberries, to me they looked like mulberries. Whatever they were they made won-derful pies. The Belgians would not eat them, which seemed strange to us for those thrifty people were not given to wasting anything that could be put to any use. The story we heard was that there was some superstition connected with those berries. If there was it was even stupider than most superstitions.

Our cook made a deal with us. There was a standing arrangement that if we did without bread for a certain time we could draw an equivalent in flour. We immediately swarmed into the hedges pick-ing berries. There were six of us including the sergeant and we delivered a prodigious quantity of berries to the cook-house.

Then the cook proceeded to make the pie. First he took a dixie lid. A dixie was a cooking utensil about the depth and width of an ordinary pail but of oval shape so that it had about twice the capacity of a pail. Among its uses was the making of porridge and the boiling of tea. The lid was from two and a half to three inches in depth. Our pie was a deep-dish pie and when it was done the wonderful pastry rose up a couple of inches above the top of the dixie lid. Simple arithmetic shows that that pie was four and a half to five inches thick. We divided it into six pieces, one for each of us and nothing extra for the sergeant. That was all we had for supper that night, deep-dish berry pie and tea. I close my eyes and I can taste it still. That is one thing about the kind of life we lived at the front, the highlights stand out so vividly.

Ibid., pp. 99-100

What a civilian might take for granted, a First World War soldier might treat as a treasure.

A delicacy regarded more highly even than toast was fried bread. At the horse lines we could get it with our breakfast. We lined up and went by the kitchen with our mess tins. At the first stop we got porridge, thick he-man oatmeal, without sugar or milk. Next we got our bacon, on top of the oatmeal. Then we got a slice of bread and our tea. The bread was usually dry in the morning though sometimes there was jam. At supper we had margarine, occasionally even butter. If it happened that there was jam and you wanted fried bread you scraped the dab of jam from the slice of bread onto the porridge. Then you had a clean piece of bread for frying. The sergeant-cook supervised that. He stood beside a large pan of bacon fat, a pan about three feet square and four to five inches deep. I doubt if it was ever emptied. In it was an accumulation of the fat from many mornings of bacon frying, less only the amount withdrawn in the frying of bread. The fat was piping hot and at least three inches deep. You dropped your slice of bread into the bacon fat and it disappeared. The cook stood beside the pan with a large sieve-like spoon in his hand fishing out slices of bread. Whenever he got a slice that was done he gave it to the first man in line and then started fishing for another.

A slice that was done was a rich brown, crisp through and through and fit for a king. No king with a soldier's appetite could ask for anything better. One morning I had something extra. There were civilians near us and one old lady had a hen that so far no soldier had succeeded in stealing. Occasionally she had an egg for sale. Once I was the lucky purchaser. I paid her a franc and a half for that egg, thirty cents, a day-and-a-half's pay. The next morning I carried it tenderly to the cook. He broke the shell on the edge of the pan and dropped the egg into that three inches of bacon fat. My heart was in my mouth. Would he ever find it again? I got my fried bread and waited while he fished around for the egg. Finally he found it and I left with a well-fried egg nestling on top of my slice of fried bread.

Ibid., pp. 106-7

And much was done—or winked at—to ensure a decent meal for oneself and comrades.

Chickens were in the public domain. Any chicken that wandered near troops met an untimely end. Even those that stayed sedately at home on their roosts were not safe. I love to think of one incident near Wallop, in England. There are three Wallops, Nether Wallop, Middle Wallop and Upper Wallop. We slept in an open field between Middle Wallop and Upper Wallop on our march back to Witley Camp from the firing range at Lark Hill. After we were properly rolled up in our blankets under the guns two of our boys went scouting. Presently they returned so laden with chickens that they could hardly walk. The cook was roused, the travelling kitchen was fired up and we had a midnight chicken dinner. One of the neighbouring batteries barbecued a calf that night. Their meal cost them much less than ours cost us.

It was not until we got back to Witley that we realized just what we had done. The bill for the chickens was made out and in due course was paid out of our battery fund. Our battery fund consisted of our share of the canteen profits, augmented by regular contributions from the Mothers' Comforts League. The League met regularly in Toronto, knitted socks, read to each other their sons' letters from the front and raised money in various ways, including monthly dues. The contents of those letters sometimes drifted back to France not infrequently causing embarrassment, as when we heard that one of our number, who had not yet been up the line, had had a horse shot under him during furious fighting of which none of the rest of us had ever heard.

The saddest part of all was that those chickens were from a pen of pure-bred, prize, white Wyandottes. They cost the battery fund eighty pounds, nearly four hundred dollars in those days. In those days, too, a dollar was a dollar. I hope our mothers did not know that the money they scraped together to buy us comforts was used to pay for stolen chickens at almost forty dollars per chicken. I also hope that they did not know that when the major would announce on parade the receipt of a draft from the League and asked what we wanted done with it, the answer would be an almost unanimous shout of *Beer*.

Ibid., pp. 29-30

Another substance of which the soldier of 1914-18 came to have intimate knowledge was mud—mud beyond imagining, even in an age of unpaved roads.

The mud of Passchendaele was in some ways a good thing. Many shells were smothered by it when they burst and there was not nearly the danger from splinters flying great distances, which we often experienced on other fronts. Some shells, particularly small ones, were completely smothered. One of my friends was standing by his bivy one day when a percussion whiz-bang landed directly under him. He rose in the air on a cushion of mud and landed on the other side of his bivy. He got up unhurt, scraped away what mud would come off easily and shook his fist eastward, demanding of those SOBs what the hell they thought they were doing. Psychologically, a little profanity was a great relief. One of our boys lost an arm in Vimy village. The men who took him away reported how he went back over the ridge, shaking his remaining fist at the Germans and cursing them in language, which, when reported to us, was the wonder and admiration of the whole battery.

Ibid., p. 65

To conduct war in such an environment placed men in conditions that can only be regarded with pity and awe.

When we left the duckboards it was to go through mud knee-deep. Progress was slow, as each man tried to avoid sinking deeper than necessary. We stopped and the sergeant waded over to an 'island' of broken timbers and got a heavy coil of large rope. It was soggy and muddy, all he could carry. We kept on and arrived at a battery of five guns. The battery horses had drowned in mire as they tried to move the guns to the left where a slight rise afforded more solid ground, so now thirty men of the 42nd took hold of the rope and tried to pull a gun. It was soon evident we could not move the guns in the usual fashion, as the mud gripped the wheels like glue, so we turned them over and over until they were at the new emplacement.

It was tremendous labour. Each man had to keep getting a new footing, and often we sank in mud and water of gruel thickness until the slime rose above our hips. The only thing solid underneath was a huddled dead man, and we stumbled over five or six during the morning. The job had to be completed before we went back to the tents, but there were just two thirty-man teams, so it was almost three o'clock when the last gun was in the new position. At that moment over came two big black-winged German Gothas and dropped bombs. Their aim was bad. They missed us by one hundred yards, but some ammunition mules were packed in line on a shaky 'board road' made of planks and one bomb made a direct hit on a broad mule rump.

The Gothas flew off, and we saw men pull three dead mules into the mire, an addition to the many carcasses beside the way with legs stiffened toward the sky and bodies distended so that they afforded footholds for rats. Shambles of heads and entrails were shovelled into the mire and then the ammunition train went on. We had stood knee-deep in the slime and watched proceedings, and now we turned and made our way toward the duckboards. We had just reached sound footing and were trying to stamp off clinging mud when we heard shells coming. The Hun was still after the battery. He seemed to have uncanny knowledge of the slope. Most of the shells went into the mud to raise small harmless geysers, but one gun was wrecked by a direct hit and two gunners were killed. We watched dispassionately from two hundred years away, as if we had no part in such actions, then went back to our tents, sodden, shaking with exhaustion, plastered with mud, and were cheered with messtins of hot mulligan and hot tea. The rations were up and better than usual. After eating we had energy enough to scrape mud from our kilts and bare knees, but only to a degree. No man tried to get clean. It began to rain again, to get colder. Some hardy spirit ventured forth and found where we could get water, as we had been issued plenty of tommy cookers. So we made tea by the messtin around six o'clock and ate again.

It was impossible to escape the leaks in the rain-soaked tent. The sagging floor pooled with icy water. We put our ground sheets over our shoulder, kept our helmets on and sat on our equipment, doubled to keep us from the wet floor, jammed together in a huddle about the tent pole. Through the night we sat there in the dark, unmoving, sleeping in fitful snatches, wakened by someone starting to fall over, not speaking, our brains numbed by the awfulness of everything, each trying to attain the comatose state that answered for sleep.

At daylight we made and drank messtins of hot tea. More rations arrived and we ate. Around nine o'clock orders came for us to put our equipment on, ready to move. There was still a slight drizzle as we waded over to the duckwalk. We proceeded slowly as we were continually meeting men, some walking wounded cases, going back. One dared not yield too much right of way, because to step from the wooden bath mats might mean immersion to the waist. On and on we went, with the occasional halt as we waited for guides or runners. At noon we reached an area dotted with rusting derelict tanks and stood there, sideways on, as the remnants of a relieved battalion edged by us, men who looked like grisly discards of the battlefield, long unburied, who had risen and were in search of graves. Not one of them spoke, nor did we.

Will R. Bird, *Ghosts Have Warm Hands* (1968), pp. 71-3

And then there was the wildlife attracted by millions of men compacted together with their refuse—and the shattered remains of unburied bodies—in the torn earth of the trenches. Rats, for example.

We tried many things to get rid of them. Shooting at them was soon forbidden because there was no way of telling where a ricocheting bullet might come to rest. We tried other methods. We would scatter pieces of hardtack at night on the ground outside the gun-pits. When we heard the rats gnawing the biscuit we would rush them with electric torches to blind them and then vie with each other in seeing how far we could kick them. The old army boot was an ideal weapon for such warfare. Twenty- or thirty-foot kicks were common.

Perhaps our warfare had some success. I do not remember much about rats in the last year of the war. Perhaps we just got used to them.

Ernest G. Black, *I Want One Volunteer* (1965), p. 8

And the soldier's eternal companion, the louse.

Located in some spots in our uniforms cooties were infuriating. Artillerymen wore riding breeches that fitted closely at the knees. A few cooties lodged in the tight part where they could not be reached, just inside the end of the knee, would drive one to distraction. A favourite place was in the ribs of woollen socks, just behind the ankle. There they were hell on earth. You could take the sock off and search it carefully but when you put it on again the pests were still there. A common sight at night was some cursing gunner running the flame of a candle along the seams on the inside of his uniform where the little white nits turned the khaki grey. They would snap and crackle like popcorn but one never seemed to get all of them.

The hot-stove league existed long before the day of hockey broadcasts. If we had a stove with a top on it we would sit around it in the evening talking with our tunics open, while we fished out our guests and dropped them on the top of the stove. A big greyback exploded with a very satisfactory *pop*. If the stove was a brazier and had no top we just dropped them in the flames. That was not quite so good because then there was no *pop*.

One of our signallers with a statistical turn of mind (he taught mathematics after the war) made a personal census at the Somme. He was at the observation post and at the time had nothing to do and nothing to read. Boredom was not the least of the horrors of war. He killed time by stripping off and making a count. I have forgotten the exact figures but they were something like this: undershirt, four hundred; drawers, three-hundred and eighty. That would be far from a complete count, however, for newly hatched ones were almost invisible. And being young and ambitious with their way to make in the world, those little ones gave the most trouble. The census did not include his socks or his uniform.

Ibid., pp. 10-11

Uncomfortable as the mud and the clothing alive with lice were, they could nevertheless find their parallels in a Canada that was still rough and growing. It was the act of fighting, the actual clash of human with human, that marked the true nightmare of war— what it was intended to be.

We went up the slope. It extended much farther than we had thought. Some distance ahead three Germans rose from a covert back of a log and shot at us before turning to run. They missed by a wide margin, but Sparky, who was a crack shot, dropped to one knee and sniped one neatly. The fellow seemed to fling his rifle over his head as he went down. Sparky shouted with elation as if it was his first battle, and raced up the hill to look at his victim. Others were firing and another of the trio went down before he could reach the crest of the slope. The third German got away.

When we reached the top of the grade we looked down on a field of grain. A deep ravine lay beyond and we could see camouflage that told of gun emplacements. We were now in extended order, the men in good spirits. We swept down through the grain, and all at once a German popped up directly in my path. He rose so suddenly that I shot without taking aim. Experience had taught me to carry my rifle under my right arm, steadied by my left, a finger on the trigger. Only a pressure was required to beat the other man.

As the German dropped he gave a fearful groan, and to my dismay I saw he was a wizened old chap with steel-rimmed spectacles and a scraggly beard. Probably he used to do mean chores around the battery position, maybe as a sanitary man, and in all probability he was trying to surrender. He had no weapon of any kind. I wanted to stop and see if anything could be done for the poor fellow, but Tommy shouted to look out for Germans ahead.

They had appeared from dugouts and were sprinting like mad toward a cutting in the high bank. Our 'C' Company men were on our left and a bit ahead of us. They bagged the lot neatly. The leader of the Germans, who tried to escape, was a fat officer with an Iron Cross dangling over his paunch. He had been remarkably agile for his size but was grabbed, and two men tried to get his decoration. All this I saw without stopping as we ran down the hill.

Will R. Bird, *Ghosts Have Warm Hands* (1968), pp. 143-4

To attack and hold small patches of muddy terrain became the aim in 1914-18. And death became a commonplace.

As we lay shivering there in the darkness, the mind had every opportunity to run riot. I believe Thiebot, a dark-skinned Channel Islander, and one of our 'tough guys' who always took a great delight in taunting and scaring the 'drafts' with the remarks that they would last like a 'snowball in hell' when Fritz got after them, and so forth, took a very serious, religious view of things, going even so far as to say that he knew he was going to get it, and turned over personal effects to one of his comrades. His premonition turned out correct for he was dead in No Man's Land a few hour later.

Shivering to the bone, we were glad to get the news about 3:30 A.M. to move out to the front line preparatory to attack. Stretching our limbs, we moved upwards, jumpled together with other units, to near the junction of trenches, when Charlie Knight appeared on the scene from the left trench in a great state, his face covered with blood, and his hands holding his chin and neck, elbowing his way, passed us in hot haste, his eyes staring wildly out of his head. It looked as if he had been hit a moment before and had not yet realized to the full what happened.

A few yards further on we became choc-a-bloc. It was impossible to move backward or forward. The trench was a jumble of soldiers. Our wrath as usual began to rise and imprecations were showered upon those in charge. The next moment saw those in the lead climb out of the trench into the open on the left, trying to make for our jumping off position in the line. The ground was a quagmire of shell holes and one had to move rapidly to keep up with his predecessor. Fritz, nervous and apparently under the impression that we were going to pull something off, was firing wildly over No Man's Land, and the bullets whistled around as we scrambled from shell hole to shell hole. Joe Saunders who was following a few paces behind me, was shot in the abdomen. Breathing heavily, he expired a few moments later, Fardell watching over him. Poor Joe, who was a 56th man, often remarked that Heiny would never get him. His death thoroughly angered us. It looked as if word had been given to every unit to make for their positions at the same time with the resultant jam that caused us to get out in the open in the vicinity of the front line. In the end we got into the trench, moved along a bit and got stuck once more. As it was becoming light, word was finally given to back up and remain where we were, mixed with the men of the 29th Battalion. Behind the parados, in shell holes, lay a number of 4 Platoon. My own platoon, No. 3, lost several in the scramble for position.

Two or three hundred yards ahead, and slightly down a slope, Fritz's line threaded its way along our front. The ground over which the attack was to be made was an expanse of pasture land torn by incessant shell fire and dotted closely with shell holes. Of growth there was nothing to be seen excepting tree trunks alongside the road running back from the enemy trench. There was the usual formidable support line, Sugar and Candy trenches, and the Sugar Refinery stronghold, several hundred yards in the German rear.

Our artillery preparation, I understand, took place the day before and ceased during the early morning of the 15th. I cannot recollect particularly heavy gunfire, and the concentration was certainly not on Fritz's front line in our vicinity, for when we entered it, it was absolutely intact. The opposition Fritz put up also pointed out that he had been severely left alone by the artillery until the last minute.

Whatever Fritz's thoughts were, they certainly were not of jubilancy. Since July 1st, regiment after regiment of Huns had been flung in the breach to stem the ever forward march of British battalions. From week to week and in some cases, day to day, he was recoiling backwards, squelched by an avalanche of iron and ground into the mire. With desperate efforts, goaded by the High Command, he tried to hold on, but all in vain, and unposted letters taken from the dead and captives bitterly told the tale of despair. Their letters were full of hunger, cold and death, with upbraidings of their airmen, who as one said, were spending their time in the theatres of Lille.

It was the same repetition in each letter—the British gunners are shelling their positions and communications so persistently and methodically that they dare not move backward or forward. No food or reserves are reaching them and they are gradually being killed off. The cry was, will we ever be relieved, will we ever emerge alive?

Reginald H. Roy, ed., *The Journal of Private Fraser* (1985), pp. 202-3

At Passchendaele the horror took on new dimensions as the attacking men struggled in hideous mud.

At 5:48 A.M., zero plus eight minutes, the 4th CMR went over the top and straight into a living nightmare. It had begun to 'drizzle' by now, and Lieutenant-Colonel W.R. Patterson was alarmed to see that the Canadian artillery barrage 'was erratic and not uniform', as he later reported, 'causing a number of casualties in our left leading company'. Shelled by their own guns, raked by German machine-gun fire, the Canadians found themselves struggling through what one 4th CMR man called 'porridge, a ghastly, dreadful porridge, thigh-deep, in which if you got it on the shoulder blade with a bullet that merely knocked you unconscious for two minutes you drowned. We lost lots of men who simply drowned because they were knocked over or stunned and couldn't get recovered before they'd sunk in the mud.' It was a horror that would be repeated countless times on this battlefield.

Daniel G. Dancocks, *Legacy of Valour* (1986), p. 128

Nowhere was there glory—except perhaps in the human capacity to remain sane amidst the unspeakable.

Every man sitting or squatting in that trench knew two things. First, that McIntyre had no sure idea of where the pillbox was. Second, that he had had too much rum. He told us it was not far to the pillbox, and that the main attack was to be on a strong point called Graf House, that one party was to be on the bank of the Gravenstafel-Mosselmarkt Road to protect our advance. There would not be any barrage. We were to work up a road as quietly as possible and to reach our objective at two A.M. The Stokes guns were moving into position and would send over salvos if they received a signal.

When he had finished talking, McIntyre climbed out of the trench and had another session with Clark. Then he called to me. 'You are to follow close to me all the way,' he said. 'When we have our objective I want you to take the message back to company headquarters. I can't trust it to a runner.'

'How far is it up the road to the pillbox?' I asked.

McIntyre said it was about one hundred and fifty yards. Clark said it was twice that far, and to the right of the road. McIntyre said he was wrong. He had seen the map. It was left of the road. Never through the war was I more sickened and discouraged than at that moment. The whole affair was cock-eyed. We were new in the sector. None knew the terrain. None knew what defences the German had or his strength. The place after dark was a swampy wilderness without anything to use as a guide. Half the men had never been in an attack, and that included the officers. Furthermore, in those few minutes I discovered that Clark had also had too much rum.

Word came to get ready. Every man was to have two Mills bombs to throw if need be. Baillie came and shook hands with me, a long hard clasp without a word spoken. Then I was amazed when Ira Black came and whispered he was glad we were on our way. The waiting was deadly and now we would have action and get from the hateful swamp when it was over. Then a sergeant came with a jug of rum and every man who would take it had a stiff jolt.

At least we found the road. It wasn't much. Shell fire had almost erased it in spots. We started in four little parties, McIntyre leading on the left. I was crawling directly behind him and told him if I saw anything of the enemy I would pull his foot. Lugar was back of me, then Charlie Hale, Stewart, Mickey, Tommy, Brown, and Johnson. On the other side of the so-called road was Clark, and back of him were Baillie, Ira Black, Jennings, a big man who disliked the French but who was religious and often got the boys to sing hymns, Neath, and Flynn. The rest of the twenty-five followed in two groups.

There was quite a drop of bank on our left. McIntyre did not look left or right but kept scrambling along as fast as possible. I peered over the bank from time to time and suddenly saw three or four Germans raise their heads no more than twenty yards from us. I seized McIntyre's foot to signal him. He yanked it away and spoke angrily. The Germans fired instantly. A bullet creased the top of Lugar's head, slicing his scalp and causing him to be temporarily insane. Hale and I had to hold him down by main force, as had he raised he would have been shot. In our struggle Hale raised up higher than he thought and was likewise creased with a bullet. Now it was Stewart, the stretcher bearer, and I holding Lugar, but he began to quiet and the moment I could let go of him I threw my grenades over the bank. Both exploded as they went down, and the Hun shooting stopped at once.

The next thing was to get Lugar's bombs to replace mine, which I did. McIntyre had never stopped and was quite a distance ahead. Clark's party kept up with him. Brown had crawled forward and now he and I left the group and ran to catch up with McIntyre. Machine-guns opened up on all sides. The night was an uproar. We dove into the mud and saw the signal to up for the Stokes support. The German Maxim stopped firing and we jumped and started running again. There was a flaming white-hot instant—and oblivion!

When I recovered consciousness my head was splitting with pain and a terrible nausea had seized my stomach. The Stokes shell had dropped beside us, throwing me bodily across the road and knocking Brown down. He was rolled over on his back, feeling for wounds, as I saw him. All around us was a clamour of machine-guns, bombs, and rifles. I heard McIntyre shouting 'Five rounds rapid!' Then his voice shut off abruptly. I discovered my nose had been bleeding, and when I tried to get up I collapsed again with dizziness.

The burst of shooting stilled. There were no more bomb explosions. But far on our left another eruption of shooting began to dominate the night. Brown had tried to stand and had just slumped down again when we heard plunging noises in the mud and two dim figures came toward us, puffing and blowing, carrying something and grunting in conversation. They were Germans, big men, and had a machine-gun on a tripod. They went past us, apparently thinking us dead, and set up their weapon about thirty feet from us. One man yanked at a long cartridge belt, while the other grunted something. I pulled the pin from one of my grenades, held it for a count of two, then hurled it at the Germans and flattened myself in the mud.

The bomb burst between the two gunners. Not a bit of metal touched Brown or myself. One German never moved but lay on his back, dead. The other pawed at his side feebly for a time, then was still. Brown and I struggled up, went over and made sure both Germans were dead, then heard a voice calling. We found a 42nd man in a shell crater, holding his left arm and groaning. He told us he was from 'A' Company, that his group was lost and most of them had been killed or wounded. His left hand dangled, held only by a strip of skin. I cut the skin with my trench knife and bound up the stump with his field dressing, poured a bottle of iodine over it, slit a hole in his tunic and had him thrust his arm through it for support. Then I took off one of his puttees and made a tourniquet of it as best I could to stop the bleeding. We helped him from the crater and away he went, past the dead German gunners.

At that moment Clark came from somewhere behind us, trying to run and reeling all over the place, 'Come on!' he shouted. 'Let's give them hell!'

His shout ended and he pitched into the mud ahead of us. He was dead when we tried to raise him. Another figure emerged from the murk. It was Neath. He said McIntyre was lying to our left, shot through the stomach and dying, unconscious. Neath wanted to get a stretcher and carry him out. We asked him where the others were.

'The party behind Clark's never came along after the shooting started,' he said, 'and I don't think the ones behind us did. The others are just ahead a few yards in a big shallow crater.'

We went on and soon found the place, the limit of our advance, not one hundred yards from where I had yanked McIntyre's foot. Mickey and Old Bill Childs and Johnson were there, crouched low and taking quick shots at a German gun that streaked sparks a very short distance away. Its bullets tore at the crater lip. Brown gave me one of his bombs and we threw at the same time. The bursts must have been right on the gun, since there was not another shot from it.

A look around showed us three still figures on the bank beyond Mickey. They were all dead: Baillie, his premonition proved correct, and Ira and Jennings, lying together, rifle in hand, all shot through the head by one sweep of the German gun. Back of them was another dead man, Sam Burnett. He had been with one of the rear parties. Neath came with a stretcher and Childs helped him get McIntyre on it. They carried him away, and Johnson went with them as relief in the carrying.

Suddenly I was sick again and vomited severely. Brown and Mickey stayed with me. There was comparative quiet now in our sector, but heavy firing to both our right and left. Machine-gun bullets whined about so that we had to crawl, and when we were back a distance we found The Professor lying on the road bank, riddled with bullets. He was plastered with mud and had lost his glasses and steel helmet. Evidently he had got lost in the darkness and there he lay, after years of study and culture, a smashed cog of the war machine, with not a hope of burial save by a chance shell.

Ten yards on we came into a light vapour rising with the chill of the night. Over on the high bank of the road, we saw Stewart stooped over someone. We called to him softly and told him to get down in the ditch. He did not answer and went on bandaging someone who was lying perfectly still. There was the report of a German rifle. Stewart pitched head-first across the man he was bandaging, so that his kilt fell over his back, and lay there, dead, while the sniper shot again and again, as if venting a crazy hate. The wounded man was still. I had lost a bomb and we had none, but we wormed back to a spot on the roadbank and from there all three of us fired at the rifle flashes. They stopped instantly. We started back. Mickey was at the limit of his endurance. He was not rugged and we had to rest him now and then, so it was an hour before we were back in the trenches. And there I suddenly lost consciousness again.

When I came awake it was late in the morning. I was lying in a corner of the trench, plastered with mud, and Mickey was beside me. Brown was curled like a dog in another corner. Mickey told me I had been violently sick twice and then had lain as if in a coma. He said there had been a heavy shelling of the area. I became aware of the acrid reek of explosives. None of the other survivors were near us. Not a runner had appeared. We huddled there until noon, then I roused up and peered over the side of our refuge. A few yards away were three green-scummed pools. White chalky hands reached out of one, and from the farther one a knee stuck up above the filthy water. In another bit of old trench, where the parados had disappeared, a soldier stood rigidly, feet braced apart. He had been killed by concussion, and his body was split as if sliced by a great knife. Some German bodies were lying on a bank and one, bare-headed, looked as if he were reclining on one elbow. A shell came as I looked and erupted almost beneath the body, and the dead man stood straight up a heartbeat, as if saluting, then tumbled down on the other side. I lay down again and saw that neither Brown nor Mickey were moving. They were huddled side by side, mud-splattered, sleeping.

Night found us still in our cover, and I got up and explored until I found Old Bill and Johnson. A runner had told them a relief was due but there had been no orders. The attack had been a flop. Lieutenant Crood's party had got into Graf House, but he had been killed and they had had to withdraw. All the 42nd losses had been for naught. Sergeant Ormandy had been wounded. Corporal Jimmy Hughes had gone on leave from St Jean. We did not know who would have charge of what was left of Fourteen Platoon. Then a corporal from Thirteen Platoon came and told us we were to go back to Ypres, the 16th Battalion was relieving us. We went with him and met our relief coming in by our old trench, and heard that Glenn Lunn had been killed.

All that drag back was a hideous nightmare. The track was worse than when we came in, and the shelling was incessant. We moved with infinite slowness, every step a struggle, a physical effort, a vast noise over us and all about us, a rolling clamour that dulled thinking and helped us forget some of the frightfulness of the night before. We went back to the Watou area and there were given trousers to replace our soaked and muddied kilts. A big draft came and refilled our ranks, and then came the dread word that we must make a second trip to Passchendaele.

Will R. Bird, Ghosts Have Warm Hands (1968), pp. 80-5

Perhaps it is impossible for anyone who has not known war to understand fully its tragedy. Yet sometimes the observations of an eyewitness can bring us close, as with this moving account of the raid on Dieppe in 1942.

The landing craft were lowered without a hitch. Soon the dark sea was lapping at the sides and the flat bottom boats lurched into the darkness. There were dark, ghostlike shapes of other landing craft all around us, and the 'mother ship', largest of all, soon disappeared from view. Inside my craft thirty men huddled over in the shape of an embryo in the womb. But each man held tight to his weapon and ammunition.

It was 3:40 in the morning, August 19. No one was sick aboard our craft but there was an air of tenseness, of expectancy.

Suddenly to our right, and to the front of us, the sky was lit up with green, red and orange flares. We huddled down closer to the bottom of the craft, and held on tighter to our weapons. I also clutched surreptitiously my black rosary beads which I carried around my neck. I thought of what Lt Coulson had said: 'When that ramp drops, Johnny, run like hell.'

All was silent, other than the lapping of the waves against the side of the craft, and the sound of the engines.

Then in a moment a thundering over our heads, and in its wake a rushing shuffling sound, like wild geese flying in the darkness. We began to hear small arms fire. I did not understand. What was happening? What about the fool-proof system that had been worked out?

I knew some of us would be killed but not with the same conviction, that I knew that if you put your hand on a hot stove you will be burned. A burst of machine gun fire swept up into the air. Someone had nervously pulled the trigger of his Bren gun. Someone else shrieked at him and tried to wrestle the weapon away from him. Eyes wild in the half light of dawn, the Bren gunner held tenaciously to his firearm. Inside our craft, faces looked drawn and pale.

We began to see one another now. It was daylight. I heard the ramp go down. The words of Lt Coulson came back to me. Someone said, 'What time is it?' '5:50,' I said. Then I ran like hell.

It was a mile to the protection of the cliffs, or so it seemed. I stumbled on the stones that made up the beach. I stopped to pick up some Bren gun magazines that were dropped, and as I did so, a hail of tracer bullets went by in front of me.

The beach was littered with dead and dying Canadians, their equipment strewn all over. I saw Pte Armstrong of the Royal Regiment of Canada, Bren gun in hand, exposed, running wildly along the beach. He had lost his helmet and was cursing—not the Germans, but our own NCOs and officers, and naming some of them. He was firing at the cliffs above and trying to get everyone else to do the same. He was cut down by the German cross fire.

Three men set a mortar into position. A burst of machine gun fire swept across. All three fell. Lightweight ladders which we carried with us were placed against the sea wall. Twelve men made attempts to climb and place bangalore torpedoes underneath the wire atop the wall. One by one they were picked off.

I saw Joe Coffey and Sammy Adams by the water's edge. The water now had a pinkish look about it. Ernie Goode lay dead on the stones of the beach, his flesh dimpled where bullets had gone in. Hughie Clemmens from Gravenhurst, was huddled near the sea wall, his face pale in death. Lt Coulson lay dead, his body half hidden in the entrance to a dark cave in the side of the cliff.

There were groups of four or five formed together in the protection of the sea wall, like animals in a storm. I picked up a Bren gun that had been dropped but the only thing I could see to fire at was a house to the left of us. After one blast with the Bren it was met with such a hail of fire, that I ran doubled over to the entrance of the cave. I skirted the body of Lt Coulson and took shelter inside.

The thunder of the barrage from our destroyers off-shore, the big Ack Ack guns, firing at shrieking Spitfires going in low over the cliffs, a confused din, rolling against and back from the cliffs. I looked again at the dead officer. He lay peacefully on the stones.

I noted engraved in the stone wall inside the cave two hearts with an arrow piercing them; and the names Ingrid and Lionel. The year 1937. For a moment my thought dwelled on Ingrid and Lionel. Who were they? What had become of them? The same sun shone down on them that day in 1937. That was before the world went crazy. Now the sun still shone down, unmoved by the fearful harvest of death and destruction on that short strip of beach.

The barrage would stop for a minute, then could be heard the steady whisper and crackle of small arms fire. The aerial battle began to build up, adding to the awful noise and confusion.

Then I heard someone up from me say—'surrender!' Five or six men were standing with up-stretched arms, holding long strips of white bandage.

Then a foreign accent said, 'You cannot escape, brave Canadians, throw down your weapons and those of you who can walk, come this way with your hands up. We will immediately take care of the wounded.'

Then a great stillness settled down from the top of the cliffs and fell on the beach.

I threw the breech block of my gun away, against the cliff and joined the others, hands high above my head.

I could hear a plaintive call for water from a Canadian laying on his back, the bright sun beating down upon him. I could see the blue patch with the green circle on his tunic. He was from my own regiment, but I didn't recognize him. I hesitated a moment, and was prodded by a lipless and grim German soldier with an ugly Luger in his hand and two or three grenades sticking from his boot tops. He quickly saw the object of my concern. By this time the beach was swarming with German soldiers.

The man with the Luger took a few steps towards the wounded Canadian, stood for a moment with the gun close to the wounded man's head. The Canadian, not seeing nor caring who stood over him, uttered one word—'water'.

The German decided. He jammed the Luger between the grenades sticking from his boot tops, bent down on one knee, removed the man's water bottle, raised his head and gave him a drink. He lowered the head again, and made a gesture with his hand which seemed to say 'that's settled'. Then he made a motion with the Luger, towards my watch. I looked at the hands, then took it off and handed it to him. The hands said 10:20 A.M.

It was August 19th, 1942.

John Patrick Grogan, *Dieppe and Beyond* (1982), pp. 13-16

For the soldier of 1914-18 there was little opportunity for the sweeping, mobile campaigns envisioned by the generals at the war's onset. But a wild moment did come for the Canadian Light Horse at Cambrai in 1918.

The glorious charge over the top which the Canadian Light Horse was to have made has materialized—in all except the glory. And this morning we of the Fourth Troop have one horse left on the line to show for the troop's mad charge. . . . Mr Sharpe and the rest of the 4th Troop, A Squadron, were ordered to follow C Squadron over as a patrolling outpost. Our orders were to proceed to an old farm on a sunken road halfway up a long gentle incline. There is a small bit of a river course running between the fields of plowed land—from it on the northeast the field slope gently to the crest of the rise about a kilometre away. Our orders took us out around the village of Naves, across the railroad tracks to the east end of the village and out toward the little river. We spread out into sections—Dan Reaves, Joe Scanlon, Corp. Marlowe and myself on the right, Mr Sharpe, Braggins, Tim Sheppard and Larry Bell in the centre, and the machine gun section on the left.

While skirting the village we had been galloping along through plowed fields, turnip patches, over spur railroads, steep embankments—our horses were quite tired before we came to the little narrow river. At the time we would have considered it quite impossible to jump the stream—but our objective being in sight we charged it and with a heroic struggle every horse got down, jumped and up the other steep side.

Then a mad gallop began. Dan and Joe got tangled up in a telephone line—Joe's old mare went down. Dan had to cut off the saddle to free him—the rest of us galloped on across the field and up the slope. The crest of the hill was lined with three or four enemy machine guns and as we galloped along they all opened up. Bullets began to plow up the dust and sizzle through the air. Every horse was doing his best. Every rider urging them on toward the farm, our objective.

A bullet hit old Nix near the right temple—he went down like a stone. I came down on my head—Nix turned over right on top of me. Quivered all over and never moved again. My helmet had rolled away somewhere. I attempted to get out from under my horse but had a hard struggle to free my feet—at last I raised his legs and got out. I lost no time in getting around behind the horse's body out of the hail of bullets. As I looked around I found that I had no broken bones—only a battered head and a sprained wrist.

Only a few minutes had elapsed but the rest were just mounting the objective to the road. Joe had cut off his saddle—pulled out his sword—mounted the old mare bareback and dashed to the field past me. He made the objective too. I saw the boys get to the road—then horse after horse fell down and men rolled off . . . it was a miracle indeed that anyone of us came out at all as such a mad adventure was never seen before.

Daniel G. Dancocks, *Spearhead to Victory* (1987), pp. 175-6

But for most the 'Great War' provided no hell-for-leather rush at the enemy. Rather, it was the slow trudge forwards against a hail of

machine-gun fire or shelling, bayonets at the ready. Here a Japa-
nese-Canadian infantryman remembers a chilling incident with a
hakujin (white) comrade.

At 5 A.M. on April 10 we received a cup of rum and drank a toast. At
5:20 orders came to start moving.

The battalion commander, armed only with a swagger stick,
shouted, 'Canadian 50th! Advance! Follow me!' The Japanese platoon moved forward in a single line with the machine-gun section.
The enemy artillery continued heavy shelling and their machine-
guns clattered into action.

A shell exploded near our platoon. I heard a Japanese cry, 'I'm hit!'
It was Narita. He had terrible head wounds and died very quickly.
The platoon commander was also killed by the same blast. Tada was
killed later in the day. Sato and I were fortunate and got through Hill
145 without a scratch. Later we wrote to the relatives as we had
promised our dead comrades.

During the battle a German charged me with a bayonet. I parried
and went for his chest. I missed and the bayonet got him on the
wrist. I was about to make my second thrust when I heard him cry,
'Mother!' I thought of my aged mother in Japan and stopped. I made
him my prisoner. He was an eighteen-year-old boy straight from
high school.

We had one unfortunate incident during the battle. Hirokichi
Isomura found a severely wounded German soldier crying for water.
Isomura gave it to him from his water bottle. A *hakujin* pushed
Isomura aside and stabbed the German with a bayonet. Isomura
cried, 'Why did you do that?' He would have died anyway!' When
we came by, the two were about to go at each other with bayonets.
Fortunately, we were able to separate them.

Roy Ito, We Went to War (1984), p. 57

An unseen enemy was often ready to take deadly advantage of
stupidity or the wrong move.

Each morning a sergeant brought a rum issue just before light. I did
not take mine and Laurie did not take his. A dozen or more of us in
the draft never drank or smoked. This morning an officer was with
the sergeant. He came in and stood beside me as MacMillan had his
turn off and asked many questions while the sergeant was at the post

on the right. He told me his name was Larson, that he was from Bear River, Nova Scotia, and thrilled with the front line. He wanted to know how near the Germans were.

I told him and he said it sounded unreal to him. It had become light as he talked, and when I put up the periscope it was shot away by a German sniper. 'That fellow must be very near,' said Larson. 'I'll take a quick look.'

'Don't!' I yelled and grabbed at his coat. He stretched up in spite of my protest. The bullet entered his forehead and went out the back, breaking the strap of his helmet and carrying it to the rear of the post. I lowered the body to the trench floor and covered the face with a clean sandbag.

MacMillan was shocked. 'Too much rum!' he said.

The sergeant came from the other post and he was stunned. He said he would report what had happened and was hardly away when we heard a shot on the left post. The sergeant had given old Dundee two extra rum rations, mine and Laurie's, and the Scot had seized his rifle and started to clean it, saying he was going to get the sniper. The weapon went off in his hands and the bullet struck the frozen side of the post, chipping bits from it. One struck Laurie on the foot and stung badly.

MacMillan tried to calm Dundee but he refused to listen. The rum had him wild. He raised up to aim his rifle, and the German shot. Dundee's head was turned so that the bullet took both eyes out. He tumbled down, clawing at his face and groaning.

Something had to be done and quickly. Sellars would not go for help. So I shed my equipment and crouched low as the sergeant had done. It was hard to keep that way, but when I raised ever so little a bullet burned the back of my neck like a hot iron. I reached the trench and got a stretcher bearer and stretcher. We were careful going in and arrived safely. But Dundee was in a bad state. We had to tie him on the stretcher, as he would not listen to anyone. Getting the stretcher and its load to the trench took almost half an hour. The stretcher bearer was ahead, pulling the stretcher, and I pushed from the rear. Finally it was done. Then I crawled back and sat all day beside the dead officer.

Will R. Bird, *Ghosts Have Warm Hands* (1968), p. 17

There is almost a surreal quality to the following account of Canadians in action during the Second World War.

Together with CSM Ponsford of Charlie company I had gone up to Able about noon to see what was going on and we got there just in time to see Captain Graydon shot. There was little we could do here, but Ponsford pointed out to me a big house in the distance, on the hill crest by the village, where Baker was marooned. Seeing as I did not have much to do right then I took a notion to go up to Baker.

I cut down a road past Charlie and hiked along. There were no friendly troops here since the division on the left had not been able to keep up with our advance. It gave me a nice feeling to be walking over those sunny fields munching some figs I had picked. Breakfast had been quick, skimpy and long ago. I crossed a deep drainage ditch and went along for a peaceful mile, as if there wasn't any war at all, through vineyards, orchards and ploughed fields. Finally I reached the foot of the hill from the far left and I started up it, keeping my head down to look for mines. Then CRACK and a bullet snapped by my head so close I smelled it. I did not wait to see if I was hit, but made a flying leap for a deep ditch fifteen yards away. I landed crawling and must have looked comical, all arms and legs, tommy-gun dangling about my neck, jumping along like a bear with a burned backside. It was comical for the joker who had fired, and he whanged away four more rounds but missed with all of them. I laid low for a spell, and he started to chuck mortar bombs at me and the 'canaries' whistling and sizzling about did not reassure me at all.

Finally I moved off up that ditch and pretty soon found two lost men from Baker company. I pointed them to the rear and crawled on, to bump into four nuns. They had pillow cases full of stuff slung over their backs, and boy, were they excited! Chattering away a mile a minute, they lost no time in social visiting but disappeared down the hill.

For a while I crawled on the road, on my belly, checking it for mines, then I cut off straight up the hill and ran for it through an old orchard. I carried on, huffing and puffing and wondering where the house was when a Jerry popped out of a bush and ducked behind another one. He had an MG 42 in his hand but his back was to me. I dropped behind a convenient tree and started to breathe again.

As I lay there wondering if it was any use praying, a voice in unmistakable Canadian Army language hailed me, so I upped and ran to the left to a seven-foot stone fence that I cleared without touching anything but the top row of stones. I landed in a lean-to at the back of the Baker company house, and the guy who had yelled at me gave me almighty hell. He said he was one of the few men still standing, and would I please not call attention to the fact by wandering around that hill and getting Jerry to start the war up all over again. At the house I found Capt. Lazier and CSM Forshee. They were somewhat surprised to see me and borrowed my water bottle. While they were drinking, a Jerry stretcher-bearer came bustling round the corner waving his Red Cross flag. I was startled, but everyone else seemed unconcerned. They told me he had been around most of the day and had arranged a kind of truce at the moment, and was making sure everybody abided by it. The situation was such that the Jerries couldn't throw Baker out of its houses, and Baker couldn't move the Jerries with the few men it had left in one piece.

I walked over to the Jerry and asked him if I could bring up a vehicle to evacuate our wounded, but he wouldn't hear of it. It was a pretty wild conversation since I spoke no German and he spoke no English; all we had was vino-Italian. While we argued, a broken-down Sherman tank about a hundred and fifty yards off, cut loose with its machine gun.

Everyone cursed and got a horrified look on their faces, particularly the Jerry. Then there was an almighty BANG as a *Faustpatrone* exploded on the tank and two Jerries popped out of a bush and charged the tank head-on, firing machine pistols. One of them hopped on top and emptied his mag down the hatch, then the two hauled a wounded man out, and still at the double, carried him fire-man fashion over to us and plopped him down before dashing back to their bush. The Englishman was badly hit, with a shattered left knee and eye amongst other things. I can still see his ginger hair and the way he tried to grin as we and the Jerry tried to help him.

The place was full of our wounded and there was no time to waste so I said good-bye, and took off down the hill, staying under cover pretty well, and getting back at last to BHQ. I told Colonel Cameron the story and he suggested I might borrow an amoured half-truck from the tank medical section and try to rescue the wounded.

Off I went again, and bumped into a platoon of the 48th Highlanders under Sgt Jim Harker. He and his platoon razzed me cheerfully for going the wrong way, but I told them that was the usual thing for an RSM and when we parted they wished me the best. Too bad they couldn't have used it for themselves; they ran into trouble that night and Jim and most of his men never came back.

A flock of 75-mm. shells straddled the road, and I dived into the ditch again. Something banged me on the shoulder and I grunted, sure I had bought it. Then a very haughty Limey voice asked what I was grunting for. The voice belonged to a tank officer who had leapt for the same ditch, gouging my shoulder nicely with his big foot.

He told me where his RAP was and when I got there and explained my needs, the Limeys jumped to help. Only they insisted on stripping me of my weapons and equipment and tying a red cross brassard on my arm before we started.

The trip back up that hill was pretty quick. I rode on the outside to con the way and wave the Red Cross flag. I held it in my teeth and it at least kept my teeth from chattering as we approached the place where I had seen the Jerry machine-gunner. He was still there holding a *Faustpatrone* in his hand at the 'ready' position and staring at us as if he didn't believe his eyes. We went past fast, and he never even budged. We swung into the village and up the main street to the Baker company house.

In no time we had a load and were heading down the hill, feeling a little naked with our back to the Jerries. But nothing happened so we unloaded and came back up, this time with an ordinary ambulance following.

We were met at the top of the hill by a Jerry corporal looking very mad, and waving his gun at us and yelling 'kaput!' It was pretty clear we weren't welcome, but our driver had a spare pack of cigarettes and I passed these to the corporal. He was looking at my rank badges the way all corporals always do, in that 'you've-got-nothing-on-me-this-time' sort of way. The cigarettes mellowed him a bit and he let me look into the big house, but what was left of Baker company seemed to have vanished. There was a dead lieutenant, but we could do him no good so we left him.

We could hear tanks rumbling in the distance, and it was getting dark so the driver suggested we get out before an attack began and we got caught in the barrage.

At that the German pricked up his ears and wanted to know if there was going to be a shoot. We said, 'Damn right—we're going to blow this village off the map!' He frowned and began to look really peeved, so we got the hell out of there.

It hadn't been a bad day. We had evacuated twenty-six of our men and the Limey tank men. Max Lerner, our own MO, bawled me out for not bringing the wounded to him, but he said it with a smile. He had a busy enough day as it was. He was always busy for he kept the most forward RAP of any unit in the Div.

Farley Mowat, *The Regiment* (1973), pp. 218-22

That Canadians could be ferocious in battle was proved at Otterloo in 1945.

Shortly after midnight a German patrol burst into Otterloo, shouting wildly and spraying the street ahead with automatic fire. They were the vanguard of a group of some 800 enemy commanded by the colonel of the 952nd Volksgrenadier Regiment. Using tracks parallel to the main road, the Germans probed forward trying to find routes through or around the village. When they ran into opposition they called down artillery and mortars and attempted to burst through with every weapon firing. Soon the forward batteries of the 17th Field were in action, firing over open sights, fuses set at 'zero' so that their high explosive shells exploded as they left the muzzle. In F Troop, Lieutenant Alexander Ross issued orders that rifle ammunition would only be used for a sure hit, 'as a result when the enemy arrived in strength, only visible targets were engaged, that is at about four yards'. Within minutes the troop was completely surrounded and cut off as the enemy attack swept on towards the left battery position.

In the rear the 60th Battery's guns were growing hot as they answered calls for fire from their hard-pressed sister batteries. Soon they themselves came under mortar fire, then Sergeant Edward Knight saw enemy soldiers appearing out of the dark. He shot the first to approach his gun, then his pistol jammed. He grabbed the next and strangled him with his bare hands while one of his men dispatched a third with his rifle butt. 'While all this was going on he still continued to pass fire orders to his gun which remained in action the whole time.'

At divisional headquarters everyone from the General down was involved in the battle. Matthew Halton of the CBC, who was there, compared it to an Indian attack on a wagon train even to the extent of saying, 'Nearly everybody in the headquarters has at least one notch to carve on his gun. Some have as many as ten.'

For more than six hours the confused battle went on. There was little the Canadians could do in the darkness but stand their ground. At daybreak the enemy made a final attempt to break through and this time the Canadian reaction was violent. Major-General Bert Hoffmeister brought the four tanks of his protective troop into action with the Wasp carriers of the Irish Regiment and obliterated a final enemy thrust.

Soon the fighting was over and the Canadians began to count the cost. A patrol from the 17th Field Regiment approached the site where F Troop had been surrounded, expecting it to have been wiped out. They found Ross and his men cleaning their guns and having breakfast. For six-and-a-half hours the troop had beaten off attack after attack and had not lost a gun to the enemy.

In all the Canadians had suffered less then 50 casualties while three guns and several vehicles were destroyed. Some 300 Germans had been killed or wounded, another 250 captured. To quote Matthew Halton, 'Man for man, those gunners and headquarters soldiers had out-fought the Germans. They killed more of the enemy than I have ever seen in such a small area.'

Jeffery Williams, *The Long Left Flank* (n.d.), pp. 287-8

Before they are in action, men give little warning as to whether they will be brave or cautious, hesitant or cowardly. Brave men a-bounded in the ranks of Canadians at the Leopold Canal in 1944.

At 1:30 A.M. on 22 September Sergeant Clarence Crockett of C Company led the eight volunteers of his patrol across a semi-demolished footbridge to an island in the centre of the canal. With darkened faces and carrying only weapons, ammunition and grenades, they moved in complete silence across the narrow strip of land to the lock gate.

With infinite care the patrol inched their way along the narrow top of the 90-foot-wide gates, knowing that at the least sound machine-gun fire would sweep them from their path. As they drew close to the far bank Crockett was appalled to discover that the last eight feet of the gate was missing. The only connection to the shore was a six-inch pipe above which the Germans had strung a single taut strand of wire as a hand grip. Moving sideways, Crockett edged his way along it to the bank. Then with every sense alert, he began to crawl forward.

'Halt!'

Crockett saw the German sentry almost as he spoke. In an instant he had him on the ground and despatched him with his knife. As his men moved up on either side of him, two enemy machine guns began lacing the south end of the lock gate and the island in the centre of the Canal. Crockett could see that any delay in dealing with them would be fatal to the battalion's crossing. Without hesitation he and his men stormed the first gun in its concrete emplacement, killed its crew then destroyed the second with one round from a PIAT. Moments later the leading platoon of C Company arrived to help.

All day the Highlanders fought to expand their bridgehead, beating off German counter-attacks which were supported by accurate shell fire, which their frustrated artillery observers could do nothing to suppress.

By 7 P.M. the Engineers had completed a bridge and crossed to fight alongside the Highlanders. During that night the Germans attacked again, but by morning Le Régiment de Maisonneuve were also over the Canal and the bridgehead was secure.

Their failure to stop the Canadians crossing convinced General Otto Sponheimer of the 67th Corps that he must pull back without delay to the next main obstacle, the Antwerp-Turnhout Canal. When the newly arrived 49th Division crossed the Albert Canal at Herenthals, they were unopposed.

Sergeant Crockett's gallantry was the key to the success of an operation which enabled two divisions to advance up to 16 kilometers. The Regiment recommended him for a Victoria Cross but Montgomery turned it down, commenting that it was a 'very good Distinguished Conduct Medal'.

Ibid., pp. 94-5

The pity of such bravery was that it so often brought its owner death. This citation —'For most conspicuous bravery and outstanding devotion in attack' — appeared in The London Gazette *in January 1918.*

When his platoon was held up by uncut wire and a machine-gun causing many casualties, Pte [James] Robertson dashed to an opening on the flank, rushed the machine-gun and, after a desperate struggle with the crew, killed four and then turned the gun on the remainder, who, overcome by the fierceness of his onslaught, were running towards their own lines. His gallant work enabled the platoon to advance. He inflicted many more casualties among the enemy, and then carrying the captured machine-gun, he led his platoon to the final objective. He there selected an excellent position and got the gun into action, firing on the retreating enemy who by this time were quite demoralized by the fire brought to bear on them.

During the consolidation Pte Robertson's most determined use of the machine-gun kept down the fire of the enemy snipers; his courage and his coolness cheered his comrades and inspired them to the finest efforts.

Later, when two of our snipers were badly wounded in front of our trench, he went out and carried one of them in under very severe fire.

He was killed just as he returned with the second man.

Canada's V.C.'s (1956), p. 93

When ordinary men were able to perform the extraordinary, their humility was often equally remarkable.

As the losses mounted, the attack bogged down, and not solely because of the mud. The Germans had more than a little to do with it; their pillbox defenses appeared to be marvelously effective on the 4th CMR front. Indeed, the battalion's attack foundered in front of a pillbox supported by a pair of machine-guns in a nearby shell hole. Khaki-clad corpses sprawled in the mud attested to the deadly accuracy of the enemy fire. No one, it seemed, could get to within fifty yards of the pillbox.

With failure staring the battalion in the face, a single young soldier saved the day. Private Tommy Holmes was an unlikely looking hero: just nineteen, his boyish countenance highlighted by a beaming smile, he looked like he should have been at home attending school and playing softball rather than being here, in this abattoir in a foreign land. It was his first time in combat, but he acted like a veteran. Jumping up, he slipped and slid through the mud, scrambling from shell hole to shell hole, bullets dancing at his feet. Word of his one-man attack soon spread. 'What's going on?' someone would ask. 'Some crazy guy!' would be the reply. 'Look! Look at him!'

They watched in amazement as young Holmes leap-frogged closer and closer to the enemy machine-guns. Finally he was within bomb-throwing range. Holmes had only one Mills bomb with him— his aim would have to be good. It was. He lofted the grenade into the air with impressive accuracy: it landed between the two guns and the ensuing explosion wiped out both crews. But Holmes wasn't finished yet. He worked his way back to his admiring comrades, secured another bomb, then returned to deal with the pillbox. Still under heavy fire, but somehow unscathed, Tommy Holmes made his way around it, then threw the grenade into the rear entrance. Moments later, nineteen Germans emerged with their hands in the air.

Private Holmes later was awarded the Victoria Cross, the Empire's highest award for bravery in the face of the enemy. Holmes, however, took his heroism matter-of-factly. Afterward, when asked if he realized what he had done, he shrugged, 'Well, no. I thought everybody did that sort of thing.'

Daniel G. Dancocks, Legacy of Valour, pp. 128-9

Like every nation, Canada has had its share of those who find a fighting rage rise within them and are carried along on the wave of its energy.

Private H. Badger, who was 'looking for a good fight', recounted that he was one of the first to reach the foremost enemy positions, 'and was indeed very disappointed when they surrendered without wanting to fight'. Forging ahead alone, Private Badger took on a pair of pillboxes. Jumping from shell hole to shell hole, firing his rifle with remarkable accuracy—'I emptied my magazine and only missed twice (fault sanded bolt)'—he manoeuvred into position to bomb the nearest one, then called on the defenders to surrender. Several Germans emerged 'with their hands in the air', but Badger cold-bloodedly dispatched them: 'There was no mercy in me and I bayoneted six Fritzies as fast as they came out.' The other pillbox surrendered shortly afterward, and this time Badger took prisoners, an officer and five other ranks. One of them pointed out a nearby strongpoint so Badger marched everyone over there and demanded its surrender: two more officers and seven other ranks were added to his collection of prisoners. Within minutes, 'other Fritzies came running up to me', and Badger found himself holding three officers and twenty-one other ranks. Before he could lead them to the rear, a Canadian shell exploded in their midst, killing two Germans and wounding a third. Badger was also hit by shrapnel, 'on the left shoulder, right neck, and right leg'. Despite his painful injuries, Badger escorted the Germans back to the nearest prisoner cages, en route putting them to work collecting Canadian wounded and carrying them to an aid post.

Ibid., p. 168

Perhaps the most arresting tales of courage arise out of circumstances wherein the man—in this case, an officer who served Canada with remarkable distinction—did what he did simply because it was the logical thing to do.

Rockingham was not noted for caution. Large, strong and self-confident, he was the picture of a fighting commander and his face wore the scars of war. In Normandy, while commanding the Royal Hamilton Light Infantry, his headquarters had been practically wiped out. A sniper's bullet killed his signaller, then a second creased the bridge of his nose. Rockingham, who had seen a whiff of smoke from a barn, seized a Sten gun, dived for cover then stalked the sniper and shot him, not the conventional way for a battalion commander to behave. When asked why he had not sent someone to deal with the problem, he replied that there wasn't anyone else and, besides, he knew where the bastard was.

Jeffery Williams, *The Long Left Flank* (n.d.), pp. 63-4

This Canadian crew kept rolling in their armoured car and trusted to luck. It did not fail them.

Approaching the farming hamlet of Bierville, Sergeant Ross Bell ordered his driver to move slowly until they reached the church which was marked on his map but which he could not yet see. Carefully he scanned the château grounds on his right, then the scattered houses opposite. The only sign that enemy were nearby was the empty street ahead, so unlike Morgny which they had just passed through, where cheering French civilians had waved them on their way.

Past the château gates and the new village hall they crawled, alert for any sign of danger.

Around a curve to the right, beyond the duck pond, they saw the church with the road dividing in front of it. There was no one in sight. A few yards further and they would have a clear view of the road they had been ordered to reconnoitre. The driver edged the car forward.

It was then that Bell saw the wreck of Lt Laird's Staghound and the glint of sunlight off German helmets behind a hedge, too late to reverse out of the ambush.

The gunner too had seen the enemy and the co-ax Browning was firing as Bell ordered the driver to take the left fork at top speed. He looked back, half expecting to see an anti-tank gun taking them in its sights but there was no sign of life. He swung round to look at the road ahead as they came to a low rise.

Less than fifty yards away, on a curve in the road, was a column of Germans with three anti-tank guns.

Hastily the driver and the bow gunner closed their hatches, as did Bell and his gunner in the turret. Moments later the car crashed into the infantry. With guns blazing it ploughed through them, smashing the anti-tank guns off the road and leaving behind the screams of the crushed and wounded enemy.

At nearly fifty miles an hour, the armoured car was driving deeper into enemy territory and Bell began to search the road ahead for a turn which might lead back to his squadron. Ahead lay another village where a road to the southeast would take him in the right direction. It was as they neared the junction that he saw, coming toward them—menacing, deadly—a Tiger tank with its 88mm gun.

There was no alternative but to keep going, hold their fire and trust to luck. Apparently the driver of the German tank had not yet recognized the Canadian armoured car for the giant fifty-six ton vehicle was beginning to ease over to the right of the road to let it pass.

Bell's eyes were glued on the '88', watching for it to begin traversing toward them. A single round would reduce the Staghound to a flaming wreck. But it did not move and in a few seconds, they were past.

Ahead in the distance lay a wooded hillside where they might find cover and plan their next move.

The road now began to descend in a gentle curve through a steep-sided ravine. The car had just entered its shadows, when Bell and his crew saw coming toward them, a horse-drawn convoy of wagons and anti-tank guns. Again they charged, firing their Brownings and reducing the convoy to a rearing, screaming shambles. Men fled from the wagons and attempted to scramble up the steep, slippery banks, only to slide back into the path of the Staghound chewing its way through the mass of men and horses. Before the carnage was over, the driver's periscope was obscured by blood and debris and Bell was directing the steering of the car from the turret.

At last they broke free from the convoy and a mile further on, came to a halt on a track leading into a wood. Wearily they opened their hatches, in time to see a civilian wearing an armband and a blue beret step from the bush.

It was the young Canadians' first contact with the French Forces of the Interior, the 'FFI', and it could not have been better timed for their ammunition was virtually spent.

Next day, 31st August, they rejoined their regiment, the 12th Manitoba Dragoons, probing ahead of the Army on its way to the north.

Bell and his crew had accounted for nearly three hundred enemy dead or wounded, 70 to 80 horses and several anti-tank guns.

Ibid., pp. 44-6

The experience of Sergeant Bell and his Staghound crew was one of success fuelled not so much by a lust to fight as by the need to get to safety. Somewhat more chilling is this description of a kind of fighting hunger experienced in the First World War.

I fire away madly till my magazine is empty; then fling down the rifle and hurl my bombs at them—the trench is chockfull of dust and smoke. Mac had come up close behind me, his shots thunder right into my ears. . . . From behind they are throwing bombs by the dozen, without minding in the least who or what they are hitting. They shout and yell: 'Give them hell, boys!' . . . Jack comes up from behind with a fresh supply of Mills bombs. . . . 'Here you are, Fritzie boy, damn you!' . . . Ah, they have had enough, they are done for, the bastards! A couple of survivors dash off from the post, and we rush after them, tear our hands and kilts on the wire, jumping across the overturned machine-gun and the dead or dying gunners, running, panting, and perspiring along the dry, hard trench, corner by corner . . . and then we reach the next machine-gun post and throw ourselves against it, yelling and roaring, with bombs and bayonets, battle-mad—regardless of everything in the world, our whole being intent on one thing alone: to force our way ahead and kill!

Daniel G. Dancocks, *Spearhead to Victory* (1987), pp. 78-9

With fighting came the prospect of taking prisoners—and then the question of what to do with them.

Some Germans were captured with ease that was often startling. In one case, a group of thirteen allowed themselves to be taken by two Canadians who were virtually unarmed! Captain W.W. Murray and Sergeant Alex Sample of the 2nd battalion set off later in the day to seek a suitable location for the battalion headquarters. Finding a dugout that seemed appropriate, they heard a noise from within. Drawing his revolver, Sergeant Sample leaned inside and fired a shot down the stairs. 'Kamerad!' came the cry, and thirteen German soldiers trooped out with their hands in the air. Covering them with his revolver, Captain Murray's delight diminished considerably when it occurred to him that he was holding an empty weapon: he had forgotten to load it that morning.

'Sample,' he anxiously whispered, 'how many cartridges have you left?'

'None, sir. I just had one in my revolver, and that was the one I shot down the dug-out stairs!'

But the prisoners were passive, and the captain and the sergeant, without a single bullet between them, led their captives to the rear.

Even an Anglican priest bagged some prisoners. Honorary Lieutenant-Colonel F.G. Scott, the first Division's chaplain, was en route to the front when he passed a shell hole from which three dusty and dishevelled Germans emerged, hands held high. Canon Scott patiently tried to explain that, as a noncombatant, he could not accept their surrender. It was to no avail, so Scott reluctantly marched them away, handing them over to the first Canadian troops he encountered.

Ibid., p. 42

And on occasion it was possible neither to kill nor to take prisoner, as this First World War soldier found.

The sap was no more than three feet deep. I moved along it leisurely and was out a good hundred yards from our trench before realizing it. Then I found an enlarged place with a badly rusted trip wire around it. Lying there, wondering who had arranged the trap, as it was now filled with weeds, I saw tall grass further along become agitated. Instantly I got down into the enlarged place, ignoring the trip wire. I kept to one side and released the safety on my Lee Enfield.

After a wait the head and then the shoulders of a young German officer appeared. He had even features and a small brown moustache. There was more of the trip wire in his path, and he put down his Luger pistol and carefully removed the strands. At that moment I raised up, my rifle ready.

The look on his face cannot be described. He seemed utterly paralyzed, incapable of action. A long minute passed, and another. Neither of us moved. I had my finger crooked on the trigger, ready, and he saw that I had. He paled and his eyes seemed to dilate. Then he smiled!

I had fully intended taking him prisoner or shooting him if he tried to get away, and yet as he backed off quickly I did not do a thing. Back he went, foot by foot, still smiling, not hurrying too fast, but always moving, and I started toward him. He did not hurry faster and had another grin as I picked up the Luger. Then he was gone around a turn and as he vanished he gave a little half-wave, half-salute.

I hurried back after first hiding the Luger in my gas-mask carrier. I called myself names and yet did not say a thing to Tommy, beyond telling him there had been an old post out there with trip wire. In the dugout I could not bring myself to tell Wilson since the others would hear. I went to sleep, alternately sorry and thankful that I had not shot the German, and next day we were relieved by the 58th Battalion.

Will R. Bird, *Ghosts Have Warm Hands* (1968), pp. 50-1

The stand of the Princess Patricia's Canadian Light Infantry at Kapyong, in a confused and savage struggle during the Korean War, showed well the Canadian capacity to grit the teeth and simply not give in.

'It was getting late by the time we got into the positions we were going to occupy,' recalls another Canadian. 'I was with a fellow by the name of Ray Orford from Westville, NS. I remember not digging our trench too deep that night. We went down maybe two feet, just enough to get underground.

'We spent the night in our shallow trench, sort of sitting down with our head and shoulders above ground. Early next morning, before daylight, a lot of firing broke out ahead of us. We heard that the Australian battalion had made contact with the Chinese and was being hit hard from a couple of different sides.

'I remember that from my position I could see a lot of tracers flying back and forth. At that point I decided that we'd better dig that trench a little deeper.'

'I don't think you ever dig a hole deep enough,' says Gary Gurney. 'I don't care if the damned thing is two feet deep or twenty; it's never big enough.'

All during the day, Monday, April 23, the ROK troops surged to the south. Then, shortly after 10 P.M., the battle of Kapyong began. The Chinese, who had been right on the heels of the fleeing Koreans, first attacked the Australians on Hill 504. From their vantage point across the valley, on the higher 677, the Patricias watched the war, and waited.

Wave after wave of Chinese stormed the hill, were tossed back, and surged forward again. 'The attack was so intense,' recalls Jim Stone, 'that I decided to change my deployment and ordered "B" Company, commanded by Major Vince Lilley, to move from their position, which was partly dug in, and dig several hundred yards to the right, where they could overlook the valley of the Kapyong. As it turned out, the move was a fortunate one, because it helped bridge the gap when the Australians had to withdraw.

'I was listening over the Brigade radio and I heard the Australian commanding officer shouting that his command post was under fire and that he was going to have to pull back. This was after several hours of intense contact. The Chinese were all around him. His headquarters was gone and he had a lot of casualties.'

The Australians had stood their ground all night and well into the following day. US tanks who were supporting them had fired almost point-blank into the mass of attacking Chinese but were unable to stop them. Finally, at 5:30 in the afternoon on Tuesday, April 24, as the smoke of battle drifted across the shallow Kapyong River, the Australians were forced to retreat.

The Patricias now stood alone.

According to the official history of the war, the Canadians had by now deployed 'to cover the north face of hill 677, with "A" Company on the right, "C" Company in the centre, and "D" Company on the left. "B" Company occupied a salient in front of "D" Company.'

Then, in the way that men who fought in Korea all remember, the Chinese signalled their first attack on the Canadians. 'They started blowing bugles and whistles,' recalls one man. 'Then there was screaming, shouting, and they were coming through the brush towards us.'

From then on, the next few terrible hours were a complete blur. Men who were at Kapyong recall some parts of the night, but have completely forgotten others. 'I remember the attacks. I remember being surrounded. And I remember being more terrified than I ever was before or since,' says Gary Gurney. 'But it wasn't until I was in Winnipeg in 1976 at the twenty-fifth reunion of the battle that I really knew about the whole thing. I learned more in Winnipeg than I ever knew or learned at Kapyong.

'I think every man who was at Kapyong was a better man for it,' he adds. 'But I sure wouldn't want to go through it again. It was three days and nights of absolute hell.'

The Chinese moved forward in waves. Some would fall but there were always others who came on. They slipped through the darkness with the ease of a panther through trees. Softly, stealthily, deadly. One minute a Canadian would be firing at shadows in the brush in front of him. The next moment he would have to fend off a bayonet attack from the rear. Over all, the sound of curses, screams, Bren gun chatter, half-sobbed prayers, acrid smoke, flashes of flames, bursts of fire, shouted warnings . . .

Bruce MacDonald of Peterborough, Ontario, and another Patricia manned a Vickers machine-gun that night. They positioned themselves so that their range of fire covered one of the easiest approaches to the hills. The Chinese realized this and scores of them moved up the draw towards the two defenders. One, twice, three times they were driven back. Then, in a final, suicidal assault the enemy overran the Vickers gun and slaughtered the Canadians who used it. Two Korean houseboys who were there sobbed in the gloom when they realized their soldier friends were dead. No one remembers what happened to the youngsters when the position was overrun.

At one point during the battle, a moving platoon from 'B' Company stumbled into a series of grenades placed on trip-wires around the Tactical Headquarters position. One man was killed on the spot and a second wounded when one grenade went off. A second flipped loose from its trip and rolled, smoking, along the ground into the middle of the platoon. For what seemed an eternity but in reality was only a second or two, everyone froze, and stared at the device, paralysed in mid-step. Then a young corporal yelled at his men to hit the dirt, grabbed the grenade, and started to heave it out of the way. There was a blinding flash and the explosive went off, blowing the corporal's hand away but saving the lives of the others. Later on, Corporal S. Douglas was awarded the Military Medal for what he had done.

The horror went on.

'Wayne Mitchell was number one on the Bren,' said another soldier. 'I was his number two. When we were overrun he was hit by shrapnel but he never gave up his gun for the rest of the night. We sat there and held then off as long as we could. I don't know how long we were there before we got the order to move out. I had three shells left, so I dropped back and fired them off. Just as I jumped up I fell over a Chinaman who was running up the side of the hill. He got me in the neck and then ran into the end of my bayonet.

'I was swung completely around. When I got my bearings I started back, I went as far as I could, then got weak and lay down. I tried to get up but I couldn't, so I crawled back. I was afraid they would shoot me, so I kept hollering. Mitchell recognized my voice and came out. Soon as I saw him I never talked for three weeks. Later I met him in hospital. He knew my rifle because I have a couple of notches carved in it. He told me, "You got him. The rifle was still in him."'

Mitchell himself was lucky to survive the night. His first wound had been in the chest, but as soon as he had it dressed he went back to the fight. Even after he was wounded a second time and losing blood, he stayed at his post. Finally, after it was safe to do so, an American helicopter flew him out. Later on, in a ceremony witnessed by many of the men whose lives he saved, Private Wayne Mitchell had the Distinguished Conduct Medal pinned on his shirt by Brigadier John Rockingham.

There were other brave men fighting that night.

The Commander of 'D' Company was J.G.W. (Wally) Mills. His position was somewhat north and west of the others—and was perhaps the most exposed on the hill. During the evening and on into the night, hundreds of Chinese moved up, completely surrounded Captain Mills and his men, and then, in savage and desperate hand-to-hand fighting, moved over the entire area the Canadians were defending. To Mills and those around him, there seemed no hope.

'Wally Mills called me and said the Chinese had infiltrated and overrun his position,' recalls Colonel Stone. 'He wanted to pull out. I told him to stay there, that nobody could pull out. "If we ever lose this hill," I said, "we lose it all." "Will you fire artillery right on top of my position?" Mills asked me. "Are you dug in?" I asked. When he said he was, I told him to keep his head down and get ready. I got in touch with the artillery and our own mortars and we fired right where he was in this wooded area. He didn't have a single man wounded but it certainly got rid of the Chinese around him.'

Captain Wally Mills was awarded the Military Cross for his actions that night.

Twenty-two-year-old Ken Barwise, a six-foot-four-inch PPCLI private, won the Military Medal. Just before the Chinese attacked his position there was a loud bugle call, then the sound of sticks being beaten together, and, as the first enemy soldier materialized out of the murk, the piercing sounds of shrill whistles. Within seconds the Chinese were less than fifty feet from Barwise, Sergeant Vern Holligan, Jim Waniandy, Private Peter Boldt, and others.

'We opened up with our Brens,' said Waniandy to Bill Boss of Canadian Press. 'We saw them (the Chinese) falling all over.'

'They kept coming all night in waves,' Barwise is quoted in a story in the *Vancouver Sun* on May 12, 1951. 'They must have been crazy, or glory happy.'

During the course of the night, Ken Barwise slaughtered six men in vicious close-quarter fighting: two with grenades, two others with their own guns, one with a machine-gun he retrieved from the Chinese, and a sixth with his own rifle. The former sawmill boom man had succeeded as a soldier. He never looked upon himself as a hero.

As the grim night wore on, fears that the Patricias would be annihilated gradually subsided. They held on until morning, and although they were heavily shelled during the following day, they were never attacked as they had been only hours before. With dawn, however, another problem arose. They were completely surrounded.

'Our supply route had been cut,' says Jim Stone, 'and I had no way of knowing how long we might have to hold our position or how aggressive the enemy might become. We were pretty well out of food, water, and ammunition. Around 4 A.M. I called for an air drop from Japan. We ordered what we wanted and sure enough, six hours later four C119s dropped, by parachute, everything we requested, including mortar ammunition.'

To the men on the ground, the air drop was unforgettable.

'It was the most beautiful sight I can ever remember seeing,' says one man. 'I was so hungry my stomach was in knots. Then all of a sudden down came these big flying boxcars. They made a pass and then came back and made the drop. It was tremendous.'

'We had Corporal Bishop in my platoon,' recalls another man. 'He had a metabolism like you wouldn't believe. We were issued two rations, two C rations per man. Bishop sat down on the edge of his trench and ate two C rations. There were three meals in each one. They he went around seeing if anyone had any ham or lima beans they didn't need.'

The battle was over. The supply route was opened and the gallant officers and men of the Princess Patricia's Canadian Light Infantry moved back into reserve. They had fought well at Kapyong, so well in fact that their gallantry was later recognized by the American government, who awarded them, as well as the Australians and a US tank battalion, the Presidential Citation for 'outstanding heroism and exceptionally meritorious conduct in the performance of outstanding services'. This was the first and only time Canadians have won this award.

While no one may ever know the long-range plans of the Chinese in the actions of April 1951, it may well be true that, had it not been for the gallant stand the Canadians at Kapyong, the UN lines might have been breached and Seoul might have subsequently fallen. 'Kapyong was not a great battle,' says Jim Stone. 'But it was well planned and well fought. We were surrounded by the enemy. We could have run, panicked in some way, or surrendered. We stayed, fought, and withdrew in a soldierly fashion. In the circumstances, the Presidential citation was earned.'

The Pats lost only ten men at Kapyong, with twenty-three wounded, but the Chinese were not so fortunate. When the guns at last stopped firing, over fifty shredded corpses littered one section of Hill 677. Many others were removed later. No one knows how many were wounded.

John Melady, *Korea: Canada's Forgotten War* (1983), pp. 74-8

To be able to hold on has always required a core of steel in the character.

In plain view of certain stretches of our trenches in the St Eloi area, there was a big white house that had survived apparently un-damaged for nearly two years. All else around this white château was desolation, including the nearby village of Hollebeke. Not a tree was standing. Yet there, not six hundred yards behind the German line, stood this beautiful reminder of peacetime. A three-storey building in that Flemish plain, it obviously housed enemy observa-tion points. Nobody could understand why we had spared it so long. Someone in authority decided that the château must go.

Two twelve-inch howitzers of the corps heavies were ordered to eliminate it. We at 13th Battery had been given notice of the shoot. That bright May morning, I had a grandstand seat for it—our new O. Pip in the second line. I don't know where the 'heavy' observer was but he couldn't have had a better view than mine. With bino-culars, ignoring the discomfort of my broken nose, I could see every detail of the building. Bright sunlight made its desolate setting more repulsive than ever.

Almost on the dot of the time set for the shelling, I heard overhead the fearful runaway roar of the first big projectile.

It took eight rounds to level the target. Looking at the smoking mound, I thought it was a little like murder.

I could not take my eyes off the ruins. There was movement in the debris, the occasional glint of a steel helmet. The concrete masses of several pillboxes could be seen in the rubble.

Everything was surprisingly quiet. Observation balloons were up but there seemed to be no retaliation.

I was about to call the battery when a large part of Belgium fell on me . . . You never hear the big one that is really close. This time it was just like Vierstraat, the shocking impact that hit before the noise. I couldn't breathe . . . or move . . .

The two signallers and an infantryman dug me out with their bare hands.

It seemed forever before I could gasp my lungs full of air, though it was only a few minutes before I was breathing normally again.

More shells came over, sweeping along the trench away from us. The first one—it must have been a 5.9 or bigger—had caved in the parapet on me. For a minute or so, I had been buried alive yet I hadn't a scratch on me. Only my tin hat was missing. I had worn my chin strap behind my head. If the strap had been under my chin, my head might have been missing with the helmet.

Raymond Massey, *When I Was Young* (1976), pp. 180-1

How could a human being find the strength to survive being shelled in the trenches of 1914-18?

In February I experienced my closest call so far in the war. For a couple of days the Germans were firing heavy shells which were exploding in the rear area of our position. We presumed they were trying to knock out our mortar as we were causing extensive damage on their position. After we had fired another six rounds we all heard a shell coming and knew by the sound it was coming close. I was about one hundred feet from the rest, crouching low against the trench. The shell hit our gun emplacement which demolished everything. If that shell had been one minute sooner we would have all been killed. Some of our ammunition was also destroyed by the blast. The concussion from that blast shot through the trenches ripping my tunic down the seam from the collar to the bottom. Most of the seams in my pants were severed, a heavy piece of shell casing buried itself in a frozen sandbag six inches from my knee and a part of a falling sandbag hit me in the head. I was just getting to my feet when our officer rushed in from the communication trench. I had a little cut on my head but it was not serious. The first thing he said after learning no one was seriously hurt was, 'What in hell happened to your clothes?' After realizing it was the result of a concussion he said it was hard to believe we were still alive.

Gordon Reid, *Poor Bloody Murder* (1980), p. 146

Trench warfare meant as well the experience of gas—poisonous gas, drifting on the wind, used as a weapon. Canadians withstood this too. But not without cost.

We stood to at three A.M. Saturday morning. Shortly after eight-thirty A.M. when it was fairly light we noticed far away on our right, a German balloon which hadn't been there the day before. As we watched it, four red flares were dropped making it quite a pretty sight. Our gaze must have been lingering on this a little too long for when I turned, men were leaving the trenches on our right. A great wall of green gas about fifteen to twenty feet high was on top of us. Captain MacLaren gave an order to get handkerchiefs, soak them and tie them around our mouths and noses. (Some were able to do that and some just urinated on their handkerchiefs.) Some managed to cover their faces. Others, myself included did not, owing to a scarcity of the necessary articles. Even with these precautions it was hopeless to try and stand up against the stuff, so we retired choking, coughing and spluttering. There was a hill behind us. We went up to it in small groups. A few shells burst over us, but not enough to do any harm. Anyway the Germans couldn't see us owing to the gas.

At the top we came to one of our reserve trenches held by some of the 7th Battalion (British Columbia) into which we dropped pretty well all in (tired). We hadn't been there long before the shells started coming again. For about seven hours they shelled us most unmercifully: the shells dropping all around, some hitting the parapet, some just going over causing a great many casualties. As far as the Highlanders were concerned we were worthless anyway because we just lay in bundles at the bottom of the trench, choking and gasping for breath.

Sometime in the early afternoon the order came to retire, so having had enough of things by this time they thought of getting me to a hospital. One of my men gave me a hand. Later on another fellow joined in from somewhere, so between the two they coaxed, dragged and pushed me over the most uncomfortable four miles I had ever gone. I wanted to lie down every twenty yards to get my breath back.

Ibid., pp. 80-1

There have been moments when the power of the enemy, the lack of training, the poor equipment—all the entries in the tactician's lexicon—combined to defeat the Canadians, as at Hong Kong in 1941, when the Royal Rifles of Canada and the Winnipeg Grenadiers were overwhelmed by the Imperial Japanese.

On Friday night Private Dennis Murphy awakened in a crowded hospital ward. He was lying under a wool blanket, wearing shorts and socks. His head and right leg were bandaged, and it took him several moments before the grogginess lifted and his surroundings fully registered.

'How are you feeling?' an attractive blonde nurse asked, looking at him from the foot of the bed. 'A headache? Any dizziness?'

'I'm feeling terrific now that I've seen you,' the former announcer said flirtatiously. 'What place is this?'

'Bowen Road Hospital. You've been unconscious for hours. We'll have to make sure you don't have a concussion.'

'What's wrong with my legs?'

'Nothing serious. A couple of nasty cuts.'

'Oh, good.' Murphy grinned as the nurse walking away. 'I'll be able to take you dancing Saturday night.'

The light banter disguised Murphy's true emotions. He had seen awesome things at Wong Nei Chong Gap. The Japs were determined to roll straight on to the south coast and, by God, the Grenadiers were just as determined to hold them back. Captain Allan Bowman had died rushing a Japanese patrol with a blasting Tommy gun. Captain Bob Phillips, one eye knocked out, had fought until his ammunition was gone. Lieutenant Len Corrigan had seen a Japanese officer charging with an upraised sword and, wrestling him to the ground, had strangled the man to death. Awesome things that made Murphy feel ashamed. He had been inexcusably naive in treating the war lightly. While he had been en route to the Gap, thinking only of getting a poker game going, his countrymen were dying. His strongest desire now was to regain his health and return to the front. He had to pour everything he had into the war; he owed it to the heroes, dead and alive.

'What happened to you?' a bearded Rajput in the next bed inquired.

'Grenade. I guess the impact floored me. We were on night patrol and, I swear, the Nips have cats' eyes, for they spotted us in pitch darkness. I didn't even get off a shot.'

As the Rajput went into a lengthy description of his experience at Lye Mun, Murphy's mind drifted. He had heard that a Grenadier detachment was preparing to storm the high ground at Mount Butler, a mile northeast of the spot where Lawson had been killed. Murphy had friends in the unit and he was curious about how they were doing.

Scrambling down the steep hillside, banging into boulders and shrubbery, those same Grenadiers were in rapid retreat. They had achieved their objective, taking Mount Butler in a bloody battle in which thirty-five comrades died. Now, three hours later, the platoon was on the run, trying to escape several hundred dogged pursuers.

Private Stanley Baty's leg and shoulder throbbed with pain from collisions with the granite rocks, but he did not dare stop to examine them. The enemy was too close.

'Don't panic,' Sergeant Major John Osborn loudly cautioned. 'Stay together and keep calm. We'll get out of this okay.'

Baty thought Osborn was an incredible man. Very strict, all rules-and-regulations—but nerves of steel. Leading his men up the mountain, he had felled six Japanese with his bayonet and, afterward, he had repelled Japanese attacks by scooping up live grenades and flinging them back. Now, hurtling down the western slope of Mount Butler in broad daylight, fleeing an overwhelmingly superior enemy force, Osborn retained his cool, efficient demeanor.

The twenty-two-year-old Baty was anything but cool. He had quit a good-paying job cutting firewood for a Winnipeg fuel supply company to join his three brothers in the Grenadiers. At Camp Shilo, he had met Charlie Smith, a Regina smelter worker, and the two had become such fast friends that Baty called him 'my fourth brother'. Now Charlie was dead. On Mount Butler he had stood up to draw a bead on a Japanese soldier carrying a flag and had been struck in the forehead by a sniper's bullet. Charlie's death and the wild rush toward the Grenadier line near the Gap had Baty's mind in a turmoil.

At the bottom of the slope the platoon quickly reassembled. Baty noted the terror in some of his companions' eyes: yet not one bolted. Osborn's strength somehow glued them into a tight unit. Taking a Bren gun from a profusely sweating soldier, Baty said he would guard the rear.

The platoon moved swiftly up the ravine. The only noise was the heavy breathing of the more exhausted soldiers and the scraping of their boots on the hard ground. 'I think we've lost 'em,' someone said. 'There aren't any Japs comin' down the hill.'

The platoon had eluded the hunters from the summit, but other Japanese units were in the area. As the platoon approached the end of the ravine, a hidden Japanese soldier tossed a grenade from somewhere above. The explosive thudded to earth three feet from Osborn and six or seven soldiers.

'Clear out!' the sergeant major shouted. In an extraordinary act of self-sacrifice Osborn flung himself on the ground, covering the grenade with his body. The blast was instantly fatal. (Osborn was posthumously awarded the most prestigious medal in the Commonwealth for bravery, the Victoria Cross.)

The platoon was stunned speechless. But the fear of more grenades suddenly tearing into their ranks prodded the men onward, half running, half walking. The ravine opened onto a narrow, dry slough. Ten feet into the clearing, Baty tripped and pitched onto his face. The fall probably saved his life. From hidden vantage points in the surrounding hills the Japanese directed machine-gun and rifle fire into the slough. Everyone near Baty was cut down. Forsaking the Bren gun, Baty crawled to the side of the clearing to where the other fourteen survivors gathered, hugging large rocks for protection. For twenty minutes the two adversaries exchanged bullets. When the ammunition was almost depleted, the Grenadiers decided to surrender. One man rose, waving a white handkerchief. He was shot dead. 'We've had it, boys,' Baty muttered. 'Those buggers are aching to do us in.'

Ten minutes later the ammunition ran out. The thirteen men removed their rifle breeches and threw them as far as they could. Then, believing it was the last move they would ever make, they stood together, their hands over their heads. Popping up everywhere, dozens of Japanese soldiers walked slowly toward them, pointing rifles.

They did not shoot. Reaching the platoon, a Japanese officer pointed a sword at a man standing beside Baty. Two soldiers grabbed the man and hustled him off to one side, where he was bayoneted. His death was, Baty assumed, a graphic warning that if the others did not behave they would suffer an identical fate. The soldiers stripped them of watches, rings, and wallets, then the prisoners were marched north.

At twilight the platoon was placed inside a one-room building. Two hundred Canadians, British, and East Indians were packed into a poorly ventilated space so small that no one dared to sit, lest he be trampled. Many prisoners, wounded and moaning, were pressed upright against the walls. During the night a stray British mortar shell banged through the roof, killing several men. With no food, sleep, or water, the prisoners endured 'The Black Hole of Hong Kong' for twenty hours. Some were held up by the crush of bodies long after they died.

When the Japanese finally ordered the captives outside—one at a time and coming through the doorway on their knees—they were told they would be interned at North Point, a camp the colonial government had originally built to house refugees. A young Grenadier lieutenant, Mitchell, said he did not want to go: his brother was too badly wounded to make the long walk. He asked a Japanese officer if his brother could have medical aid. The officer barked a command and two soldiers accompanied Mitchell back into the building. The soldiers' grim expressions as they emerged moments later disclosed that they had slain the brothers.

The cruelty Baty witnessed did not prepare him for the kindness shown by a Japanese soldier en route to North Point. The prisoners marched single file, their hands linked by a long piece of telephone wire. An unusually tall Japanese soldier looped his canvas pack around Baty's neck. It was jammed with stolen food and jewelry, and the strap frequently slipped by Baty's throat, causing choking spasms. The soldier untied his hands and permitted him to tote the pack on his back. That unexpected bit of kindness was followed by an even more surprising deed. When they arrived at North Point, the soldier removed the pack, effusively thanked Baty for bearing it, and give him a gift—a small tin of asparagus tips.

Ted Ferguson, *Desperate Siege* (1980), pp. 167-71

But death did not win every time. Now and again, some inexplicable other power intervened.

As we went back and drew near the railway embankment someone called in a low voice. I went over and found two of the men from the 73rd had dug a neat bivvy into the embankment. They were very decent chaps and insisted they had made the place wide enough to accommodate the three of us. We snuggled in, and with a ground sheet pegged to hold over our heads we were really comfortable. In seconds I was dead to the world.

The ground sheet pegged over our heads was pulled free and fell on my face, rousing me. Then a firm warm hand seized one of mine and pulled me up to a sitting position. It was very early, as first sunshine was glittering on the dew-wet grass. I was annoyed that I should have to do some chore after being out so late. I tried to pull free. But the grip held, and as I came to a sitting-up position my other hand was seized and I had a look at my visitor.

In an instant I was out of the bivvy, so surprised I could not speak. I was face to face with my brother, Steve, who had been killed in '15!

The first notice from the War Office had said: 'Missing, believed dead.' After a time one of his mates wrote to say a boot had been found with his name on it. The Germans had mined the Canadian trench and blown it up.

Steve grinned as he released my hands, then put his warm hand over my mouth as I started to shout my happiness. He pointed to the sleepers in the bivvy and to my rifle and equipment. 'Get your gear,' he said softly.

As I grabbed it he turned and started walking away rapidly. It was hard to keep up with him. We passed make-shift shelters filled with sleeping men of my platoon. No one was awake. Now and then a gun fired off toward the Somme or a machine-gun chattered, but on the whole it was a quiet morning. As soon as we were past the shelters I hurried to get close to Steve. 'Why didn't you write Mother?' I asked.

He turned and the grin was still on his face. 'Wait,' he said. 'Don't talk yet.'

Then I noticed he had a soft cap on and no gas mask or equipment. Somehow he had learned where the 42nd was, and our 'D' Company, but how in the world did he know where I was sleeping?

We left the company area and headed directly into a collection of ruins that had been Petit Vimy. 'There's no one around here,' I said. 'How did you know where to find me?'

At that moment my equipment, slung hurriedly over one shoulder, slipped off and fell to the ground before I could catch it. As I stooped and retrieved it Steve went into a passageway in the ruins and I ran to catch him. Arrived there, I saw one way went right and the other left. Which way had he gone? 'Steve!' I called. There was no answer, so I dropped my rifle and gear and ran to the right. It only took minutes—two or three—to get to the far side, but there was no sign of my brother. I ran back and called again, took the way to the left, searched and searched again, called repeatedly, but could not find him. Finally I sat down on my equipment and leaned back against a bit of wall. I was tired and sweating and excited. A great desire to find our officer and get the day off took hold of me, but I realized I did not know where the officer or sergeant-major were, and if I left the immediate area and Steve returned he would not know where I had gone. Probably he had no pass and did not want to be seen. If only I had not bothered with my equipment I could have kept up with him!

Minutes went by. I got up and made another search of the ruins. The sun began to glisten on the tops of the broken walls. I settled back more comfortably on my equipment and heard the usual morning stir of guns firing registering shots. The sun got warmer. I dozed.

Suddenly I was shaken awake. Tommy had me by the arm and was yelling. 'He's here! Bill's here!'

I stumbled up, dazed, looked at my watch. It was nine o'clock.

'What's made you come here?' Tommy was asking. 'What happened?'

'What's all the row about?' I countered.

'You should know. They're digging around that bivvy you were in. All they've found is Jim's helmet and one of Bob's legs.'

'Legs!' I echoed stupidly. 'What do you mean?'

'Don't you know a big shell landed in that bivvy? They've been trying to find something of you.'

It seemed utterly incredible. I put on my gear and followed Tommy. There was a great cavity in the embankment and debris was scattered over the whole area. Mickey came running to shake hands with me. Then the sergeant was calling and I saw he was talking with an officer.

When we got nearer I saw it was an artillery officer of high rank and saluted him.

'What made you leave the bivvy?' the sergeant asked. 'The boys say you got in there with Jim and Bob.'

'I did,' I said. 'I was there till daylight.'

'What made you leave then?'

It was the artillery officer who asked the question, and I hesitated, felt it would sound foolish if I told them exactly what had happened.

'Don't be afraid,' he said. 'We're all friends.'

He looked a real gentleman, so I told him my story in detail. He made notes in a book he carried, asking my name, where I was from, and all about Steve. Then he shook my hand. 'You have had a wonderful experience,' he said.

The sergeant looked as if he did not know whether to believe me or not, but a runner came with orders for another move and I hustled to get something to eat. Neither Tommy nor Mickey mentioned the matter to me through the day, and that night we were over to the left doing working parties again until late. I slept in a bivvy Mac-Donald and I had made but it was past midnight before I could doze off.

I had seen Steve as clearly as I saw Mickey. His warm hands had pulled me from the bivvy. His voice had been perfectly natural. He had the old half-grin I knew so well. He had saved my life.

I had joined the Methodist Church when I was fourteen and had been as decent as the average. At evenings in the YMCA I loved the singing of hymns. I did not like the compulsory church service and the officers singing 'O God, Our Help in Ages Past'. But now I knew beyond all argument or theory, by any man learned or otherwise, that there was a hereafter, and there would never again be the slightest doubt in my mind about it.

For a few days I sensed that the sergeant had not believed my story but it did not worry me in the least. Then a batman let me know the officers had talked about the incident and regarded my story as the result of too much rum. This was rather amusing as I never took the ration and everyone in our company, except the officers who were new, was aware of the fact. However, in a few days the matter was forgotten by the men. And it was only as I lay ready for sleep that I thought of it.

Will R. Bird, *Ghosts Have Warm Hands* (1968), pp. 38-41

5

THE AIR WAR

'It was the mud, I think, that made me take to flying,' said the high-scoring First World War fighter pilot W.A. 'Billy' Bishop. For whatever reasons, as military aviation developed, Canadians became airmen with enthusiasm. In the early days, though, getting airborne at all could be a tricky proposition.

Monday, January 17th, 1916

Had tea and caught tender as usual not knowing that this would be a red letter day for me. Spent morning expecting a flight but without results. In the afternoon Long took me up for fifteen minutes and then asked me if I would like to go alone. I said 'yes,' and up I went.

I went up and was still climbing when I noticed that the machine was hardly going at all. I grew suspicious and hastily gave the throttle a push, causing the machine to leap forward, probably just in time to prevent it backsliding (stalling) to the ground and completely ruining my young career. I safely negotiated a turn in spite of the fact that I had to balance with one hand and hold the throttle open with the other. Sailed along, negotiated another turn, shut off and landed.

Long said I could go up again and do two more circuits and land again. He also said that he had forgotten to tell me the throttle slipped, and that he was hoping while I was up that I wouldn't kill myself before I found it out. I went up again and sailed around twice, and was again saved by nothing but the generosity of the Lord. This time I attempted to push the rudder to make the machine turn to the left when the right wing was down. This is a fatal mistake if the machine responds, but luckily the machine didn't but merely tilted over more to the right. I couldn't get it right side up, so I turned the nose down near the tree tops and managed to right the thing and climbed up again did a circuit and landed. Felt a bit shaky as I had barely avoided crossing the Great Divide.

Brereton Greenhous, ed., *A Rattle of Pebbles* (1987) pp. 28-9

That experience was by no means unique. Billy Bishop's first solo flight was nearly a disaster.

An ambulance stood on the aerodrome, and it seemed to me, as it has to many another student-pilot, that all the other business of flying had suddenly ceased so that everybody could look at me. I noticed with a shiver that the ambulance had its engine running. Were the doctors at the hospital expectantly fondling their knives? Everybody looked cold-blooded and heartless. But I had to do it—so into the machine I crawled, trying to look cheerful, but feeling awful lonesome. How I got off the ground I do not know, but once in the air it was not nearly so bad—not much worse than the first time you started down hill on an old-fashioned bicycle. I wasn't taking any liberties. I flew as straight ahead as I could, climbing steadily all the time. But at last I felt I had to turn, and I tried a very slow, gradual one, not wanting to bank either too steeply or too little. They told me afterward I did some remarkable skidding on that turn, but I was blissfully ignorant of a little detail like that and went gaily on my way. I banked a little more on my next turn and didn't skid so much.

For a time I felt very much pleased with myself circling above the aerodrome, but suddenly an awful thought came to me. Somehow or other I had to get that machine down to the earth again. How blissful it would be if I could just keep on flying. At last, however, I screwed up all my courage, reached for the throttle, pushed it back, and the engine almost stopped. I knew the next thing to do was to put her nose down. So down it went at a steep angle. I felt it was too steep, so I pulled her nose up a bit, then put it down again, and in a series of steps descended toward the ground.

About forty feet from the ground, however, I did everything I had been told to do when two feet from the ground. So I made a perfect landing—only forty feet too high. Eventually I realised this slight error, and down went her nose again. We rapidly got nearer the ground, and then I repeated my perfect landing—about eight feet up. This time I just sat and suffered, while the now thoroughly exasperated old machine taking matters into its own hands dropped with a 'plonk' the intervening distance.

Major William A. Bishop, *Winged Warfare* (1918), pp. 31-3

By the time of the Second World War, the speed and complexity of fighter action had increased dramatically. But Spitfire pilot Bill Olmsted's account of his first action has an immediacy that Bishop would have understood.

February 25 was a full day for the squadron. In the early afternoon, together with seven other Spitfire squadrons, we escorted flying fortresses to bomb Bizerte. The Forts had their own close support of P-38 Lightnings while we had a roving commission, free to do what we liked as long as we stayed in the Bizerte area. The day was gorgeous, with a radiant sun shining full power so that even at our height of 27,000 feet it felt warm, giving me a sense of well-being. Below us, at 12,000 feet, was a thin layer of patchy cloud.

Then the Forts began their bombing run. Behind them at a safe distance hovered a cloud of thirty Me 109s. I could just picture those German pilots trying to make up their minds on exactly how to attack the prickly well-armed bombers. Other gaggles of 109s and Fw 190s flitted hither and yon. Aircraft were everywhere, forty Forts, over one hundred Germans, at least thirty-six Lightnings and ninety-six Spitfires. When the fight started, it looked as thought it would be a real free-for-all.

I was flying number 2 to Gray when he suddenly announced, 'Bouncing, chaps. 190s below. Tallyho.'

I had all I could do to follow his sudden move. Some 8,000 feet below us I could see a large gaggle of Fw 190s quite unaware of our presence. At well over 400 mph, Gray closed in on the last 190. I saw smoke from his guns trail over his wings as he fired, but the 190 stooged along, unhit and unaware of what was happening behind him. The CO broke left, and I climbed up the back of the enemy, firing wildly with no strikes. I pulled away to the right, missing the German by only a few feet. I could look into his cockpit almost as if I were sitting beside him. He did not have a smile on his face, although he should have, considering he was still alive and unhurt. It was one of the few times I saw Gray miss when he fired in anger.

I pulled up vertically, since I had so much speed, feeling that altitude would be a good move. As I got to the top of my loop and started to roll out, I saw a great black cross and the stubby nose of a Messerschmitt 109 fewer than one hundred yards away directly in front. Again I fired a long burst before I pulled the stick back and dived vertically toward the ground. Missed again! As I dove I saw a 190 flying carelessly along on top of the cloud layer right below me. Again I lined up my sights when within range and fired, only to miss again. This was my first fight and the sweat was pouring off me. I figured it was time for a breather and dodged into the clouds with a sigh of relief.

I could hear the CO on the R/T telling the squadron to pull out and head for home. I knew the sky above was a mass of whirling aircraft, many short of ammunition and all anxious to head for base. I set course for Tingley and tried to figure out what had happened.

Although the fight had lasted only a couple of minutes, as far as I was concerned, it seemed much longer, as though time had stood still. I had fired at three different enemy aircraft and missed them all.

Bill Olmsted, Blue Skies (1987), pp. 51-3

The aviators of the First World War often seem to have shared the spirit of 'play up, play the game' associated with that era.

We continued to patrol our beat, and I was keeping my place so well I began to look about a bit. After one of these gazing spells, I was startled to discover that the three leading machines of our formation were missing. Apparently they had disappeared into nothingness. I looked around hastily, and then discovered them underneath me, diving rapidly. I didn't know just what they were diving at, but I dived, too. Long before I got down to them, however, they had been in a short engagement half a mile below me, and had succeeded in frightening off an enemy artillery machine which had been doing wireless observation work. It was a large white German two-seater, and I learned after we landed that it was a well known machine and was commonly called 'the flying pig'. Our patrol leader had to put up with a lot of teasing that night because he had attacked the 'pig'. It seems that it worked every day on his part of the front, was very old, had a very bad pilot, and a very poor observer to protect him.

It was a sort of point of honour in the squadron that the decrepit old 'pig' should not actually be shot down. It was considered fair sport, however, to frighten it. Whenever our machines approached, the 'pig' would begin a series of clumsy turns and ludicrous manoeuvres, and would open a frightened fire from ridiculously long ranges. The observer was a very bad shot and never succeeded in hitting any of our machines, so attacking this particular German was always regarded more as a joke than a serious part of warfare. The idea was only to frighten the 'pig', but our patrol leader had made such a determined dash at him the first day we went over, that he never appeared again. For months the patrol leader was chided for playing such a nasty trick upon a harmless old Hun.

Major William A. Bishop, Winged Warfare (1918), pp. 47-8

Yet when the killing did occur, there was nothing held back.

On the 25th of March came my first real fight in the air, and as luck would have it, my first victory. The German retreat was continuing. Four of us were detailed to invade the enemy country, to fly low over the trenches, and in general to see what the Boche troops were doing and where they were located.

Those were very queer days. For a time it seemed that both armies—German and British alike—had simply dissolved. Skirmishes were the order of the day on the ground and in the air. The grim, fixed lines of battle had vanished for the time being and the Germans were falling back to their famous Hindenburg positions.

The clouds had been hanging low as usual, but after we had gotten well in advance of our old lines and into what had so recently been Hunland, the weather suddenly cleared. So we began to climb to more comfortable altitudes and finally reached about 9,000 feet. We flew about for a long while without seeing anything, and then from the corner of my eye I spied what I believed to be three enemy machines. They were some distance to the east of us and evidently were on patrol duty to prevent any of our pilots or observers getting too near the rapidly changing German positions. The three strange machines approached us, but our leader continued to fly straight ahead without altering his course in the slightest degree. Soon there was no longer any doubt as to the identity of the three air-craft— they were Huns, with the big, distinguishing black iron crosses on their planes. They evidently were trying to surprise us and we allowed them to approach, trying all the time to appear as if we had not seen them.

Like nearly all other pilots who come face to face with a Hun in the air for the first time, I could hardly realise that these were real, live, hostile machines. I was fascinated by them and wanted to circle about and have a good look at them. The German Albatross machines were perfect beauties to look upon. Their swept-back planes give them more of a bird-like appearance than any other machines flying on the western front. Their splendid, graceful lines lend to them an effect of power and flying ability far beyond what they really possess. After your first few experiences with enemy machines at fairly close quarters you have very little trouble distinguishing them in the future. You learn to sense their presence, and to know their nationality long before you can make out the crosses on the planes.

Finally the three enemy machines got behind us, and we slowed down so they would overtake us all the sooner. When they had approached to about 400 yards, we opened out our engines and turned. One of the other pilots, as well as myself, had never been in a fight before, and we were naturally slower to act then the other two. My first real impression of the engagement was that one of the enemy machines dived down, then suddenly came up again and began to shoot at one of our people from the rear.

I had a quick impulse and followed it. I flew straight at the attacking machine from a position where he could not see me and opened fire. My 'trace' bullets—bullets that show a spark and a thin little trail of smoke as they speed through the air—began at once to hit the enemy machine. A moment later the Hun turned over on his back and seemed to fall out of control. This was just at the time that the Germans were doing some of their famous falling stunts. Their machines seemed to be built to stand extraordinary strains in that respect. They would go spinning down from great heights and just when you thought they were sure to crash, they would suddenly come under control, flatten out into correct flying position, and streak for the rear of their lines with every ounce of horse power imprisoned in their engines.

When my man fell from his upside down position into a spinning nose dive, I dived after him. Down he went for a full thousand feet and then regained control. I had forgotten caution and everything else in my wild and overwhelming desire to destroy this thing that for the time being represented all of Germany to me. I could not have been more than forty yards behind the Hun when he flattened out and again I opened fire. It made my heart leap to see my smoking bullets hitting the machine just where the closely hooded pilot was sitting. Again the Hun went into a dive and shot away from me vertically toward the earth.

Suspecting another ruse, and still unmindful of what might be happening to my companions in their set-to with the other Huns, I went into a wild dive after my particular opponent with my engine full on. With a machine capable of doing 110 to 120 miles an hour on the level, I must have attained 180 to 200 miles in that wrathful plunge. Meteor-like as was my descent, however, the Hun seemed to be falling faster still and got farther and farther away from me. When I was still about 1,500 feet up, he crashed into the ground below me. For a long time I heard pilots speaking of 'crashing' enemy machines, but I never fully appreciated the full significance of 'crashed' until now. There is no other word for it.

I have not to this day fully analysed my feelings in those moments of my first victory. I don't think I fully realised what it all meant. When I pulled my machine out of its own somewhat dangerous dive, I suddenly became conscious of the fact that I had not the slightest idea in the world where I was. I had lost all sense of direction and distance; nothing had mattered to me except the shooting down of

that enemy scout with the big black crosses that I shall never forget.
Ibid., pp. 51-5

*By the Second World War, accounts of air fighting could be extreme-
ly technical, which was important both for record-keeping and for
understanding what exactly had taken place.*

While patrolling with squadron over North Weald enemy sighted on
left at 1705 (approx.) enemy a/c 2 in vic formation stepped from
12,000-18,000 ft., attacked middle section of '110s and two enemy
a/c broke off to attack. Succeeded in getting behind one enemy and
opened fire at approx. 100 yds; enemy a/c burst into flames and dived
towards ground. Next attacked He.111 formation and carried out
beam attack on nearest one opening fire at approx. 150-200 yards.
Port engine stopped and a/c rolled over on back, finally starting to
smoke then burst into flames and crashed to earth. Lastly was
attacked by Me.110 but succeeded in getting behind and followed
him from 10,000 ft to 1,000 ft. Enemy a/c used very steep turns for
evasive action but finally straightened out. I opened fire at approx.
30 yards, enemy's starboard engine stopped and port engine burst
into flames. Enemy crashed in flames alongside large reservoir. No
rear fire noticed from first two enemy but last machine used large
amount.
Hugh Halliday, *No. 242 Squadron The Canadian Years* (1982), p. 94

*But less terse accounts suggest that air combat was still a wild and
confused business.*

One passed immediately under me heading for the tail of the last
section of bombers. I opened up full throttle but he pulled away from
me. But this time I was opposite the tail end of the bombers. Just
then another Me.109 attacked the last section of the bombers and
turned to the starboard side. I moved over and had a good 2 seconds
burst at him starting from about 150 yards until he pulled away from
me. I saw white smoke coming from him and he turned slowly away
more to the starboard and back toward the way from which he had
come. Then saw bullets hitting my wings so took certain evasive
action and shook him from my tail. I then moved back to my former
position near the tail end of the bombers about 500 feet above. While

THE AIR WAR

watching another Me.109 (old type—square wing tips) came up to attack bombers, so I turned on to him and at about 200 yards opened fire and slowly closed in on him and saw white and black smoke pouring out and he dived steeply towards the ground, completely out of control. I then found I had another on my tail and after shaking him off saw another coming up on the bombers so turned and took a quick shot but he turned away and I saw no definite result. I resumed my original position and saw the bomber formation safely over the English coast.

Ibid., pp. 128-9

Air fighting was in general chaotic, and never more so than when it was evident that, with your aircraft disintegrating under you, your life hung on a combination of quick thinking and blind luck.

Attacking the first lorry I opened fire at three hundred yards in a medium dive. The vibration of my guns shook the bomb free, so that it struck the truck when I was less than fifty feet above the vehicle. It blew the truck to smithereens, knocked me unconscious, and blasted my aircraft several hundred feet upward. My Spit slowly rolled onto its back, and when I regained consciousness two or three seconds later, I was heading for the ground upside down. Death was only seconds away, although I was too dazed to think clearly. The trees below looked enormous. Suddenly, instinctively, I moved the control column hard and the aircraft righted itself, pulling out of the dive just above the tops of the trees.

In a few moments I realized that my plight was desperate. I wondered whether or not I should bail out while I still had an opportunity or try to fly back toward base. Then I found that there was no choice, for struggle as I might the coupe top would not open.

Setting a rough course for Volkel, I surveyed the damage from the cockpit. Both wings were badly buckled from the force of the explosion and had been blown or bent upward an extra foot and a half. Every panel in the aircraft had been blown off, with the ground clearly visible through great empty holes in the wings. Pieces of brown canvas from the covering protecting the truck cargo were streaming from the jagged metal pieces of my aircraft, and the fuselage was buckled and twisted while the tail unit fluttered and vibrated, threatening to break off. Both ailerons were sticking almost straight up in the air. While I was subconsciously recovering from the dive, Providence had made me move the control column the only way it would work. The cockpit had been badly stoved in and none of the cockpit instruments read correctly. The radio and oxygen equipment, normally situated behind the seat, were rattling on the floor of the Spitfire, completely shattered. Some of the control cables had been completely severed; there was no elevator control, and the rudder remained the only control which worked normally. It took both my hands, one foot, and all my strength on the control column just to prolong what little flying capability remained.

Using full engine power I staggered through the air at 140 mph and climbed about two hundred feet per minute. From Munster to safety was almost one hundred miles. I was certainly on my own, for though the pilots herded about me, without a radio I had no idea what was happening other than my own immediate problems. Several lifetimes seemed to pass before my derelict aircraft crossed our lines at some 15,000 feet.

Upon reaching the comparative safety of friendly territory I thought that since I would have to bail out, how clever it would be to jump right over our field and save me a long walk home. That opportunity disappeared because the smashed coupe top would neither open nor jettison. I released the control column so I could use the strength of my back and legs for added leverage against the confining cover. At last it released and blew away. Now there was the question of how best to exit from the machine. All the methods of abandoning an aircraft flashed through my mind; diving over the side while flying as level as possible finally won out.

Before I could make the final decision, the engine apparently ran out of oil. It was making strange noises as it lost power, indicating that it might blow up at any moment. At the same time the tail assembly started to flutter and vibrate so violently I thought it would fall off. With the loss of engine power the Spit became totally unmanageable and it entered a steep spiral dive. With helmet already off and straps released, and radio and oxygen lines unhooked, I pushed myself headfirst through the side door, into the slipstream.

The Spit's dive was now so steep that the pressure on me meant I was stuck, pressed against the plane's metal skin, staring at the tail. The fuselage was rippled and bent horribly. How did the machine ever fly, let alone last for one hundred miles? I had a few moments to think of these things, for I was completely stuck, unable to move. Then, after a seeming eternity, the rapidly increasing wind pressure suddenly plucked me from the side of the aircraft, flinging me free. For a silly moment I felt that I was being chewed up by the propeller, a totally impossible act since the engine was pointing down and I was well behind it. This ridiculous impression was to invade my dreams for years afterward.

Hurtling through the air at nearly 300 mph, staring alternately at the sky and then at the ground, I thought it a wonderful feeling to be free, with no sense of falling or of speed. The gentle, almost somersaulting motion of the fall allowed the air to fill my clothes and dry my sweat. It felt as though my whole body was being caressed with velvet—soothing, peaceful, wonderful.

After dropping free for several thousand feet, allowing my rate of descent to decrease somewhat while the various thoughts had raced through my head, I looked down to my left side, saw the D-ring of the ripcord, and pulled it. I looked at the metal ring, thinking what a queer-looking object it was, and since it had done its job, I threw it away as being of no further use. There was a sharp jolt as the pilot 'chute caught in the air, pulling out the main canopy with a force which jarred every bone in my body. I must have been falling at great speed to receive such a jolt when my downward momentum came to a shuddering halt. I felt angry and helpless drifting down and extremely weak from having fought the controls of my aircraft for so long. I was completely drained. I watched with no emotion as my aircraft crashed in a tiny Dutch field, but later I would thank that remarkable aircraft for lasting long enough to bring me safely home.

My worries were not over, for I was a mere two miles from the German lines, toward which a very brisk wind was blowing the parachute at a good rate of speed. With thousands of feet still to drop there was a very real chance that I could still end up in enemy hands. My recourse was to pull the shrouds of the chute to speed up the rate of descent as well as counter the wind drift. Tugging desperately on the silken cords, I pulled down the edge of the canopy and the rate of descent increased dramatically. Below was a small village that had a church with a wicked-looking spire, and I could imagine it spearing me, bottom first. I could see people, small as ants at first, running from every direction to converge on my probable landing site. Cars, trucks, and jeeps twisted through tiny lanes, each trying to be first to reach me when I finally landed.

Too late I released the shrouds to slow my rate of descent, starting a violent swinging motion which I did not have time to stop. Although I missed some tall trees I was hurled against the side of a sloping slate roof, with the lower half of my body smashing through it as easily as if bursting a paper bag. Within a minute a crowd of Dutch civilians gathered about the building, curiously watching a helpless airman stretched flat on the slope of the roof. The owner and his wife had been eating lunch when I smashed through their roof, but they seemed to accept this as an everyday occurrence!

A short, stocky British army captain succeeded in rescuing me, giving me and my rolled up 'chute a seat in his jeep while the escorting Spitfires flew low and dipped their wings in a farewell salute. My landing site was the tiny village of Veghel, only six miles past our base. Arriving at the captain's mess, he urged half a bottle of Scotch into me and as the liquid warmed my body, aches and bruises seemed to disappear and muscles and nerves relaxed. I was safe, unhurt, and life seemed very, very sweet.

Bill Olmsted, *Blue Skies* (1987), pp. 228-31

For the fighter pilot, it was at least possible to release some tension through active participation in the fight; for the bomber crews of the Second World War, the need for formation flying and careful bombing runs while under the threat of fighter or anti-aircraft gun attacks produced tremendous strain.

The tension of waiting to fly was obvious in everyone and suiting up in the crew room gave a clear indication of the stress everyone felt. I think most aircrew were superstitious. I know I was. We dressed in the same order for each trip. The right flight boot must be put on first. The same heavy socks must be used. Personal pieces of clothing, like a girlfriend's scarf, must be carried. A rabbit's foot or a stuffed toy would be pushed into pockets. Each had his own talisman. Mine was a hockey sweater that I had worn playing for a Toronto team. I wouldn't fly without it. I still have it today and my children wonder why I keep this ragged thing around.

Most crews had a ritual of things they did while standing around the aircraft waiting. Many urinated on the tail wheel for good luck. Others chainsmoked. Some checked the bricks and bottles they would throw out over Germany as their individual contribution to Hitler's woes. Bottles were supposed to make a screaming noise as they fell, and so scare the hell out of the Germans below. Some of the stones had been sent by fathers in food parcels as personal additions to the cause. Occasionally, men vomited before boarding. Eric, our navigator, was one those. An extremely nervous kid, his hands shook so much you wondered how he could hold a pencil and draw a straight line. He always did. He was one of the sharpest navigators on the squadron.

J. Douglas Harvey, *Boys, Bombs and Brussels Sprouts* (1981), p. 53

The way the Bomber Command aircrews dealt with the crushing weight of fear says much about their courage.

The fear of flying operations was a constant with most aircrew. It had to be. My own fear was easier to carry because I was captain of the aircraft, young enough to accept all the guff we had been brought up to believe. 'The captain always goes down with the ship', and other fairy tales. I might be terrified—but I mustn't let my fear be known to my crew.

One evening, over some beers, Eric asked, 'Why do you swear so much when we get into trouble over Germany?'

I was completely stunned by his question. 'Swear? You're kidding!'

'No, really, every time we get caught in the searchlights or get hit by flak or have a fighter up our ass, you start cursing.'

I found his remarks hard to believe and I sat there conscious that I was afraid to examine the question. 'Maybe', I said, in an attempt to change the subject, 'it's because I love those bastards so much.' But I made a mental note to check it out. Sure enough, Eric was right. Whenever we got into a tangle with the enemy and I began throwing the bomber around, trying to get away, I found myself cursing the Germans. 'You rotten bunch of bastards. You sneaking, yellow sons of bitches.' I kept it up until we got free.

While Eric recognized my behaviour patterns, I don't think he knew his own. He would throw up before boarding the bomber for each operational trip. Never on training flights, just on ops. One moment he was standing with the crew waiting for the time to board, and the next minute he was bent over the tail wheel vomiting. His hands shook continually, and since he was a small kid, very pale and blond, he looked like a nervous, fluttering chicken. He never mentioned his obvious nervousness, neither did the crew. Once in the air he was efficiency itself, keeping the aircraft on track and on time. We never failed to find the target or base on return. I thought he was the greatest and so did the crew. Eric compounded his reasons for nervousness by marrying a lovely English girl when we were halfway through our operational tour. He then had more than himself to worry about.

The operational word for nerves was the twitch. You could see it at the bar anytime. Facial muscles would twitch involuntarily without the owner's awareness. Some of the guys were funny to watch and I always stood next to the guy with the most pronounced twitch. Some would flutter an eye, some would stutter slightly as their mouths jumped around. Some had a jerky arm or leg that would twist and leap. When two or three guys with a decent twitch got together it was a hilarious sight. One senior officer would begin to speak and after about six words his jaws would lock open. His eyes bulged out and he would gurgle and gargle trying to speak. It was funny to see; but not so funny when you were standing in front of his desk, desperately trying to understand the order he was fighting to deliver. These manifestations of the stress caused by operational flying were always understood and allowed for by other aircrew. It was, in effect, a badge of honour.

Each flyer had his own particular fear. Some, like myself, dreaded the searchlights. Some hated the German fighters. Some even hated flying. I didn't fear the fighters, figuring naïvely, that I could handle a one-on-one situation. Bob Young, who came from Niagara Falls, would tease me constantly about how I would meet my end. 'A night fighter will get you for sure.' Unfortunately, it was a night fighter that got Bob during a raid on Düsseldorf. When he failed to return I began to think more seriously about the fighters. But in truth, it was the bloody searchlights that terrified me. It wasn't until my third Berlin raid that I met my personal fear face to face.

I had just settled the Lanc into a straight and level bombing run, bomb doors open and vibrating as I followed the course directions of the bomb aimer. Berlin was sixty miles of flame, smoke, bursting shells and bombs, and, it seemed, millions of glaring searchlights sweeping the sky. I could spot dozens of bombers below, converging on the Pathfinder flares, some already in flames and plunging down. I held the Lanc steady as Steven dropped our bombs, every nerve in my body screaming to turn off the target and flee this inferno. I had just closed the bomb doors when I went blind. Absolutely blind. Terrified, I realized we had been coned. The world was a dazzling white, as though a giant flashlight was aimed directly into my eyes.

I couldn't see my hands on the control column, couldn't see the instrument panel, couldn't see outside the cockpit. I was naked, totally exposed, helpless. Foolishly I told the gunners to keep searching for fighters, but they were as blind in their turrets as I was in the cockpit. I could tell the flak hadn't started up the beams because we weren't being rocked by bursts. That meant the searchlights were illuminating us for fighter attacks. Paralyzed with fear, I tried to get my brain working. I had seen enough bombers coned by searchlights to know it was useless to turn and twist hoping to break out of them. We were a very bright and shiny target in the apex of fifty or more beams that were radio directed. They weren't going to let go easily.

Instinctively I reacted by shoving the nose down hard and jamming the throttles forward. My brain was screaming at me: the shortest distance between two points is a straight line. Dive. Outrun the lights. My speed built up rapidly as I hurtled down, the controls stiffening. I had no idea of my direction or even if I was turning. I tried to keep the controls centred. Cupping my hands around the airspeed indicator to block the light, my chest holding the control column forward, I got a reading of 350 miles an hour. The altimeter needle was whirling backwards so fast my panicky brain failed to register a reading. Fearful that I would fly us into the ground I began easing back on the stick. I was covered in sweat and trembling with fear. In my mind's eye I could see fighters racing in for the kill. The Lanc roared over the blazing city and after an eternity, finally out-distanced the lights.

Bang. The window in the nose was blown out by a burst of flak that peppered the fuselage and engines. A howling wind blew maps and charts and dust into the cockpit, as Steve tried desperately to block the hole. Abandoning the hopeless task, he crawled back to the navigation section. We were now below 4,000 feet and I asked Eric for a safety height. He told me to climb to 20,000 feet and we began the long trek home, frozen by the frigid air blasting in through the nose.

Eric later estimated that we had been coned by sixty searchlights. It seemed more like 250 to me. He had, amazingly, timed how long we had been held by the lights. Seven minutes. Only a navigator thinks like that.

Now, at last, I had confirmed that my fear of searchlights wasn't totally irrational. Each light was more than two million candle power. Not all beams were radar controlled, usually only the master beam, which was so white it had a bluish tinge. It did the job of illuminating the bomber. Then the manually operated slave beams clustered together on the aircraft. Going into Ruhr Valley targets, the lights stretched for endless miles, from city to city. You could be coned by lights from cities you weren't attacking. Often a bomber flying beside you would be coned. It would twist and turn, with the flak streaming up to it, and you would pray that the lights held it long enough for you to creep safely past.

I was never able to overcome my fear of the lights. On practice raids over English cities I would deliberately fly into masses of searchlights, hoping to find some sure way to escape. I had Ken, in the mid-upper turret, concentrate on the wings to see if he could tell when they were level with the horizon. But none of our experiments worked and I found I was just as terrified whether they were English or German searchlights. My fear, however, did make me more sympathetic towards those who could not continue to fly.

Ibid., pp. 160-3

Eventually the statistics would tell, and the bomber crew would confront the nightmare they dreaded.

While the Germans were battling fires, we were being encrusted with ice. As I struggled with the ice-laden bomber to gain altitude it was clear we wouldn't get above 17,000 feet. By dropping the nose slightly and then pulling back on the controls it was often possible to nudge the bomber up fifty feet at a time. But our Merlin engines were in danger of overheating. The glycol gauges showed the temperatures of the coolant already in the red, and my sharp pulls on the controls threatened to stall the aircraft.

Thunderstorms were all around us. Lightning was tearing and streaking through the cumulus nimbus clouds, lighting the sky and making it possible now and then to see what a wild night sat outside the cockpit window. A thing called 'Saint Elmo's fire' crackled and danced all across the inside of the windscreen and all over the flying panel. Sparkling blue flames leaped and snaked, making it difficult to concentrate on the instruments. With each lightning bolt I could see the massive thunderclouds, surrounding us, some a rosy red from the reflected fires sweeping the city.

Our wireless operator, Ray, an English lad, was positioned near the rear door of the aircraft throwing out bundles of 'window'. He could hear me cursing the weather and talking to Eric, the navigator, about the way the aircraft was behaving.

Suddenly Ray began to scream, 'Turn back, skipper, turn back! We're all going to be killed! Please, skipper, turn back!'

His screams threw panic into everyone and put the hair on the back of my neck straight out. I yelled at him over the intercom to shut up but he kept screaming, his screams getting louder and louder and more hysterical. I ordered the bomb aimer to go back with a fire extinguisher and stop the screaming. Plugging into a portable oxygen bottle, Steve started to crawl towards the rear of the bomber. 'Hit the bastard over the head,' I ordered.

The screaming continued to grow louder and more frightening and I found it hard to concentrate on flying the Halifax as it wobbled under its load of ice. Suddenly the screaming stopped, and I thought Steve had managed to quiet Ray. But Steve came on the intercom to report that the rear door was open and the wireless operator had baled out. He had jumped without unplugging his intercom which explained the sudden silence.

I shut my mind to the problem as I continued to wrestle with the Halifax. For the last twenty minutes I had been watching a huge cumulus nimbus thunderhead as the lightning outlined its monstrous swollen form. Its anvil shaped top, thousands of feet above our flight level, was drifting across our path.

I knew instinctively that if I got into that thunderhead our wallowing bomber would be in terrible danger. Trying to keep on course and yet avoid the storm, I was inching my way around the storm cloud, or so I thought. Ice on the windscreen and the blue flames crackling on the inside of the window made it difficult to see, and the darkness of the night blended with the black form of the clouds.

Without warning we plunged into the cloud and the bomber stalled. With one wing down, because we had been turning, the aircraft started into a spin, the instruments gone wild and the altimeter needle racing backwards. I knew I might never recover from the spin and ordered the crew to bale out.

Eric was screaming at me to drop the bombs. The harder I pulled back, the tighter the spin became. I slammed the bomb doors open and pulled the bomb jettison handle. The sudden opening of the huge bomb bay doors acted as an airbrake and with the stick hard over and full rudder, the Halifax slowly straightened into a dive. I got control at 5,000 feet but we were still bumping around in the thunderhead.

I called the crew to find them still on board. No one had been able to bale out. The force of gravity in that wild plunge had pinned them into their seats. They all responded as I closed the bomb doors and tuned to a compass heading for home.

We had dropped our bombs about ten miles short of the target, which seemed much closer at the lower altitude. The fierce winds associated with the thunderstorms were fanning the flames and the entire city was a Dante's inferno. The ice began melting off the wings at our lower altitude and great chunks started to pound the fuselage, thrown there by the propellers. As our speed slowly returned to normal, I began to climb up to a safer altitude for the long run home across the sea.

It felt strange to head for home without one of the crew. No one mentioned the subject but they must all have wondered if Ray had made it safely to earth. We maintained radio silence and waited until we were back at base before talking about it. Utter terror had obviously seized Ray and overcome his normal reactions. As we flew over the sea I tried to reason what had caused him to jump. He had never exhibited any abnormal behaviour on any previous flight and had performed his chores efficiently and without bitching.

But then, as I sat there in the dark, I began remembering things Ray had said, at least once a day. 'I'll never let you down, skipper. I'll always do my part. You can rely on me, skipper.' At the time I used to wonder why he would say those things, but never really gave it much thought. We were all young kids busy trying to get some fun out of living and trying not to dwell on the raid. We were all frightened, although no one mentioned it. We might fear the future but we were all in the same boat and there wasn't anything we could do about it.

Ibid., pp. 44-6

Canadian F-86 Sabre pilot Andy Mackenzie experienced his own terrifying version of the fighter pilot's fear when he lost his aircraft over Korea and fell into enemy hands.

'When I got to Korea, I was based at Suwon with the American 51st Fighter Interceptor Wing. I arrived there about the middle of November 1952. For the first two weeks they checked me out, took me up over the parallel, showed me where the enemy were, and so on. My first four sorties were uneventful. Then, on December 5, I left on my fifth.'

It would be his last.

'They gave me what I later realized was a tremendously bad briefing. I was told that if anything were to go wrong, they didn't know what would happen to me because nobody had ever come back to tell them. They didn't tell me there were any prison camps in North Korea. I believed all of our fliers who were shot down were dead. The Americans know there were seven prison camps along the Yalu River but they didn't tell me. They said they didn't know.

'I still admire the Americans, but they lied to me.'

At noon on December 5, sixteen Sabres, four flights of our planes each, roared down the runway at Suwon. Flying in the number 2 position was MacKenzie as Cobra 2. Even the code name seemed to be a premonition of trouble. 'I hated snakes then and I still do.' he says today. 'Perhaps I should have expected problems.

'After we gained altitude, we headed straight for the Yalu. That day we stayed about five miles south of the river, although a lot of guys had flown over it on other occasions, although they generally stayed rather quiet about where they had been. We weren't supposed to fly into China but a lot of chaps did. A lot of them shot down MiGs in China but they were later deliberately vague about the exact location.

'The radio transmission discipline in Korea was terrible. In World War II we didn't say anything unless we had to, but in Korea everyone was on the air at once, babbling away, telling jokes and so on. I remember one fellow who got lost over China. He panicked, I guess, and he started crying on the radio—asking his mother to help him, all kinds of baby stuff. A British exchange pilot heard a lot of this and finally had enough. "Oh, for Christ's sake," the Brit yelled on the radio, "shut up and die like a man." The fellow who was in China shut up but I don't know whether he died or not.'

As MacKenzie's flight headed east, some few miles south of the Yalu, several of the pilots noticed jet contrails. This was the sign they had been hoping to see. Obviously Chinese jets were in the vicinity.

'Suddenly I saw two MiGs shoot under me,' recalls Andy MacKenzie today. 'They were going into North Korea, so I knew they'd have to turn and come back. I decided to follow.'

MacKenzie transmitted his decision to his flight leader, but because of radio interference only part of the message was heard. The next thing he knew, the flight leader was asking for cover as he went after a group of MiGs up north near the Yalu. MacKenzie turned to follow.

'Because I was so far behind,' he says, 'I had to try to catch up. The only way to increase my speed was to dive down and then zoom up. Because the leader was climbing and I was diving. I figured I could increase my speed enough to catch him. I would be going seven hundred miles per hour or so and I figured I could zoom up to where the leader was. As I did this I dropped down through the other three flights of our own airplanes. Just as I went to pull up, there were tracer bullets coming at me. Then all hell broke loose.'

One of the tracers blasted the canopy away over MacKenzie's head. When this happened, the explosive decompression tore his instrument panel to shreds, causing the pieces to fly out of the cockpit. A second bullet sheared off part of the right wing, while a third thudded into the fuselage, wrecking the hydraulic control system. The plane shuddered and went into a wild screaming, spinning dive. MacKenzie slammed the control column to the left in a vain attempt to stop the spin. Then he pulled the ejection handles and blasted himself out into space.

A split second before he did so, he saw the American who shot him down.

As soon as MacKenzie was free of his plane, the terrible slipstream tore at his body. Because he was falling at seven hundred miles per hour, his face was horribly contorted, his helmet and goggles disappeared, his arms and legs flailed wildly. The watch on his wrist was ripped off and he went careening, out of control and unconscious, towards the rocky hills of North Korea, forty thousand feet below.

'When I came around, I was still a long way up but I was dropping like hell, so fast I couldn't control my hands. When I was at last able to do so, I got the chute out above me. That was a beautiful feeling. In all my years of flying, I'd never bailed out, but when I had to, the damned thing at least worked. But then it was cold, so terribly cold, but at least I was alive, scared as hell, half frozen, still excited from all I'd just come through, but alive, alive. I started looking around to see where in hell I was.'

'. . . I could see the Yalu River off to my right, and the sun shining on the mountains all around me,' he recalls. 'And it was so quiet. One minute there was all the roaring and excitement of battle; the next I was hanging under the parachute and there wasn't a plane in the sky. I thought I was completely alone. Then I happened to look down, and a few feet from where I was going to land, I could see an old Korean woman picking up sticks. She glanced up at me with a rather blank expression on her face but then turned and went on about her business. I didn't believe anybody could be so stoic. She hardly even *paused* in her work.'

John Melady, *Korea: Canada's Forgotten War* (1983),

pp. 120-2, 127-8

The Canadians in the air war obviously combined great technical skill with quick-thinking judgement. Still more evident is the courage that must have been required to put one's life on the line so irredeemably high above the earth.

6

THE HORROR OF WAR

There can be no celebration of war. It is the pit, the nightmare of human existence in which the suicidal human acceptance of conflict becomes a disease, eating away all who are infected by it. There is in the Canadian soul a loathing of that disease, as the introduction to this collection suggested; it is perhaps why Canadians, so good at making war if they must, are even better at preventing it. The horror of what happens when peace is lost is the most vital lesson that can be read in the sad, proud eyes of Canada's veterans each November at cenotaph services. They know the course of the disease, and its obscene suffering. This recollection of the convoy-escort war at sea of 1939-45 is a chilling example.

I still have a vivid mental picture of one interminable period during this action which gave me nightmares for many years to follow. Ships had been torpedoed and were sinking all around us. No effective attacks were being made against the U-boats because we could not find them. A great many of the torpedoed ships in the convoy refused to sink and were still battling fires around the periphery of where other actions were taking place. In the middle of this fiery furnace, three large ships carrying passengers were torpedoed and, curiously, all three were hit in such a manner that they broke in two halves. One half of one of these vessels sank before I saw it myself, but five halves of the other ships were still afloat and one could see a cross-section of six or seven decks, all brightly lighted—some with the main power still on and some of these 'half-ships' with corridors illuminated by emergency lighting. Through binoculars, I could also see that there was a considerable amount of panic on board amongst the passengers. Men, women, and children were rushing down the corridors towards the severed stumps of their vessels—those reaching the edge and looking out into the black sea trying to push back and those behind in the lighted corridors pushing forward. In this manner, many people lost their lives. Tumbling and being pushed from behind, they cascaded into

160

the sea as though leaping from the windows of tall burning buildings—not just from one of these, but from all five of the remaining halves of the three torpedoed ships, which were slowly settling into their watery graves.

Of course, the crews of all vessels under attack made valiant attempts to launch life boats and rafts, and it was only the very stupid who were not wearing life jackets of some sort, so despite the number of immediate casualties, the sea was full of survivors. As I have said, the night was very dark and, in going about our duties of driving off the U-boat attacks it was inevitable that we should plough through great numbers of these unfortunate souls. The most dreadful decisions were forced on some of us as Captains of escorts, such as having to decide whether to drop a pattern of depth charges on a suspected submarine contact with full knowledge that the massive explosions would kill many survivors still in the water, or whether, on the other hand, it was a justifiable risk to stop and try to bring back some of our countrymen on board and out of the cold and oily sea. On the night I am describing, I tried it both ways.

Killing one's own countrymen by depth charging a suspected submarine in the vicinity of survivors was an excusable necessity that could quickly be dismissed from one's mind because our duty was to sink submarines before they could sink more ships. Other decisions were sometimes more difficult.

Trying to pick up survivors on a pitch-black night in a rough sea, with ships sinking all around and a convoy still under attack, was not easy. On quite a few occasions, with scrambling nets hung over the side and with all spare hands standing by to reach down and pull these oil-soaked and choking human beings from the sea, there would be some measure of success—but also some misses and near misses. Sometimes it was even worse.

Even from an open bridge, I could not see through the darkness what was going on in the water around my ship. Relying partly on instinct and partly on reports received from the Fo'c's'le Officer and the Officer on the quarterdeck aft, manoeuvering Stonecrop to achieve the maximum return for our efforts was a tricky and blood-curdling business. A 'hail' from the foredeck:

'Two rafts with survivors fine on the starboard bow, sir.'

'Very good, thank you. Am approaching now.'

From the telephone on the fo'c's'le: 'A great bunch of survivors dead ahead, sir, in life jackets. Go astern, go astern.'

'Half astern, sir. Engine half astern, sir.'

Voice from the foredeck: 'We have swung 'round, sir, and we're now bouncing on the rafts. Can you manage to back out of this?'

'I'm trying my best. You just do what you can manage.'

Voice on the quarterdeck telephone: 'About twenty survivors dead astern, sir—no, there are more than twenty, a great number. Go ahead. Go ahead, for Christ's sake, we're cutting them up in our screws!'

'Very good. Coxswain, stop engines.'

'Stop engines, sir. Engines stopped, sir.'

Some were rescued, many were not. Fortunately, Mother Nature has so arranged things that our minds can only accept so much horror at a time, and some automatic reaction within the brain permits even the most sensitive to write off the losses and get on with the job. The fact was that, whatever happened, many survivors pulled from the sea were so filled up and choked with bunker fuel oil that they did not last long in any case. Oil floats, and swimming above the water does not keep one's head above the oil. These memories come back to haunt.

Jeffry V. Brock, The Dark Broad Seas, vol. 1 (1981), pp. 125-7

The following passage describes the grim experience of torpedoing from the victims' point of view.

Suddenly a terrific shock struck the ferry, shuddering through the staterooms, throwing passengers from their bunks. As they ran to the decks in night clothes, water was already pouring into the ship from all sides.

Margaret Brooke was stunned for a few minutes by the crash. Yet while her body was momentarily helpless, her mind realized what must have happened. They had been torpedoed—almost in sight of shore. She and her Nursing Sister companion, with others of the service personnel, had not got to the War. The War had come to them.

As she shook off the effects of the shock, Margaret realized that Agnes was urging her to the lifeboat on the port side. The two girls staggered and rolled with the plunging of the stricken ship. But the lifeboat had been blasted away.

Life belts were the only hope, Margaret realized, and snatched at them as scalding steam gushed from the engine room. Deftly fastening the life belt around her, she saw Agnes was in trouble and could not cope with the safety device. Margaret pulled the shivering girl to her and fastened her snugly into the belt. By that time, in less than five minutes, the gallant little *Caribou* was settling on her way on the bottom of the Strait.

The two girls were tossed into the cold churning water, while the

Caribou plunged down, bow first, carrying her gallant Captain, his two ship's Officer-sons and all but about a dozen of his crew.

Survivors related that the Master of the doomed *Caribou*, in a last ditch attempt to destroy the destroyer, steered the sinking vessel directly at the now surfaced U-boat. But the *Caribou* slid under the waves before her ice-breaker prow could ram the Nazi submarine. And a great suction pulled and flung the survivors struggling in the cold water.

All this happened in a matter of minutes in the darkest hour of pre-dawn. The torpedo struck at 2:40 A.M. Atlantic Standard Time. Passengers clung to flotsam, found rafts of debris, and some crowded into the remaining intact lifeboats. As the U-boat surfaced, she capsized several of the frail rafts and her hull smashed into a lifeboat.

Meanwhile, the two Naval Nursing Sisters floundered in the surging waves. An overturned lifeboat floated within reach.

'Come on, Agnes, we can hang on here and wait for rescue,' Margaret gasped.

But already Agnes was weakening. Margaret hauled her within grasp of the slippery craft. By this time, about a dozen others were clinging to the rough ropes on the boat and striving desperately to get a hold on the up-turned vessel.

Minutes dragged into hours. The sea roughened as daylight approached and the plight of the ill-clad people was terrible. Waves slapped at and curled over the overturned lifeboat. One by one the freezing survivors were washed off.

Nursing Sister Brooke anxiously watched her comrade and tried to bolster Agnes' visibly sinking strength.

'The rescue boats are coming, Agnes', she cried. 'It won't be long. Hang on.'

But Agnes began to slip, her hold weakening rapidly. Margaret wriggled her own numb body closer to Agnes, tightened one hand's hold on the rope and grabbed at her friend with the other. She was just in time, as Agnes had developed a cramp forcing her to let go.

Naval rescue craft on patrol were steaming to the scene, among them HMCS *Grandmere*. The first grey streaks of dawn lightened the eastern sky. Still Margaret Brooke held her almost helpless companion. Her own strength was failing and her arms trembled and ached with the double strain. Still she clung desperately to life, and the life of her friend.

With the rising sea waves roughened and washed over the capsized vessel. Just as dawn came a huge breaker swept the two nursing sisters apart. Emerging weakly from the onslaught, one arm almost frozen to the rope, Margaret looked for Agnes. She called her name but no answer came back.

Searching the rocking waves, Margaret thought she glimpsed the other girl being washed away.

Willing her almost unconscious body, she made an effort to reach Agnes, but all her attempts failed and no sound came from the engulfing water.

Margaret Brooke was not able to tell how she was finally rescued. She knew only that after Agnes had drowned, she, herself, sank into numb oblivion. Later she was told that a sailor had dived into the water, loosened her desperate grasp on the life boat, and took her aboard the rescue ship.

The toll was heavy in that attack in home waters. Of 237 lives, 136 were lost.

In his statement following the disaster, Canadian Navy Minister Macdonald said, 'It brings the war to Canada with tragic emphasis.'

Of Nursing Sister Agnes Wilkie, the Minister said, 'She was the first of our Nursing Sisters to lose her life in this War and she died, in truth, in action. The Navy and Naval Nursing Service will treasure this young woman's memory.'

Of Nursing Sister Margaret Martha Brooke, RCN, the nation, on 1 January, 1942, declared her to be a Member of the Military Division of the Most Excellent Order of the British Empire, 'For gallantry and courage. After the sinking of the Newfoundland ferry, SS *Caribou*, this officer displayed great courage while in the water in attempting to save the life of another Nursing Sister.'

Mabel Tinkiss Good, *The Bridge at Dieppe* (1973), pp. 59-62

As dreadful as the slaughter may have been in action between armed opponents, there was a special horror to the random violence that struck where somehow it should not have.

Returning one evening to *Stonecrop*, berthed in Albert Dock, the air raid sirens started their wailing warning as darkness fell, and I quickened my pace through the old business section of the city, through streets of stone and masonry buildings. I could hear the bombers overhead and distant explosions as they unloaded their deadly cargoes. It seemed to me that the bombs were getting closer and I took refuge under the deep-arched stone entrance of a building. It had started to rain, and a few people were rushing past along the street. I could hear what sounded like an approaching stick of bombs falling sequentially in our direction. Grabbing the arm of a young girl in uniform who was passing, I quickly pulled her close beside me under the sheltering doorway. The stick of bombs passed, one creating an enormous crater in the roadway opposite our shelter. Masonry bits and metal shards were flying in all directions, shattered glass was in the air, and in the ensuing sudden silence I could hear the tinkling sound as it fell.

Dazed and shaken I flexed my arms and legs to check working parts and felt my face and neck, which were sticky and blood-stained. Turning to see how my temporary companion had fared, I discovered that our companionship in this emergency had, indeed, been very temporary. She was no longer there—or rather, no recognizable part of a human being was there. Not even 'a bracelet of bright hair about the bone'. She had disintegrated. What I had first believed to be blood stains from my own injuries, I quickly realized had been from hers.

I crossed to the bomb crater and vomited. Next, going to the rain-filled gutter, I scrubbed my exposed head and hands as best I could. Seeking no other shelter, I vomited again and slowly dragged myself homewards, allowing the heavy rain to wash me down.

Arriving back on board, sodden and soul-sick, I stripped, bathed, and, wrapping my outer garments in a bath towel, dropped them over the side into the harbour. It was time to buy a new uniform anyway.

Jeffry V. Brock, *The Dark Broad Seas*, vol. 1 (1981), p. 70

Sometimes the only response possible was a kind of rough, unconsciously self-protecting pity, as in this recollection from the Korean War by Canadian infantry officer J.A. Dextraze.

'We would attack a village, level the place, and then go on to the next one, the next, and the next. One day we were approaching this place and I called for an air strike. A few hours after, I moved into the village with my scout car. The whole place was a burning, shattered, smoking ruin. Almost everything was destroyed. As we went along, we were passing buildings that were almost all gone and I could hear somebody crying. I told my driver to shut off the motor and we listened, and then we walked toward the sound. In what had been a house was a grandmother, a grandfather, and a mother lying dead with a little baby trying to feed at the mother's breast. I went inside to take the baby in my arms. As I did so, a bigger brother, of about six or seven, who had been hiding in a corner, came and started beating on me. While I held the baby, one of my signallers took the little boy. We brought both of them back with us.

'I gave the baby to my medical officer and the padre and they

placed him in an orphanage. The little boy stayed with me for
months. We took some of my shirts and pants and cut them down
so he could wear them. I grew very attached to the little fellow, and
he would sit and wait for me, morning and night, and bring me tea
and so on. I missed him when we had to say goodbye.

'The boy was eventually placed in an orphanage and he was
educated. I paid for his education, but lots of our soldiers did the
same thing. Most of us sent money for these kids. It was always sad
for me to see this type of thing, to see a cripple without a crutch,
and so on. Such things bothered all of us. Canadian soldiers are
tough, but we are not tough inside. Whether we're French or English,
we are all basically very sensitive. Canadian soldiers are really all a
bunch of emotional bums.

'I remember another day when we were in North Korea and lots
of refugees were coming down. I had been in the rear for something
or other, and as I was moving back up towards my battalion, I came
to a crossing in the trail. There was one woman there, all alone,
sitting on the ground with a little boy and girl of four or five, I
suppose, with her. She had a baby in her arms. The two little ones
were sitting.

'There was a bag of rice that she had been carrying on her head but
the bag had fallen and the rice was all spilled in the dust. I stopped
and had my interpreter ask her what she was doing there. She told
us she had given up, that she didn't want to go on any more; she
didn't want to live any more. She said she had nothing but her rice,
and now it was gone, and she wasn't able to feed her children any
more, to keep them alive.

'That bothered me a lot because the woman was so terribly
pathetic, so totally discouraged. I knew we had tons of rice and here
was this poor creature, ready to die because she had none.

'We brought her back to my headquarters, fed her, and gave her the
things she wanted. She stayed with us for three months.'

John Melady, *Korea: Canada's Forgotten War* (1983), pp. 98-9

*Very few veterans ever claim to have completely come to terms with
the direct, personal business of killing. Simple acceptance of duty
could turn in a moment to revulsion, as it did for this First World
War sniper.*

We watched all the morning and much of the afternoon and saw
nothing. There was no need to be impatient, he said. He had

eighteen kills to his credit and had taken months to get such a bag. It was dull and chilly but the next morning there was sunshine and we were out early. I was no more than in position than a German in full pack rose almost waist-high at a place in their trench. The sight was so amazing it took me a moment to discover that during the night our guns had knocked down some of the German parapet. The German was evidently a new man in the sector and unaware of the nearness of our lines. He was looking around as I scored my first hit. It was not a great shot, the distance was not more than one hundred yards and I had cross-hair sights—but I had really killed a Hun.

'Good stuff,' praised Pearce. He rubbed his hands gleefully and noted down the facts in his record book, but had not finished when a second German, also in pack, rose in the same place. I shot him as soon as he appeared, as my finger was taut on the trigger. Hardly had he fallen than a soldier without any pack and a rifle in his hands stepped up on the piled earth. I could count his tunic buttons through the telescopic sights and shot him through the left breast. As he pitched down from view two more Germans suddenly appeared at a spot to the left. They did not have packs and neither wore a helmet. One had an immense head, almost round, and he glared and pointed a finger. His mate was dark and his hair close-cropped. He had binoculars in his hand. I shot him and as he went down the binoculars were flung in a high loop over his head.

The fellow with him was aiming a rifle in our general direction. Pearce gripped my shoulder. He had been watching with the glasses outside the plate. 'Shoot!' he rasped. 'You won't get a chance like this all day.'

I drew back and handed him the rifle. A queer sensation had spread over me like nausea. 'Go ahead yourself,' I said. 'I've had enough.'

He seized the rifle and took quick aim. I saw the dark flush that spurted over the face of the big-headed man as he sank from view, one hand clawing at the sandbags. Then, over on the left, a German got up and walked overland carrying a big dixie. He was clearly a cook and his actions indicated that a new battalion was in the line. Pearce shot him and the dixie was flung away, spilling some liquid. Then an officer stepped into view at a blown-in part and waved to someone. He sank down as Pearce shot him, and pitched forward. No other Germans appeared but we could see their shovels as they cleared the damage our shelling had done. Pearce shot at a helmet twice and twice a spade waved a miss. Then we went back to the dugout and Pearce said I would have to explain myself to Sergeant Cave.

Cave looked at me oddly as I told him I had had all I wanted of sniping. He said I had had too big a kill for the first time, that if I had only shot one German I would have been all right. Then he informed me there was to be a raid the next day, April 1, between Durrand and Duffield Craters, and that I was one of the snipers who must get on top of the parapet as the raid started and shoot any German who tried to get away overland. After the raid he would talk to me again.

Will R. Bird, *Ghosts Have Warm Hands* (1968), pp. 30-1

Later in the same book, Will R. Bird describes with deep sadness a death he was powerless to prevent.

It was quite warm at noon and we enjoyed a good hour of rest. In the afternoon as we came around a turn in the road we saw a path on the left and walked over to see where it led. To our amazement there was a pile of short logs, recently cut, and a German soldier, a rather slight fellow, was seated on them eating his lunch. His big helmet was beside him on the logs and his rifle learned against the pile. His back was toward us. Since we were treading on moss and old leaves that were damp in the shade we made no sound whatever, but as Tommy and I stood to whisper to each other we were shoved aside and Giger pushed by us, breathing with short, eager intakes. He was almost running and had reached the logs before the German looked around.

'Kamerad!' The German's arms shot high above his head. But Giger didn't hesitate. He drove his bayonet into the German's middle with all his strength and almost sprawled over him as the man went down. At that split second a second German arrived. He had evidently been answering a call of nature, as he was buttoning his trousers. When he saw Giger's work with the bayonet he leaped to the end of the log pile and seized a woodman's axe lying there, swung it in one motion and, before Giger could straighten, cut him down with a fearful blow on the neck and shoulder. Then the Hun ran like a deer—and no one fired a shot after him.

There was nothing we could do for Giger. As we reached him he raised the wrist with the hair-ring charm around it, and died with a gaze of startled incredulity.

Ibid., pp. 202-3

To be responsible for the death of another human being in war was a part of one's duty. On occasion, as in this memory from Canadian

*artillery officer Raymond Massey, the weight of that duty could be
unexpectedly heavy.*

Once, at a Vierstraat O. Pip, I was watching the road from Wyt-
schaete to the German front line when I saw a tall figure in a long
greatcoat walking down the road. Although he was six hundred
yards from me. I could see through my telescope that he wore a
monocle and, as his coat was open, the ribbon of the Iron Cross in
his jacket buttonhole. He stopped at a pile of rubble we had registered as a machine gun post. He stood there peering at our front
line, an audacity that was scarcely believable. I couldn't understand
why our snipers hadn't picked him off.

I ordered number one gun to stand to, gave the target number, and
ordered one round of high explosive. The tall officer stood there
motionless.

I heard the shell whining overhead. It was right on target. There
was a burst of yellowish smoke and rubble—and no tall officer. I
don't know if it got him but I felt rather sick. Some people said the
field artillery was an impersonal service.

Raymond Massey, When I Was Young (1976), pp. 137-8

*Many men attempted to ward off the pain of loss by cultivating an
artificial indifference. But the death of a friend could pierce any
armour.*

We met incoming men and there was considerable shelling. I had
Hughes by the arm and fairly dragged him through the mire. Then
we came to a ruin where a man sat on a fragment of wall. I went to
him and asked if he could spare a drink of water. He did not answer.
He was not wounded, but absolutely everything in his mind was
dead. I took his water bottle from his equipment, took it to Mickey
and Hughes in turn, then took it back and replaced it. We went on
down the road and there came a salvo of 'whizz-bangs'. As the last
soul-tearing smash crashed in my ears I saw Mickey spin and fall. I
let go of Hughes and jumped to him. He had been hit in several
places and could not live ten minutes.

'Mickey—Mickey!' I called his name and raised him up and he
nestled to me like a child.

'I'm through,' he said. 'I don't want to kill people anyway. Tell my
mother. . . .'

His voice was so low I could not hear, but his lips still moved. Little white-faced Mickey. I held him in my arms until he stiffened, then laid him by the roadside and took his paybook from his pocket.

Will R. Bird, *Ghosts Have Warm Hands* (1968), pp. 92-3

In other cases there was nothing but ruthlessness. Or was it realism?

There has been quite a scrap in this push and the 4th Machine-Gun Company are full of incidents relating thereto. One of their crews took possession of a cellar and found ten Germans therein. Four hours later they found a Fritz minus his boots under a bed. This Heiny acted rather peculiar. He struck a match and as he had no cigarettes or pipe the conclusion drawn was to attract the attention of the enemy. He was told to desist. However, he did the same thing a second time so the officer was advised. He came upstairs and promptly plugged him with his revolver.

Reginald H. Roy, *The Journal of Private Fraser* (1985), p. 304

A particular horror of the First World War was the fate of the animals that suffered along with the men. Here a soldier describes a mule trapped in the mud.

[The] poor thing kept sinking down and down, inch by inch, and we were frantic. And finally the transport officer of the 18th Battalion decided there was only one thing to do, and when [the mule's] head was just above the mud the officer pulled his revolver out of his holster, and I will never forget the look in that poor brute's great brown eyes when he looked at the officer, and the officer shot him and then cried like a kid.

Daniel G. Dancocks, *Legacy of Valour* (1986), p. 110

And then there was the burial of the dead.

Four or five men were asked to volunteer for a burial party, the inducement being 'no fatigues tonight'. Needless to say, the burial party was more inviting than the fatigue and I clinched the matter. It turned out the dead man was Sgt Kemp. He was wrapt [*sic*] up in a blanket, which was tied with signalling wire. We carried him to the cemetery on a stretcher. The minister officiating said a few words. The grave was a double one, the other fellow had already been buried, that is a few inches of earth were thrown over him. This had to suffice till Kemp was interred, when the grave would be filled in. When we arrived the grave contained several inches of water, coloured red by blood. Kemp was buried in this mess. As soon as the body stirred in the liquid, it just about made us vomit, the effluvium being terrific. We found out later we were a bit previous in volunteering as no one went on fatigue that night.

Reginald H. Roy, *The Journal of Private Fraser* (1985), p. 71

For those wounded or scarred, the men horribly burned, the only bright light in such tragedy was their courage.

The ones who had been burned in their tanks were the hardest to live amongst. Ears, noses, hair, eyebrows, all gone. The nose, two tiny holes in a mass of scar tissue. The skin drawn tightly over the cheekbones and the mouth twisted and drawn up tight. Ears shrivelled into tiny corkscrews. Heads completely bald forever. I shrank from them for weeks, ashamed of my behaviour, but so deeply disturbed that I could not act or talk normally with them.

It was they who pushed the socializing. They would land on the end of my bed, clutching a deck of cards in a clawlike hand. 'How about a game of knock rummy?' the twisted little mouth would say. Try as I would, it took weeks of close association before I was able to meet their eyes. Their courage and spirit, their complete lack of self pity, was overwhelming. Oh, the joy when they got their first hairpiece. Strutting around the ward with a hand mirror, they would pose and posture, slicking down an imaginary end with a wet finger.

'How about it? Don't I look great? How about that colour? No grey hair for me, chum. Wow, wait until the girls see me now.'

J. Douglas Harvey, *Boys, Bombs and Brussels Sprouts*
(1981), pp. 200-1

But if death was one's fate, one could be brought to it by strange quirks of pure chance.

War shows what silly things the life of a soldier hangs on. The night before we left England, one of our men named Knights, who had extraordinarily big feet, was unable to get a pair of boots to fit him. At the last minute, an hour or so before the regiment embarked on the ship, in came a new shipment of boots. Among them were a pair big enough for Knights. As a result he went over with us and was the first person killed at Armentieres. If the boots had not come in he would have been left in England. It shows what one's life depends on.

Gordon Reid, Poor Bloody Murder (1980), p. 77

And in some cases the timing of death was particularly tragic.

On November 11, 1918 we passed through the outskirts of Mons in daylight. We were about four to five miles east of Mons. We didn't know anything about the armistice, until about ten-thirty A.M. We captured a German dispatch rider on horseback, who had their dispatches explaining the armistice.

At eleven A.M. we got into this little village. As we approached it, German machine guns opened up and we got into a ditch. I was in 'B' Company. Another Company came up a parallel road. The roads converged. I think it was a Corporal Price, who didn't get down and walked across the road. He was the last Canadian killed in action in World War One.

Ibid., p. 242

Some men revealed unsuspected depths of perception before their lives were snuffed out.

My first leave was in August, 1917, after more than thirteen months at the front. I remember telling that to an American soldier in front of the Eiffel Tower in Paris. As I stood gazing up at the Tower, he kept circling me, taking me all in: the pipe-clayed gunner's lanyard I had put on for leave, my leather bandolier well polished with even the brass fasteners brassoed; my two blue service chevrons, one for each year, the second one put up as soon as the second year started; my riding breeches and spurs, which had not yet lost their rowels. After he had taken me all in he stopped in front of me. 'You been to the front?' he asked. I told him, yes. 'How long?' he asked. I told him. He was struck with astonishment. 'And you ain't dead yet,' he said.

My first leave was shared with one of my drivers for whom it was his only leave. He was the Speedy that I mentioned in my introduction. In civil life he had been an hostler in a livery stable. In Paris he displayed an unexpected susceptibility to beauty. I can see him yet, standing in the Hôtel des Invalides looking down at the tomb of Napoleon, almost breathless with the emotion that that miracle of colour and lighting evoked. He was with me when I got into the Chamber of Deputies. There were four of us together, and seeing a guard we applauded the guardhouse. After some debate one of the guards conducted us across the square to the main entrance, where he turned us over to a most imposing individual. He wore a tricorn hat, knee breeches and silk stockings. On his shoes were large silver buckles and there was a heavy silver chain around his neck, which came down in several loops to his belt line. I was never quite able to decide if he was the head porter or the equivalent of the gentleman usher, Black Rod himself. When we left him we were in great perplexity trying to decide whether he was the kind of person one could, should or dare tip. We debated it aside and then it was put up to me to find out. I turned to him with a gesture toward my pocket and asked if it would be permissible. The smile and the sweeping gesture with which he deprecated the idea makes me think that probably he was the gentleman usher. Few people in France scorn a tip.

The last thing we saw there was the chapel attached to the Palais Bourbon, which in due course was converted into the Chamber of Deputies. We viewed it from a gallery. Not many people would say that it is one of the most beautiful chapels in the world, but to soldiers fresh from the filth of the battlefields it was breath-taking. For a moment Speedy stood motionless and then started saying in a half-whisper, 'Jesus Christ. Jesus Christ.' There was nothing either religious or irreligious in those words; they were simply the expression in army idiom of his deep emotion in the presence of beauty. Seldom have I met a man who was so deeply moved by beauty as that little hostler from the livery stable who, a few months later, smothered in the mud of Passchendaele.

Ernest G. Black, *I Want One Volunteer* (1965), pp. 171-3

Particularly in this century, Canadians have fought for good against evil, to end rather than to begin war, to do away with hatred rather than to enshrine it. It is a cruel irony that so many have joined their enemies in the final equality of death.

Months later, a grisly sight greeted the British defenders of Pas-schendaele. In the spring of 1918, the ground thawed and many of the thousands of dead who had been buried, deliberately or other-wise, in the mud of the previous autumn rose to the surface.

Burial parties were formed, and the bodies were reinterred. The Newfoundlanders holding the line discovered among the corpses the remains of 'a big Canadian who had grappled with a big German. Both had fought desperately, and had died in the mud in each other's arms.' The Newfoundlanders tried to separate them, but it was impossible—their death struggle had been cemented by rigor mortis. Unable to pry them apart, the soldiers buried the Canadian and the German together. Mortal enemies in life, in death they now shared the same resting place.

Daniel G. Dancocks, Legacy of Valour (1965), p. 184

7

THE HUMOUR IN WAR

There was little to laugh about in moments of terror. But humour could surface abruptly at the most unexpected times, acting as a kind of safety valve. This recollection comes from the First World War.

A very amusing incident occurred during this lively bombardment when two of our gun crew tried to escape the shelling which very nearly got them. They occupied one of the dug-outs adjoining the communication trench about twenty-five yards away. A shell exploded within fifteen feet of them, throwing a fountain of earth up in the air to fall on the top of their dug-out. We said to each other, watch Aimoe and McCormick get out of the dug-out in a hurry, but there was not a stir. In a few minutes another one came over and just missed them. In a flash McCormick rushed out of the dug-out, down the trench towards us and turning sharply into the short trench leading to the emplacement, threw himself into it. He was immediately followed by Aimoe who had his tunic on his arm, his braces streaming in the wind and he was in such a hurry to get round the bend in the trench that he did a perfect Charlie Chaplin on one foot. No sooner did he land in the emplacement when a third shell exploded right in front of it wrecking the emplacement and tossing the gun out of the way and scattering corruption all over them. It was a scream to see them, consternation and fright written all over their features. Scrambling from the emplacement they literally flew up the trench a couple of hundred yards away, finally taking refuge in a deep dug-out in the battalion's quarters. They did not put in an appearance for quite a while afterwards. Although it was a serious situation and their plight desperate, it was impossible to refrain from laughter.

Reginald H. Roy, *The Journal of Private Fraser* (1985), pp. 239-40

Some things were funny without meaning to be, in a grim sort of way.

The area is being subjected to a furious bombardment. Telephone wires are broken down and the Colonel decides to send a message by runner. The runner answers the summons and stands to attention while he received his orders. Then he turns about to go out into the barrage.

Before he ascends the dug-out steps the Colonel calls to him, 'Well, good luck to you, runner, and . . . ah . . . before you go . . . ah . . . by the way . . . ah . . . who's your next of kin?'

Arthur E. Wrench, *In Lighter Vein* (1976), p. 134

Even a wounding could raise a smile . . .

When we first arrived in France in the early summer of 1916 groups of us were sent up the line to be attached to batteries in action for a few days to get the feel of things. Some of us went to a Second Division battery on the shore of Dickebusch Lake a short distance south of Ypres. Most of the guns in the area were under direct observation by the Germans on a sizable knoll just south of the salient. Not only could they see us but on clear mornings they probably knew what we had for breakfast. From time to time, even when the front was quiet, they would take a shot or two at us just to show that they knew where we were and that we were not forgotten.

The first morning we were there I was outside the gun-pit when the daily shoot took place. It was a pleasant summer morning and there were a number of gunners outside with me. I got my first lesson in what to do under shellfire. At the sound of the first approaching shell almost everyone went flat. I was the last one to go flat, from pure ignorance. The only one who did not go down at all was a battery corporal who took shelter instead of going flat. Taking shelter was an excellent protective movement if the shelter was adequate. The shelter the corporal took was not well chosen and is not recommended; it was a nice bushy hedge but rather insubstantial. He ran into it with his head down and his rear end up. That is where he got the Blighty, in the seat of his pants. It was a lovely Blighty, a nice splinter in the fleshy part of his rear end, nothing to do any permanent damage but enough to get him to hospital in England and a furlough before he came back to France.

Ernest G. Black, *I Want One Volunteer* (1965), pp. 6-7

. . . or challenge the wounded man's powers of explanation.

It was after the battle of Ypres when many wounded were returned to home hospitals where they received numerous solicitous visitors.

One dear old soul went around the wards speaking to each soldier in turn and inquiring of each the nature of his wounds.

'And where about were you wounded my dear man?' she asked one soldier.

'Ypres, ma'am,' the man replied.

'Yes, yes, of course,' said the dear old soul, 'But where about? That is, in what way?'

'Oh, I see what you mean,' the soldier said. Then after a pause he added, 'Well, ma'am, it's like this; if you had been wounded where I was wounded, then you wouldn't have been wounded at all.'

Arthur E. Wrench, In Lighter Vein (1976), p. 158

Some men received decorations for actions that were particularly gallant, in the fullest sense of the word.

In the entire 1st Division of twenty thousand men there was only one company of French Canadians. There were one hundred and fifty of them. Their officers were nice and we were fond of them. They were a little odd in their ways. One of them was a chap called Ercoule Vare who afterwards became the Canadian Commissioner in Paris after the war ended. When the shelling at Ypres started, Private Ercoule Vare was given a few hours leave to go into the town of Ypres. He was having an affair with a Belgian tart when a shell hit the roof of the building he was in. A splinter wounded him in the seat. Afterwards the French gave out a bunch of Croix de Guerre's and Medaille Militaire's to the Canadians for their gallant show at Ypres. They requested particularly that the decorations should go to French Canadians if possible. There were so few French Canadians in the 1st division that they practically had to give one to everybody. Amongst those who got one was Ercoule Vare. He received the Croix de Guerre! When this was announced in our mess, after it came out in orders what he had received, somebody said, 'For God's sake! Ercoule Vare was wounded in the seat when he was on top of a girl in Ypres.' Eric McCuaig, one of the comical men in our battalion, admonished, 'Ah yes, but you don't realize. He saved the maiden's life!' Everybody laughed at that.

Gordon Reid, Poor Bloody Murder (1980), p. 90

With so many men only a few years past boyhood, it was often possible to get some satisfyingly irresponsible behaviour going at the drop of a hat.

The crew seemed to enjoy low flying, especially the gunners who would roar with laughter as we ran a horse over a fence or dove on a British anti-craft gun battery, scattering the crew. They always rushed for cover. Had they put a few rounds past our ears it might have taught us something. With the exuberance of youth we didn't care for the army who, as far as we were concerned, didn't do anything but march around England. We were fighting the war and didn't mind telling them so.

One nice summer day, we were low flying, just horsing around over the Yorkshire moors. We had taken off to do gunnery practice over the sea, which was only twenty minutes from base. We usually went out over the coastal town of Scarborough as low as possible. Now, on our return to base, I again pushed the nose down and started skimming the hills and plunging into the alleys. The crew chattered away, pointing out things to 'shoot up'. I found a red-tiled roof on a farmhouse which was standing on a hill, and pushing the nose down farther, I aimed just below the roof line. I wondered if I could blow some tiles off with the slipstream if I pulled up at the right moment. With the throttles wide open I roared at the house, then at the last moment I heaved back on the stick and went straight up. Several of the tiles flew off the roof and the crew laughed and hooted, describing the scene for me. Now I really got into the mood and down I went into a flat valley where farmers were cutting hay and forking it onto wagons.

Zoom, right over the wagons. The hay flew and the horses bolted. Chuckling with glee, my head turned to watch. I didn't see the shadow ahead. Crash! I flew right through the top of a huge, luckily dead, tree. The windscreen in front of Jock disintegrated with a bang as a bird came smashing through, hitting him in the face. I turned to look, and horrified, saw that his face was streaming with blood. My God, I've killed him! Eric ran forward with the first aid kit and began swabbing the blood from Jock's face. Only then did we realize it was the bird's blood and not Jock's. The rush of air coming through the smashed windscreen was blowing bits of bird and a swirl of feathers down the inside of the aircraft.

Blinded by the slipstream blasting in I pulled my goggles over my eyes and, thoroughly chastened, climbed up to a safer altitude. I checked the instruments to find the two starboard engines overheating. I feathered both engines and turned for base. How to explain the damage? As I settled the Lanc into a two-engined approach for landing and began rounding out, I noticed some bushes just off the end of the runway. They stood about four feet high. Ha.

Shutting down at dispersal I could see the engineering officer had gathered with some groundcrew and as the two engines died, I could hear them talking and pointing. Climbing out I joined them as they stood under the wing, pulling sticks and branches from the oil coolers, which hung beneath the Hercules engines. 'What happened?' asked the engineering officer. I turned towards the end of the runway, pointed, and said in as stern a voice as I could muster, 'Those bloody trees off the end of the runway. I've asked you guys a hundred times to cut them down. I flew right through them.' They bought it.

Without a grumble the groundcrew got busy and replaced the windscreen and oil coolers, and we flew on ops that night.

J. Douglas Harvey, *Boys, Bombs and Brussels Sprouts* (1981), pp. 61-2

Even the mildest effort at finding enjoyment could be dangerous, as a Canadian on leave from the trenches of 1914-18 found out.

Once while on leave I sort of got lost. A fellow invited me to his house for some supper. At a corner, we got to his house, shoved open the door, and his wife stood there glaring at him. He was holding our package of fish 'n chips as he tried to explain how he found me. She grabbed the food, hit him in the face with it and knocked him out cold. I found my own way back with the aid of people who guided me.

Gordon Reid, *Poor Bloody Murder* (1980), p. 35

And even the most personal of possessions could be at risk.

One of the chaps in the loft with me was Flynn, an Irishman who had false teeth. They were army issue and did not fit properly, so he took them out for sleeping. He came in late that night after having many beers in the *estaminet*. So he only took off his boots and put his teeth on the floor before dropping into slumber. Soon we were wakened by wild yelling. A rat had come up through the wall and seized Flynn's false teeth, and was dragging them to the hole in the wall when Flynn wakened. He was not quick enough. Down the

wall went rat and teeth. The shouting was enormous and Flynn
stormed downstairs where Madame and Monsieur were lighting a
lamp. There was nothing they could do, as there was no opening in
the wall. The argument and commotion lasted an hour and next day
Flynn went on sick parade to get new teeth.

Will R. Bird, Ghosts Have Warm Hands (1968), pp. 23-4

*Sometimes, when the 'system' had you trapped, the only escape was
a humorous approach. After all, if you couldn't take a joke, you
shouldn't have joined.*

I suppose there were guys in the Canadian Army who got promoted
once and then never again. Me, I reckon I held down the one spot in
the services so long I was often mistaken for a Chelsea pensioner.

At the outbreak of war when most blokes didn't know the dif-
ference between a tent pump and a left-handed housewife, I was
among the brightest of the lot. This accident could be traced to my
training as a youth with a renowned group called the Church Lads
Brigade.

The fact that I knew how to shout out with some authority
stentorian phrases such as: 'Squad . . . wait for it . . . Squad—SHAH!
Move to the right in threes, RIHOIT TAH—Byderlef'—Quick-marsh!'
followed by my bestest parade ground shriek, 'Chin up, chest out,
look to yer own height there! . . . eft, ite, eft, . . . cover down front
to rear. Dressing, dressing by the left . . . Heads up, watch them
arms—up . . . back, up back. Change direction left . . . LEHEFT WEEUL,
eft, ite, eft, . . . Squad . . . HALT!'

Beaming, the powers that be quickly promoted me out of the rank
and file. And it was there that my army clock stood still. It seems
that outside of a pre-war capacity to shout 'eft, ite, eft' in a soldierly
fashion I had little else to offer in return for the King's shilling.

And so it was this way a few years later when my Old Man called
me to his quarters fronting the huge parade ground square at Aldershot.

'Smith,' says he, 'in two weeks' time we are to be honoured with
an inspection by His Majesty the King. I don't have to tell you how
important that is,' he says, fixing me with his arctic-cod blue eyes.

'I am informed,' he continues 'that CMHQ will be sending along a
photographer. They want a man to assist him with his equipment
and take down names of the men he photographs. I cannot afford
any of my good men so—do you think you can do this job without
getting yourself into too much trouble?'

Nice guy, is my Old Man. All heart and understanding—with the sympathy of a South American cobra.

Came the big day and our unit was something to be proud of. All ranks loved it, blancoing, cleaning boots and polishing brass and weapons with gusto. With their rifles smartly at the slope they marched on to the square with pride and precision, in perfect ranks, in perfect step, arms swinging, waist-belt high like linked shafts in a single machine.

I have heard some guys scoff at royalty, but I have known few soldiers who did not tingle with pride as they stood to attention to be inspected by a man so revered as the late King George VI. You could hear a pin drop as he moved quietly up and down the ranks.

There was one fly in the ointment. A big, stuffy colonel from CMHQ, acting as a sort of aide-de-camp. Everytime the King stopped to talk to a private and the photographer tried to take a picture, the colonel would poke his beaming muzzle right in front of the camera.

It was getting so our unit wasn't going to have any photo souvenirs at all except stuffy boy and his smirking Haymarket fizzogg. The photographer looks at me and I shrug at him. How do you handle a situation like this with a full colonel?

The final blow arrives when His Majesty stops to chat with a young, full-blooded Indian from Northern Ontario. This was a picture too good to miss. But—who again was blocking the view, practically hanging on the King's shoulder? The stuffy colonel, of course.

Signalling to Jake the photographer to line up the shot, I quickly step in, deliberately walk on the colonel's toe and say in my most righteous tone, 'Sir, I think we are in the way, don't you?'

His Majesty, bless 'im, lowers the corners of his mouth in a quick offguard smile, the colonel mutters something like 'sorry' and steps back a pace. Jake the photographer then gets the most wonderful shot of King George smiling at the Canadian Indian soldier.

Months later, everyone who has joined up with me is so far ahead that I begin to look an old boy from a retarded children's school. Even my mother, bless her, begins to query in her letters, nicely-like, when am I going to get promoted?

In desperation I get myself paraded before the Old Man. 'Sir,' says I, after giving him my special Church Lads Brigade salute, 'sir, if it isn't too personal, I was wondering if there was ever any chance of me getting promoted?'

The Old Man for once almost looked human. 'Smitty,' says he, 'by now you are to me what an old slipper was to my grandfather—I've got used to you. But as far as promotion is concerned there isn't a darn thing I can do about it.'

He then went on to tell me the sad tale. The photogenic colonel had not forgotten my stepping on his toe. Straight back to CMHQ in Cockspur Street he had gone and filed the longest adverse report ever to be put on any record, with words reading like 'insubordinate, insolent, conduct unbecoming,' etcetera, etcetera.

Wearily I trudged back to my barracks long condemned since the Crimean War, flopped on the creaking wooden bed and stared vacantly at 'Hut Standing Orders' which read in part:

'Boots will not be cleaned on the table.'

'Rifles will not be cleaned on the table.'

'Cigarette ash and ink will not be spilt on the table.'

'The table will not be damaged in any way.'

Defiantly, and to be recorded for posterity, I took my pig-sticking bayonet and scratched on the side, 'D.W.S. 1943.' One week later I was orderly-roomed, confined to quarters and docked ten shillings for barrack room damage. The pride and joy of the Church Lads Brigade had sunk to an all-time low.

Meantime plans for the invasion of Europe went blithely along. Men with names like Eisenhower, Montgomery and Crerar seemed blissfully unaware of the dynamic and military potential of this young hopeful.

Time flew on, the impregnable Fortress Europa broke down, and my unit was munching sour apples in an orchard this side of Carpiquet.

'Smith,' says my Old Man, 'I've got a job for you to do. We have been saddled with a British war correspondent who wants to write nice things about the Canadians in action. Get yourself a Bren carrier, and for God's sake don't let anything happen to him.'

Hours later, myself and Mr Harkley Heathcote, of a London daily newspaper, were tooling down the road towards Benouville. I wasn't feeling too happy about the assignment as the Jerries were directing their shell-fire from the Colombelles chimney lookouts. Even the burlap and canvas screens placed along the south side of the road to block their vision didn't help my jangled nerves too much.

But not so Mr Harkley Heathcote. Freshly arrived by air from London that morning he was full of mad-cap ambition. Gad, sir, his readers were going to taste the blood of battle right in his imperishable words.

Tugging at his walrus moustache he sniffed the air with the enthusiasm of a soldier let loose in a distillery.

'Take me to the sound of the guns,' he says. I gaped at him. The man was mad. He had the light in his eyes of the early Christians going to the lions.

Somewhere near Benouville, after we crossed the first bridge, the

Canadians were in the woods along the banks of the Orne. However, to get to the woods we had to cross a small clearing, definitely marked with the ominous signs of Minen.

'Forward,' says the British warco.

'Not for this baby, Mr Harkley Heathcote,' says I.

'Forward,' says he again, pointing ahead with his swagger stick.

'No, siree,' says I. 'I don't know what your plans are for after this war, but me, I hope to be raising chickens, not daisies.'

Well, fellas, with that he jumps into the Bren carrier and highballs it alone across the clearing.

Yes, it happened alright. He struck a mine. Minutes later I dragged his cut-up carcass back . . . minus a good Bren carrier. However, he lived and wrote again . . . much later.

Months afterwards I was wining and dining in the Metropole Hotel in Brussels. The Old Man was nearby, feeling no pain. This was my chance to get in the old needle about promotion.

'Sir,' says I, 'now that I've upheld the honour of the unit and shown the old esprit de corps and stuff, do you think, sir, there's any chance of me ever getting promoted before this bloody war is over?'

The Old Man sobers for a moment. 'Smitty,' says he, 'my hands are tied. Your old pal Mr Harkley Heathcote, when he got out of hospital wrote a blistering, stinking letter to 21 Army Group in which he cited you for "cowardice under fire, dereliction of duty", and God knows what else. I'm afraid that it's all on your file.'

Well, fellas, that's the sad tale of my ignoble effort to assist my King and Country—the soldier longest on the payroll with the same rate of pay since Wellington kept his batman with him for life.

Nowadays I have the promotion complex. Every time someone nominates someone for secretary of the PTA I raise my cherub face in hopeful anticipation.

Some day I'm gonna make it.

> Doug Smith, *Memoirs of An Old Sweat* (1961), pp. 151-4

When all else failed, the ordinary man in the ranks could usually count on his officers, and other gods set over them, to provide amusement. Field Marshal Sir Douglas Haig, Commander of the British Army in the trenches of 1914-18, came up to the mark admirably.

The result of Haig's verbal fumbling could be quite comical at times. He once addressed the winners of an inter-regimental cross-country competition: 'I congratulate you on your running. You have run

well. I hope you will run as well in the presence of the enemy.' Haig
had no more luck on the rare occasions he spoke to individual
soldiers. 'And where did you start the war?' he asked a private.
'Nowhere, sir,' came the predictable reply, 'I didn't start the war.'

                    Daniel G. Dancocks, *Legacy of Valour* (1986), p. 12

*Sometimes a dark humour made light of a desperate situation, as
in this anecdote about a Canadian sniper in the Second World War.*

We found a small and very brave sniper vigorously firing from two
corners of a house (he kept dashing between the two). Corporal
J.A.M. Smith, in the lead car, shouted to him. 'What have you got
up there, mate?'
   The sniper replied, 'There are about three hundred Germans just
over the railroad tracks, but I got one of them.'
   'Good,' Corporal Smith told him. 'Then I guess there is nothing to
worry about.'

                    Jeffery Williams, *The Long Left Flank* (n.d.), pp. 51-2

Certainly there was nothing to do but laugh at a mild misfortune.

Once, after I was relieved from my anti-tank gun I had a ride in a
tank. I was at the horse lines near Aix-Noullette for some time and
there was one morning I was in charge of a party grazing horses. In
the plain near our grazing horses were some tanks practising crossing a sunken road some fifteen or twenty feet deep. After I had been
watching them for some time a young tank officer came to where I
was standing. 'Would you like a ride, Canada?' he said—Canada, not
sergeant. From an Imperial that was breath-taking. Naturally I said,
'Yes, sir.'
   A tank was halted and a port at the side was opened for me to enter.
While I was getting in a mechanic opened a five-gallon drum of oil
and took some out for his motor. Away we went down the bank into
the road, with me holding onto the machine-gun at my side to keep
from rolling down to the front of the tank. We crossed the road and
started up the other side. The tank seemed to stand on end, and I
kept from rolling to the back by handing on again to the machine-
gun. The can of oil had nothing to hang onto as we climbed and
started to roll. It was not until it came to rest squarely in my lap that

I noticed that the mechanic had forgotten to replace the cap after he had withdrawn his bit of oil. By the time we were on level ground again I had between two and three gallons of heavy machine oil all over my smart Bedford cord breeches.

If entertaining the troops were a meritorious service I should have had some sort of citation. Everyone in the battery except the sergeant-major seemed to think my breeches were funny. The SM regarded me with a fishy eye and said, 'That's what you get when you put stripes on some people.'

Ernest G. Black, *I Want One Volunteer* (1965), pp. 72-3

There were, of course, endless practical jokes, sometimes regretted afterwards.

When I visited my Fourteen Platoon, I met a short bow-legged fellow they called Bunty and heard a story about him. He had made himself a bivvy under a parados, as it was easier digging there, and had so constructed it that he could sit like a Hindu statue and go to sleep. He was a heavy sleeper and was very scared of shells. Tommy found him asleep there one morning and got a dud shell that was lying back of the trench. He made a cleft in the parapet directly in front, scooped out earth between Bunty's legs without waking him and put the dud into the cavity. Then he threw a Mills bomb into the grass back of the parados. The explosion wakened the little man rudely, but there was no outcry. Tommy, hiding around the bay, had to emerge to see what had happened. Bunty was rigid, unable to move or speak. Tommy dashed to him, seized the dud and hurled it over the parapet. Bunty rallied, and got up and shook Tommy's hand so fervently that Tommy swore he would never play another trick on anyone. He was a fine boy and was truly penitent.

Will R. Bird, *Ghosts Have Warm Hands* (1968), pp. 54-5

The most satisfying means of lifting the spirits was to 'liberate' some commodity or equipment, hopefully without undue pain to anyone else. It was illegal, yes; contrary to orders, certainly; reprehensible, without doubt; and enjoyable, totally. It is a proud tradition of the Canadian in uniform, albeit an unacknowledged one.

We were comin' back to Halifax from Gibraltar. One of the squadrons in Halifax said to us: Seein' you're empty—all our ammunition decks were empty—would you fill up with some duty-free liquor from Gibraltar? Sure, we says. So we totalled up what the ships in the squadron wanted, and when we got to Gibraltar we picked up 50 cases each of rum, gin, scotch, and rye. In Gibraltar the trucks from the liquor supplier arrived and we started loadin'. We had an officer down in the ammunition locker and the rest of us in a big long line to the upper deck, passin' the cases along. I was at the after hatch, next to our mess, and I could hear him countin', 41, 42, 43, as the cases come down, and I'm countin', too, 48, 49, 50, 51.

Fifty-one?

Maybe I miscounted, 48, 49, 50, 51! Now, I'd seen the manifest and it said '50 cases.' So I pulled aside the curtain to our mess and threw in a case of gin.

'Hide this!'

The guys in the mess quickly ripped open the case, hid the bottles, and tossed the carton out the scuttle. The officer signs the book, 50 cases, right. Next comes the rye. Same thing. 51 cases; 50 on the manifest. Swish! into the mess with a case of rye. We ended up with four cases—48 forty-ounce bottles. So, anyway, the liquor was safely stowed down below, the officer signed for it, the supplier's trucks took off, and the next day we left.

Well, we started drinkin'; we had to drink all 48 of those bottles before we got to Halifax. My mess bill for mixer alone was $35! And you can imagine how many cokes that was. We cleaned the ship out of all the mix they had. We were absolutely, completely, stoned all day. Oh we did our jobs alright ... just bombed out of our minds, that's all.

When we got to Halifax I had to stay on board. Can't remember why. Maybe I was in trouble, or had a special job to do. I can't be sure. Most of the time I was in trouble, so that was probably the reason. Anyway, a signal comes in from Gibraltar: Please confirm receipt of four complimentary cases of liquor sent to HMCS Haida. Because of the large liquor order, the supplier had added a complimentary case of each brand. Well, they checked, but all they found out was that four cases of liquor had mysteriously disappeared between the upper deck and the ammunition locker. There was nothin' they could do, though one of them said to me,

'Here, what's this?' He's lookin' at my mess bills. 'Five or six bucks all the time you were in Korea, and here, in the last week—$35?! In soft drinks?'

(Electric pause.)

'... uh ... sure was hot, Sir, comin' back across that Atlantic ...'

Alan D. Butcher, *I Remember Haida* (1985), pp. 147-9

In the end, though, it was the warmth shared with those serving alongside them that helped the Canadians laugh. And got them through.

8

LEAVING IT BEHIND

*Reactions to the end of one's personal war varied from the usual
mixture of relief and joy to uncertainty, disbelief, and even regret.
Often the thought of home and loved ones had assumed such
proportions that the reality of going back to them was hard to grasp.
Usually, however, the long repressed desire to get home would soon
overpower all other considerations.*

*For many, the war's end came with the receipt of what the First
World War soldier called a 'Blighty': a wound of sufficient serious-
ness that it spelled the likely end of military service. No two
experiences were alike, but every one was a transition to a very
different world.*

I was thrown by the force of the explosion on to my face into the
gutter at the side with the rest of me sprawled around the edge. The
first thing that surged through my mind was 'Am I dead, am I dead?'
I was badly dazed and partially choked by mud and water when I
went face first into the ditch but my mind quickly cleared and I
looked around and saw my horse lying dead half over my right thigh
and pinning me down. We were tossed from one side of the road to
the other. Glancing ahead I observed the horse in front dead and its
attendant also. He was Joe Bishop, the brother of Elmer who was
killed several weeks before at Lens. Joe was taken off the gun crew
and given a supposedly safety job with the transport. Ahead of him
was Ladd. His horse was dead also and he, himself, was wounded
and trying to rise. I turned around to see how the fellow behind me
fared. I saw him and his horse motionless in death. Four horses
killed, two men killed and two men wounded was the result of the
senselessness of the officer who led us in. He certainly played us
into the hands of the enemy.

After squirming for several minutes, I managed to pull my leg from
under my horse and astonishing to say it was not sore, let alone
injured. The right side of my face, however, was burning and sting-
ing as if someone had stuck hot needles into it. It was full of tiny

bits of metal. My chin, lip, nose and the inner corner of the eye was hit, besides the cheek, ear, jaw and also the fingers. I knew from the burning that my face was plastered, but that was all as far as I felt. Ladd shouted that he was hit in the leg. Getting up, I said I would bandage him and then tried to extract the bandage from the frontal corner of my tunic, but at this moment another salvo came over and the explosions so disturbed the air that I had difficulty in breathing for a minute or two. The shells fell short and the small embankment above the ditch seemed to waver before my eyes as the earth erupted. Ladd cried out that he could not make it and sank to the ground. I shouted back that I would send stretcher bearers as soon as I could. Then, for some unaccountable reason, I got mad and swore a volley of oaths in Gaelic. I was mad not only at Heinie for getting me, but also at myself for being so easily caught and wounded in such a simple fashion.

I started down the road feeling as strong as an ox, not even the least bit sickened, and after going about twenty yards, looking down I observed my tunic and pants were streaming with blood. I never noticed until I had gone a few yards further that my right arm was shattered at the shoulder, completely twisted around and dangling. There were five other wounds, but I did not know of their existence until later. In a temper I skedadled down the road holding up my right arm as the way it was dangling I thought it would fall off.

About two hundred yards further down the road, two men from our transport approached and when I neared them I shouted rather forcibly to them to clear out. It was a picture to see their faces. They stopped, looked at me for a moment and in sheer fright turned around and ran away as if the devil was after them. My face, which was plastered with mud and blood, must have scared the daylights out of them.

Reaching the base of the ridge I walked right into the cement blockhouse and told the Red Cross men that Ladd was lying wounded at the top of the road. They went out with a stretcher but waited up the road a bit for about ten minutes until the shelling ceased and soon afterwards Ladd was brought in. I looked at the MO and recognized him immediately. He was Hart who enlisted from the Youngstown or Hanna District as a private and came to my Company. After a while he got tired getting kicked around and blossomed out as the 25th Battalion MO. His first words to me were, 'Good God, Fraser, are you still around the line?' In a few minutes an ambulance appeared and four or five of us piled in and away we went.

Our first stop was Potijze when we were given hot cocoa and the right sleeve of my tunic was cut away. The next stop was Ypres where the driver had to report. Later on a further stop was made at

the western end of Vlamertinghe where we were stripped of our
uniforms, put into flannels, tagged and had a visit from a padre who
asked for the names and addresses of our next of kin. In quick time
we were into another ambulance and whisked away to a casualty
clearing hospital beside Poperinghe. It was operated by the Australian Medical Corps and consisted of several large tents. We were
dropped off here and in a matter of minutes I was under the X-ray
machine. When an anaesthetic was being given, the last words I
heard were spoken by an elderly doctor to his assistant when he said
in soft encouraging tones, 'That's it, Donie, that's it.'

Later I awakened in a tent in a dim light where about thirty fellows
lay on stretchers moaning and groaning. A bag containing the
shrapnel taken from my shoulder was pinned to my clothes, while
the left arm was wreathed in bandages and the other wrapped the
same way but, in addition, strapped to my body. At this stage I was
very dazed and sore and if I felt strong after I was hit, I felt the
opposite now. During the later hours of darkness the noises, sighs
and groans arising from pain and distress sounded as if we were in
purgatory. Two or three times I called out Ladd's name, but apparently he was not in the tent, for no response was received.

In the morning a Red Cross train was at hand and in a short time
the carriages were filled. Two nurses came into my carriage and sat
about ten feet away on the opposite side. I could tell by the sinister
way they looked at me every now and then that they expected me
to peg out.

As the train slowly sped away and I realized that my fighting days
had passed forever, I silently said farewell to the line that had been
my home for the last two years and two months.

Reginald H. Roy, *The Journal of Private Fraser* (1985), pp. 314-16

*Canadian troops camped together in Wales after the end of the First
World War faced seemingly endless delays before they would be
sent home. Eventually, the frustration became too much.*

Around the last of February things came to a climax, which should
go down as the blackest page in the history of the Canadian Expedi-
tionary Force.

One night, around eleven o'clock, a riot broke out, starting in the
Montreal depot, from where it spread to the other sections of Camp.
Hundreds went on a wild rampage looting everything in sight
including Tin Town, beer canteens, quartermaster stores. Everything was left in a shambles. Rifles and ammunition were secured

by the rioters; girls working in canteens lay down on the floor to escape bullets which passed through the building. This spectacle lasted all night and continued the following day. Our depot number 6 was situated at the extreme end of the camp. So far, we had not observed anything but could hear the noise. We knew from the start what was going on.

Around noon, our Colonel called a parade. He told us that we were going to protect our depot so he gave orders to roll out all the beer barrels and told us, 'What you don't drink, pour out so the rioters will not get it.' NCOs were issued rifles and ammunition, and ordered not to shoot unless absolutely necessary; if so, shoot low at the legs. Soon afterward, we saw the mob coming down the main road. They stopped at our main gate and started to come in. Just in front of me was one of our officers. He walked to meet them with a revolver in his hand. A big burly fellow was leading them. The officer told them to turn about. He also told them there were armed men to stop them. The crowd just jeered and called the officer names, and started coming. The officer said, 'I'm not fooling,' and shot the big fellow on the knee. I guess it surely hurt, as he hopped around and made an awful fuss. When the rest of the mob saw that we were armed and meant business they clunked back through the gate and I think most of them were apprehended by the authorities. Of course, by this time many who began to realize the serious nature of the whole event had left the ranks and returned to their respective quarters. One man from our unit, a Corporal, was killed that day and had nothing to do with the rioting. We had a military funeral for him later. Here was a man who had come through the war, and on the eve of his homecoming, was killed by his own comrades. I never found out just how many casualties there were, but there were several.

Gordon Reid, *Poor Bloody Murder* (1980), pp. 247-8

Then the move would come: by trucks to trains, by trains to ships, and all in a bizarre atmosphere in which anything might happen.

We were off again, but for a long time the train simply crawled, as we had to wait at three places to let another train go by. Then the boys began to be uneasy. There were no washrooms on the train, and the cups of tea became a regret. Each passing hour made the lads more desperate. No one could sit still. Then windows were dropped and the boys called from one section to another. There was no passageway on the train—all were in the same predicament. Something had to be done. After much calling back and forth, it was agreed that whereas an individual might get into serious trouble, nothing would be done if the whole battalion committed the same offense. So, at a shout, one half were to find relief at windows on the north side, one half on the south side. The signal came, and a moment later we arrived at Liverpool station!

The situation was beyond description. Organizations of women were awaiting us with tea and buns, and the amazing spectacle that swept into view must be still talked about in the circles of old ladies. We on the south side faced the railway yards and were all right, but those on the north, after bitter moments of indecision, flooded the interior of the cars, both seats and floors, their only care being not to contact a fellow traveller. Our packs were in the racks.

There were many red faces and much laughter. Many boys were only intent on escaping the scene. Then away we went to the dock.

Will R. Bird, *Ghosts Have Warm Hands* (1968), pp. 246-7

The urgency of getting home took priority over everything else.

When we went home in 1919, there were two of us seated in the train together that were artillerymen. We stopped in Montreal. Two officers asked us if we were in the artillery. We told them we were in it. They said, 'We'd like you to enlist for another three years. If you enlist we'll guarantee you Lieutenant's commissions. Right off the bat. No joking about that.' I asked, 'What's the idea?' He said, 'We need instructors. You fellows have been through the war and we're short of instructors.' That was the first mistake I ever made. I should have taken them up on it. I told them, 'No, I've had all the army I want and I want to get out of it.' The other fellows with me felt the same. I would have had a nice pension coming.

Gordon Reid, *Poor Bloody Murder* (1980), p. 246

Even as the home shores approached, the returning man was still part of a special society, and often he would realize that certain things could be understood only by that society.

I got up and dressed, although it was only four o'clock in the morning.

It was cold but I wore my greatcoat, and to my amazement there were other dark figures near the rail. We stood, hunched together, gazing ahead into the darkness. Presently another figure joined us, then another. In an hour there were fourteen of us, and no one had spoken, although we were touching shoulders. The way we stood made me think of a simile. Ah—we were like prisoners. I had seen them standing together, staring over the wire to the field beyond, never speaking. And we were more or less prisoners of our thoughts. Those at home would never understand us, because something inexplicable would make us unable to put our feelings into words. We could only talk with one another.

All at once the watchers stirred, tensed, craned forward. It was the moment for which we had lived, which we had envisioned a thousand times, that held us so full of feeling we could not find utterance. Far ahead, faint, but growing brighter, we had glimpsed the first lights of home!

Will R. Bird, *Ghosts Have Warm Hands* (1968), pp. 248-9

Finally the waiting would be over. The intensity of such drama and risk, comradeship and activity, would end, abruptly. What would fill the void?

If anyone was to ask me what were my two most exciting days in the services I would list them as follows:

(a) The day I was sworn in.

(b) The day I got my discharge.

Nobody but the dullest clod could refrain from a spine-tingling thrill as you stood in front of the recruiting officer, raised your right hand, and took the oath of allegiance.

From that point on life took on an entirely new meaning.

The first night in barracks, the strange sounds.

The proper bahstud of a corporal who treated you like you were something under a microscope.

The ill-fitting uniform, with its narrow-bottom trousers, the large, black boots, the narrow wedge-cap which kept falling over your ear.

As you strolled down Main Street for the first time in uniform you were certain that everybody, but everybody in town, was staring especially at you.

You peeked self-consciously in store windows to see how you looked, and you blushed like hell when you realized that the guy you had just saluted was only the doorman outside the hotel.

I've had many self-conscious moments in my chequered career, but nothing to compare with my first few weeks in uniform.

However, the thrill to surpass all thrills was the time five years later when you knew that someday now, any day perhaps, your number would come up and you would go home.

Back to civvie street! Boy, what you weren't going to do! The very first thing would be to go to the poshest restaurant in town with your special girl friend and order the biggest, the juiciest and the most succulent steak in the house—and hang the expense.

Then, if he ever crossed your path, you were going to go up to that particular NCO, or that s.o.b. of an officer, and were you ever going to give that bloke a piece of your mind! And, if he uttered one peep—just one small bleat—you'd poke him right on the snoot.

Yes-siree, that's just what you were going to do.

I know there was one particular RSM for whom I had a fate all planned out. I wasn't even going to make with the small talk. I was just going to let him have it . . . hard.

Several years after discharge I ran into him at a Legion hall. I was having a few beers. This guy walks in. He spots me and I spot him. I spring from my seat. He strides towards me.

'Smitty!' he cries.

'Sa'hunt-major, you old son of a gun!' I yell.

Three minutes later we are downing beer like thirsty camels, with arms around each other's shoulders.

Yep, I sure kept my long-promised vow—hah! I wonder how many of you fellas did likewise?

However, I guess that's all water under the bridge now. Except at one time it was all very real with you.

Little things like points. How many of them did you have? Surely with 200 points they would be posting your name any day now for repatriation. And yet the call did not come.

Meantime, you heard through the most reliable source, Daily Routine Rumours, that some jokers with only 78 points were on their way home. You cussed the services and all those in authority for a bunch of lazy, sloppy, indifferent plugs. Guys who didn't give a damn as long as they filled their quota with any odds and sods nearby.

You stewed in the bunkhouse and wrote long, promising notes home until there wasn't anything left to write anymore.

You went on leave. One final more fling at the Big Town. But it wasn't the same. There was a gnawing restlessness to get the hell out of there and get home. What you were going home to you weren't quite certain. But home was home and that was the one place in the world you wanted to go to most.

Then came the big moment. Your name came up. You were on your way to a repat depot.

You never in all your life saw a guy fling stuff so fast into a duffel bag. Never did you salute so smartly as when you reported to the orderly room, apprehensive lest by some freak of fate any slip or misconduct on your part would take you off the roster.

Feverishly you gave excess baggage away to buddies who called you 'lucky dog'. Furtively you tucked that German Luger way down between a pair of heavy socks.

You still couldn't believe your luck. And it was only when the 60 hundredweight began pulling away from the camp and you waved goodbye from the tailboard that it finally dawned on you that you were really on your way. Or at least the first step of many steps to come had been taken.

You crossed the Channel and again you bunked down somewhere near Farnham. Brightly you went to the orderly room with that hopeful question on your lips, 'When do I sail?'

'Watch for your name on the notice board,' drones a sadly disillusioned corporal who knows he is frozen and couldn't care less when you got home.

And so day in and day out you watch that board. Drafts leave and still your name never appears.

By this time you have played all the cribbage you can stand, drunk all the nut-brown ale that the NAAFI can supply, said farewell to your English friends, and stared at the pictures in your wallet with a yearning out of this world.

And still your name doesn't come up. The hours, the days and even the weeks go by. Yet back in Amsterdam they had given you three hours to pack and hurry-hurry-hurry.

Then the lowness sets in. Your morale droops lower than a mongrel's tail. You live and breathe ship movements. Rumours fly around, despondent rumours, and you are fair game for them all.

Latest on the rumour rounds is the Lizzie. The Lizzie has been taken off and sent to the Pacific . . . the Empress of Scotland was in dry dock and wouldn't be off for a month . . . civilians were travelling ahead of troops . . . low-pointers were going home and high-pointers were frozen, etc., etc.

You ran hot and cold with each eagerly devoured rumour until fact no longer existed and fiction ruled the day. There were no facts in your life for the simple reason the authorities never told you any facts.

Then came the fateful day when you saw your name on the board. You stared at it, fascinated. And you looked, and looked, and looked, and prayed that there was no mistake.

There was no mistake. For once in its ruddy life the Army had done something right. And you didn't mind the eight-tiered bunks in the troopship's hold. You would have slept on coal sacks in a corner if it meant getting across that ocean . . . and home.

Then came the distant shoreline of Halifax. And if you didn't actually get down and kiss the dock, you did so in your mind.

No longer did the fussing, officious little tin-pots annoy you as they herded you aboard the train. No longer did you fret and fume as you waited in the long dining room queue.

No more did you swear as the old sway-backs of racked-out troop trains roared around the curves, tossing you helter-skelter in your sleeper. For the sweetest music in the world was that rackety-tack-ety-tack as the wheels ground over the rails, and each whoooo, whoooo of the engine's whistle brought you that much closer to home.

Then your train puffed into the hometown station. The bands were playing, the flags were flapping, the crowds were cheering and your heart was pounding, but you paid no heed. Somewhere, but somewhere in that sea of faces were the ones you loved.

And then you saw them—mom, dad and the girl of your dreams.

This indeed was home! The end of a road. More roads would come—but none would ever be the same.

Doug Smith, *Memoirs of An Old Sweat* (1961), pp. 46-9

And for some Canadians, memories were not the only lasting treasures from the war. Love, too, came home with them.

One evening in January 1941 a girl friend and I were walking on the cliff side of the South Coast Road, a few miles east of Brighton. We met two rifle-carrying Canadian soldiers in battle dress coming in the opposite direction. The men were on patrol.

'You can't walk on that side of the road after dark, girls,' declared one of the Black Watch of Canada types.

'Let's see what you can do about it,' I shot back, always braver when another female was present.

We made a date that night to meet the following Sunday afternoon at the same spot, neither knowing what the other looked like. That was how I met my husband in the black-out, and he has been putting up with my cheek ever since.

Joyce Hibbert, *The War Brides* (1978), p. 23

9
KEEPING THE PEACE

The Canadian military experience did not end with the ceasefire in Korea. Canada has remained firm in its NATO *and* NORAD *commitments, training for war with the fervent hope that it will never come. At the same time, beginning essentially with the experience in Egypt in 1956, Canadian troops have served the national commitment to the United Nations through participation in peacekeeping operations.*

To be a peacekeeper is to keep one's head when the antagonists you separate threaten to lose theirs; to carry the double burden of keeping the peace without full recourse to one's own weaponry; and to win the day through patience, persuasion, and a shrewd appreciation of the combatants' minds. It calls for maturity, endurance, and a quiet kind of courage. It is not always an easy role to play, and even for the best-trained troops, the first exposure to warfare can test that training.

On Saturday morning, July 20th, I received a call at 0430 hrs advising me that we were placed on 'Red Alert' and that I was to report to the joint operations centre immediately for orders. I hurried over and learned that a Turkish invasion was in progress along the north coast in the Kyrenia area.

At 0700 a dramatic illustration of the invasion occurred as I watched the Turkish airborne operation from the upper floor of the Ledra Palace Hotel. Turkish aircraft were dropping parachutists north of Nicosia. It was a beautiful, still cloudless morning and watching the sky fill with parachutes was an awesome sight, especially to our Canadian Airborne Regiment members.

Throughout the morning sporadic firing continued increasing in intensity, and punctuated by key machine-gun fire and heavier explosions. At about 1230 hrs we received three mortar rounds in Wolseley barracks, and our first injuries . . . I told everyone to start digging. One thing I did discover was that when there is danger, it is no problem to get troops digging. Getting them to stop digging however is another story. A little later in the afternoon, I had to order some dirt put back in two trenches. The occupants had dug down so far that they couldn't see out.

Fred Gaffen, In the Eye of the Storm (1987), pp. 98-9

Gradually the peacekeepers become cautious and perceptive, alert to the habits of the people they are among—and shrewdly learning how to use those habits to respond in kind.

The UNTSO officers were happy to have Canadian troops in the area as we were armed while they were not. Warrant Officer 'Turk' Deschamps and I would make tours of the UNIFIL area of operation visiting our radio detachments at the various contingents. We became quite familiar with passing through check-points. Generally, the first thing a militiaman of PLO type would do at a check-point was open the jeep door and push a rifle in at us. This procedure was, of course, intended to be intimidating. We counteracted by having my submachine gun, loaded and cocked, cradled casually in my lap pointing directly at the soldier's crotch. . . .

Ibid., p. 153

As long as the peace holds, the peacekeeper must work in an atmosphere of tension, never knowing when the murderous hatreds of over-armed and under-disciplined factions will explode. When the shooting does actually break out, the peacekeeper has to keep his wits and nerve about him to save lives.

Sgt Lessard's helicopter landed where two nuns lay literally surrounded by some fifteen to twenty Jeunesse. One sick nun was on a stretcher while the other lay on the ground. . . . Despite a shower of arrows aimed at the helicopter, Lessard jumped to the ground and without assistance proceeded to put the stretcher aboard the helicopter. While he was thus engaged he was tackled from behind by four Jeunesse who tried to drag him down. As he fought off his assailants, Lessard pushed the stretcher aboard and then reached out for the second nun who lay nearby. Without the slightest regard for his attackers he pushed the nun into the safety of the helicopter, holding off the last two attackers until the helicopter had actually started to leave the ground. Only then did he free himself completely and jump aboard. . . .

Ibid., p. 233

Sergeant J.A. Leonce Lessard won the George Medal for his actions in the Congo that day.

Perhaps the most dramatic demonstration of what Canadian peace-keepers can achieve, to their everlasting credit and the rightful pride of their country, is this incident from the Yom Kippur War of 1973.

My partner and I picked up an Israeli liaison officer and proceeded towards El Tasa. I was surprised to discover how badly the Israeli military treated the UN. But I learned that there are good and bad in every society.

When we were about ten miles from El Tasa we passed an Israeli military convoy of mixed vehicles a mile long. The only thing different from any other convoy was that it was stopped and consisted of burned out wrecks practically bumper to bumper. A couple of miles later we passed a repeat of the first except this was about one-half mile long. I was shocked to think that the Israelis had gotten themselves trapped and wiped out so effortlessly by the Egyptians. I couldn't stop to investigate as Suez city was another two to three hours drive. As we passed El Tasa there were knocked out Egyptian tracked vehicles so they had gotten that far in this sector. We then turned southwest passing the area of 'Chinese Farm' (Galan) and much wreckage.

We reached the canal where I did my first duty. There were many Israeli tanks and anti-aircraft guns and whatever located there. As I got closer I could see half of them were knocked out. In one spot six tanks were burned out so close to each other that one could jump back and forth. . . .

We crossed the canal on a floating bridge that was badly listing due to over-use, lack of maintenance, and shell-fire. Getting off the bridge we entered a new world of agricultural land. Tall date palms, sugar cane, and varieties of grass were abundant. Every 100 metres for at least one mile were knocked-out Israeli tanks. After we got free of the green belt, we were back into desert. . . .

At Suez city there was absolute pandemonium. Confusion a-bounded around Israeli Defence Forces' command headquarters. Orders were given then countermanded then rescinded. Everybody in their army from the top brass to the lowest rank had an opportunity to be seen as well as heard. Major Bill Bailey and his partner handed over the reins, wished us luck and happily sped away towards the west. . . .

My partner and I ventured out of town about five miles and

inspected some abandoned positions along the canal. As I was driving parallel on a trail through the heavily-vegetated jungle-like area, we were stopped at gun point by an Egyptian soldier. So much for the Israelis having the Egyptian Third Army surrounded. They had bypassed this area and the Egyptians were in strength. We then crossed a steel bridge over the Sweet Water Canal and met with the Egyptians. . . . The Israelis claimed the Egyptians had moved into this area after the Israelis had cleared it. Clearly this was a ruse as the Egyptians could not possibly have prepared fortifications in a couple of hours.

What I believe to be the first peace talks of the Yom Kippur War then took place. Can you imagine a small group of Israelis and Egyptians who were about to kill each other having a meeting? An Israeli officer offered an Egyptian a cigarette. He noticed the man was trembling badly. How can you kill somebody who you have just met and offered a cigarette?

An Israeli officer came out from hiding with his weapon in hand and spoke to us saying, 'You had better leave. We are attacking this position in ten minutes.' He was either a Canadian or an American Jew because he did not have an English accent. We replied: 'There is a cease-fire and there is to be no more fighting.' Soon another Israeli force moved in from the side we had entered and we were stuck in the middle. The Egyptian soldiers were in a frenzy being pushed on two sides by the Israeli army. To distract their attention, I broke open a carton of cigarettes and gave them out. It was just enough to stop them from getting nervous and pulling a trigger.

We were given until 1700 hours to get out by the Israeli Defence Forces. My partner and I moved our vehicle onto the bridge to prevent the Israelis crossing over the Sweet Water Canal. At ten minutes before the attack, we both took off our flak jackets and helmets, threw them out onto the bridge, sat on the hood of our vehicle, and began smoking cigarettes.

Around 17:30 a cigar-smoking, short, squat, grey-haired Israeli colonel arrived and then angrily left in a cloud of cigar smoke. It was getting dark. The Israeli combat team commander then told us to stay. 'After all,' he said, 'this is my fourth war and I see no need to die this late in the war especially now that you have made this cease-fire stick. . . .' The Israeli forces soon withdrew and we were the last out.

Ibid., pp. 29-32

In the steady courage of those two perceptive, resourceful men is mirrored much of what is best in Canada and Canadians.

INDEX